Rinkrats
I Have Known
AND OTHER STORIES

DONALD A. McKELLAR

Trafford
PUBLISHING

www.trafford.com

North America & international
toll-free: 1 888 232 4444 (USA & Canada)
phone: 250 383 6864 ♦ fax: 250 383 6804
email: info@trafford.com

The United Kingdom & Europe
phone: +44 (0)1865 722 113 ♦ local rate: 0845 230 9601
facsimile: +44 (0)1865 722 868 ♦ email: info.uk@trafford.com

10 9 8 7 6 5 4 3

Table of Contents

꙳

Acknowledgments

IT WOULD BE SAFE TO SAY THAT THIS COLLECTION OF SHORT STO-
RIES WOULD NOT HAVE BEEN WRITTEN WITHOUT THE HELP OF
KEN ROBERTSON, COUSIN AND AUTHOR, (*WINDCHARM -A DREAM
DELAYED*). Several of these stories were born out of long discus-
sions in front of the wood-stove at Ken's Medonte home. My
original intention was to write only three or four stories for my
own amusement, but twenty-seven stories and five years later,
Ken said to me, "I think you've got a book here."

This book represents a family affair in another sense; some
of the individuals whose stories are told in these pages are ancestors of mine. Johnny McGinnis, for example, was my great,
great, great-grandfather. Isabella Hughes was my great great-
grandmother. Alexander and Lillias Rose, other direct ancestors, were the pioneer farmers who received the gift of a cow
from the diplomat, John Rose. This goes to prove that a nation's
heritage is best told through the lives of ordinary people.

My grandfather was T.C. Shiels, a good story teller in his own
right. As a boy growing up in Lanark County, Ontario, Canada, he
had a personal acquaintance with Frank Lynch, George Howard,
John Bangs and Peter McIquham, but his favourite Valley stories
always centred around Poulin, with whom he worked on spring

drives from 1900 to 1903 on the Pettawawa River.

It was also my grandfather who, in Halifax during the Second World War, struck up that conversation with the gentleman who had photographed Alexander Graham Bell's kite.

My late father was the Boy Scout who won the prize of an airplane flight with Roy Brown in 1925. Incidentally, in 1973, while researching the story of the Sage of Aru, I wrote to the late Howard M. Brown, who was a friend of my uncle and an eminent Ottawa Valley historian, to ask what he knew of George Howard. H.M. Brown kindly responded with a long letter of personal recollections, including a wonderful description of the Sage's automobile. H.M. Brown was the younger brother of the famous pilot.

I also want to thank the Westhead branch of my family for supporting me on this project; my Aunt Marion, for her memories of Ross Smither, keynote speaker, author and cousin Tim Westhead, who patiently edited my original manuscript and to writer cousin, Jessica Westhead, who also took the time to read and comment on the stories for me.

I am indebted to four Canadian war veterans for sharing their memories of the thirties and the Second World War with me: Ken Robertson of Medonte, Ontario, Jack Pringle, of Thunder Bay, Ontario, Spencer G. Evans, of Toronto, and Allan W. Brown, of Cobourg, Ontario.

My thanks also to Mike Cresswell, Donogh O' Brien, Doug Munroe, and Don Geater for their input into the stories. And to my late friend Russ Coles, whose encounter with Dr. Banting at the CNE grounds many years ago is told here.

I'm fortunate that my friend, the late Lewis McLauchlan, wrote down his thoughts of the Klondike Gold Rush in a series of letters to me, which I have used as a source for the two stories of the Yukon.

Thanks to my cousin, Evelyn McColl, of Maxville, Ontario for permission to include poetry written by her father, M.J. Shiels in this publication.

A long distant thank you to Alex Hamilton, of Essex, England, a gifted aviation artist, who gave me permission to use "Outbound Blenheims" along with kind words of encouragement.

And may I add a special thank you to my friend, Stephen Ashmeade, whose wonderful companionship I enjoyed since he was seven, as my 'little brother'. The activities experienced by the characters in this book were based on our weekly adventures together.

I'm very pleased to include in this history some wonderful pictures of Canada's past. Numerous museums, archives and halls of fame in Canada and the United States granted me use of their images. A complete list of photo-credits and permissions appear at the end of the book.

You will read two direct quotes in these stories attributed to two famous people: Frederick Banting and Lou Gehrig. I believe the quotes to be true because I knew well the men to whom those words were spoken.

And talking about quotations, I must comment on some of the words spoken by the two characters. In "Victoria Cross Hill", Brendan refers to a painting he has seen in a book at school depicting a First World War scene. I believe he's referring to Group of Seven artist F.H.Varley's 1918 painting, entitled, "For What".

And finally, elsewhere in the stories, Linus quotes "forgotten, as a dream" , in "Black Pete's Last Fight", which is taken directly from Rev. Isaac Watts' 1719 hymn, "O God, Our Help in Ages Past", and in "Rinkrats I Have Known" he quotes Edward Young, who wrote, "Procrastination is the thief of time." I owe it to the reader to name the true writers of these words, because, although he doesn't come out and say so to Brendan, Linus thought he was quoting Dickens.

—Donald A. McKellar, Toronto, Ontario, Feb. 20, 2007

Introduction

On this road where autos speed,
In days long past, some laden steed
With heavy rider on his back,
Or provender in hempen sack;
Plodded on its weary way,
O'er rock and mire from day to day.

And years before the horseman came,
Some pioneer of sturdy frame,
A hatchet from his waist belt hung,
A flintlock o'er his shoulder slung;
And tump rope taut from heavy pack
Trudged bravely on the forest track.

Son of an Orkneyman was he,
Of Erin, Yorkshire, Normandy,
Seeking a place more free to roam,
Hoping to build himself a home
Of rocks and logs, a cabin warm
To shelter loved ones from life's storm.

On this road many feet have trod,
Surveyor carrying his tripod;
LaSalle, Champlain, the fierce Iroquois,
Lumberjack with axe and saw,
Macdonald, Brock, a great Shawnee;
They built this road from sea to sea.

M.J. Shiels, 1952

1 6 1 5

Ambush on the Iroquois Trail

"On this road many feet have trod,
Surveyor carrying his tripod;
LaSalle, Champlain, the fierce Iroquois,
Lumberjack with axe and saw;"
—M.J.Shiels

"I'M ALMOST SURE WE'RE ON THE TRAIL NOW, BRENDAN. From here, it heads north to Woodbridge."

Linus and his nine-year-old grandson, Brendan, stood on a path in a field north of Toronto; the grandfather's family-sized basset hound, the aptly named "Horse" was at their side.

"How old is this trail, anyway, Grandpa?" asked the nine-year-old.

"A thousand years old at least, probably more—who knows? It was one of the oldest Indian trails on the continent and certainly one of the most important.

"*A thousand years!*" repeated the boy.

"And we're walking on it," Linus said. "When you consider all the history of the Native population that has been lost to us, Brendan, we're lucky that at least we know the route of this famous portage. It's hard to believe, but this overland trail tells us the story of a continent. Historians say the path here at one time had been worn a foot deep."

They were hiking the Toronto Carrying Place.

9

Linus unfolded one of his maps. He loved maps.

"Think of the history this path has seen: fur traders, raiding parties, explorers, hunters, voyageurs and missionaries all took this route over the centuries."

"It sure was a busy place."

"The great French explorer, LaSalle, was perhaps the most daring of them all. We're following right along in his footsteps, my boy."

"We are?"

"It's exciting, isn't it? He walked this very ground three and four times," Linus said.

Brendan instinctively looked at his feet.

"Did I ever show you C.W. Jeffrey's famous pen and ink sketch of that amazing trail blazer? It's in a book I have at home."

"I don't think so."

Linus loved C.W. Jeffrey's artwork. "Jeffrey's drawing shows him crossing the Toronto Carrying Place in the pouring rain and he sure doesn't look very happy about it," he said. "C. W. Jeffrey made Canadian history come to life."

"All I can say is I'm glad *I'm* not carrying a canoe or something like that on this walk," Brendan commented, "and it must have been even worse in the rain."

"Here's where we are," Linus said, pointing to the Humber River on his map. "This hike is fascinating because LaSalle came right along here on his famous expedition into the interior of North America. That was his historic trip of 1681 in which he claimed half a continent in the name of King Louis XIV of France."

"Wait a minute! You mean he claimed half a continent just by walking along here? Could he just do that?"

Linus began to wonder about that himself. "There was nothing very humble about the early explorers."

"I guess they could do things like that back then," the boy said.

This is C.W. Jeffreys' famous pen and ink sketch of LaSalle, walking north along the Toronto Carrying Place, Ontario, Canada in August of 1681. Eight months later he reached the mouth of the Mississippi.

"It really is an amazing accomplishment no matter how you look at it. It all started after LaSalle's party of a dozen canoes and about fifty men and women left Fort Frontenac."

"Where's that?"

"Present day Kingston. Then they paddled along the north shore of Lake Ontario until they reached the mouth of the Humber River. Then the expedition began the difficult task of carrying their canoes over the full length of this portage."

"I'm glad I didn't have to do it," Brendan said.

Linus nodded in agreement. "It was worse north of here. There are some very steep hills ahead so it took them more than three weeks just to reach the Holland River."

"That's a really long walk."

"The Carrying Place was an exceptionally long portage; almost thirty miles," Linus said, pointing north. "This was the route LaSalle followed all the way to the Gulf of Mexico."

Brendan didn't look convinced. "You mean he traveled in this direction and somehow ended up at the Gulf of Mexico?"

"That's right. In the spring of 1682, LaSalle completed a journey to the mouth of the Mississippi where he planted the French flag and named the country Louisiana."

"But this story isn't making any sense," Brendan protested. "Wasn't LaSalle going the wrong way? I thought the Gulf of Mexico is south? How come you keep pointing north?"

"Look at this big map of North America as a whole, Brendan. Picture the continent as it would have been drawn in LaSalle's time when it was wilderness."

"But this is a modern map," complained Brendan. "How I am supposed to know what it looked like back then?"

"Just ignore the boundaries and the names we're familiar with today. You can see that Lake Superior and Lake Michigan are located in the center of the continent. If LaSalle could get to Lake Michigan, he'd be able to connect to the great river systems of the Ohio, the Illinois and the Mississippi. You can see on the map that he could follow the Mississippi southward to the Gulf."

Brendan studied the map closely. "I guess I never realized that the lakes and rivers were so important back then."

Linus drew a finger over the map of Great Lakes. "In the heyday of the fur trade the two upper lakes: Michigan and Superior were the jumping off points into the heart of our continent," he said. "LaSalle used the Toronto Carrying Place to get to the Holland River. That river took him into Lake Simcoe and then onto the Severn River. From the Severn, he entered Georgian Bay. He stayed close to the north shore of Georgian Bay until he reached Lake Michigan. It was the best route that he could have taken."

"When you look at it like that, I guess it would be a bit of a shortcut," Brendan said.

"That's *exactly* what it was, Brendan. LaSalle followed the advice of his guides. The native people of North America always traveled efficiently. They took the shortest and most direct routes. Their footpaths, like the Carrying Place, invariably followed the high, dry ground; their water routes had the fewest portages." Linus smiled at his grandson and finished by saying, "Don't argue with the wisdom gained from thousands of years of trial and error."

"I won't," Brendan promised.

"Etienne Brûlé was another of those daring young French explorers," Linus went on. "He came before LaSalle. Brûlé was actually the first European to travel this ancient trail. He came south from Huronia along here in 1615 with twelve Huron allies on his way to Lake Ontario."

"Where was he going?"

"Samuel de Champlain had sent the young explorer on an important mission into the interior."

"I've heard of *him*."

"Champlain was the Founder of New France. He had instructed Brûlé to visit a nation called the Andastes and to establish an alliance with them. Brûlé turned west when he arrived at the mouth of the Humber and rounded Lake Ontario. He crossed Lake Erie by canoe into the wilds of what is now Upper New York State."

"He must have been brave to go on a trip like that in those days," the boy said.

"When Etienne Brûlé made this trip, the area was fairly safe for the Hurons. They lived north of here on the shores of Georgian Bay. They became very friendly with Champlain during the fur trade and allied themselves with him against their mortal enemies. Do you know which enemies I mean?" asked Linus.

"They were the Iroquois, weren't they?"

"Yes," Linus answered, "the fierce Iroquois. The Hurons and the Iroquois were bitter rivals. The Iroquois hated the Huron-French fur trading alliance and were determined to use the total military might of the Five Nations to destroy it. In the fall of 1648 a war party of over one thousand Iroquois warriors in seventy canoes crossed Lake Ontario from their homeland in the Finger Lakes of New York to winter at bases near Lake Simcoe. Late in the winter of 1649 they slipped silently out of the woods and attacked Huronia. The Hurons were unprepared to defend themselves and were wiped out."

Brendan jaw dropped. *"Wiped out!"*

"The courageous Jesuits, Brebeuf and Lallamand, who lived with the Hurons were tortured and killed," Linus added. "It was a tragic end to the Huron Nation."

"Couldn't they defend themselves somehow?"

"It seems they didn't post guards or send out scouts to warn them of the approaching danger," answered Linus. "I don't think they really believed the Iroquois would attack them in winter."

"I'd sure have a lot of scouts and guards back then if I was in charge," Brendan blustered with the advantage of more than three hundred and fifty years of hindsight backing him up. "I would have been prepared for them."

"The Iroquois were the great military strategists of the eastern woodlands," Linus said. "Can you imagine those warriors coming all the way up from New York State and living off the land all winter and patiently waiting to attack? It's a scary story, isn't it?"

Brendan shivered at the thought of it. "It sure is."

Linus agreed. "When I first read about the destruction of Huronia, I thought the invasion route must have been along the Ottawa River. That was the route Champlain had taken years before. But now I doubt they would have taken the chance of being seen on a well-used fur route like that. I think it's more likely that after crossing Lake Ontario, the Iroquois portaged through the Trent Valley waterway and entered Lake Simcoe from the east. That's my opinion anyway. No one knows for sure."

"Then how do you know they didn't take some secret route that nobody knows about?"

Linus stroked his chin to help him think. "I just think a war party of that size would have used the Trent."

"It probably wouldn't have made any difference anyway, Grandpa. I think the Hurons were goners no matter which way the Iroquois came."

"I guess so," agreed Linus. "Anyway, for the next forty years The Toronto Carrying Place was exclusively an Iroquois trail."

"No wonder everybody was so scared of the Iroquois."

"They built a fortified village of longhouses at the mouth of the Humber, which they called Teiaigon. They lived there quite peacefully."

"They did?"

"Yes, they fished and grew corn and squash. Then the Iroquois too, were pushed back to their ancestral lands in New York's Finger Lakes region, to be replaced by the Ojibway."

"A lot sure happened on this path," Brendan said, beginning to appreciate the different people who had trod the Carrying Place throughout the ages.

"Over the years the river has changed course and the ravines and valleys have filled in," Linus said. "But despite all the changes, the Toronto Carrying Place remains one of the most historic sites on the continent."

"Wouldn't it be great if we found some real Indian arrow-heads on the trail?"

"Keep your eyes peeled, Brendan. Maybe we'll find some-thing. A few years ago, a man found a spear-tip in Sunnybrook Park, which is just a couple of miles from here. It was more than three thousand years old."

"*Three thousand years*!" the boy exclaimed. "Imagine how many arrow heads would have been lost in *three thousand years*. I bet we find lots."

"The man who found the spear-tip donated it to the Royal Ontario Museum," his grandfather said. "If we find any arti-facts, we'll donate them too."

"I guess so," Brendan said, "if we have to." But secretly he wished that he could keep them. He would have loved to start a collection of arrowheads.

Horse, in his role as chief scout, sniffed around to make sure there were no Iroquois braves lurking in the tall bushes along the path. This modern day expedition did not want to repeat the mistakes of the Hurons. To be prepared for an ambush they must be on their guard.

"It's a long walk, isn't it?" the boy said after a while.

"The trail is twenty-eight miles in length," Linus answered. "It ends at the Holland River. We won't go all the way, but let's go a little further before we return to the car."

"I wonder if the Indians ever got bored during this walk," Brendan said, and then added as an afterthought, "especially the ones my age."

Linus had never thought about it before. "The Hurons prob-ably had their favourite parts of the trail and I suppose there were other parts of it they didn't like. Even by First Nations standards, The Toronto Carrying Place was a long portage, so anyone walking it would have plenty of time for contemplation.

Now that you mention it, I wonder what went through a Huron traveler's mind as he trod this path back in 1615?"

Brendan knew exactly what would have been going through their minds. He knew because he had just made a decision.

You see, if he had his life to live over again, Brendan would come back as an Iroquois warrior. He could think of no other life for which he was better suited. In his dream world, he considered himself more at home in deerskin and moccasins than in T-shirt and jeans. No other "Warrior of the Long House" was as soft-footed up and down the Toronto Portage as the boy's Iroquoian named alter ego, "Young Bear". Brendan was proud that he had come up with such a great nickname.

With those thoughts racing through his mind, Young Bear bolted ahead. Brendan's baseball cap went flying in the wind.

"Hey, where are you off to?" Linus shouted after him.

The young warrior veered off the path, stopped, turned, and drew his bow, sending an imaginary arrow aimed at his grandfather.

"*Iroquois!*" Linus cried out. "*Iroquois attack! Everybody take cover!*"

Wild war whoops pierced the air. It was a classic Iroquois surprise attack.

As soon as he had shot his arrow, Young Bear dove headfirst into the tall grass and remained motionless, which was very hard for the ever-active nine-year-old to do.

He dared not move a muscle. Meanwhile, Linus stood squinting into the sun.

The whole Humber Valley fell into a deep silence.

Young Bear was very pleased with himself. Yes, the attack had gone well, but regrettably there was one lone survivor and his dog. He knew he must deal with this approaching European interloper. He peeked through the long grass and saw the figure of the famous explorer the "Black Robes" called "Grandpere".

The old explorer made an inviting target. There had been so many stories told of this man around the lodge fire that he too, had been given an Iroquoian name out of respect. That did not mean however, that he was welcome on the Iroquois trail.

Grandpere sat down on a big boulder on the side of the trail to rest. From his vantage point in the tall grass, the young warrior studied the look of the old explorer. He watched as Grandpere took off his cap and wiped his forehead with his wrist. No wonder, Young Bear thought to himself, that the man's Iroquois name, translated into English, meant "Bald Eagle".

It was then that Young Bear's keen sense of smell alerted him to more important things. Grandpere had opened a bag of salt and vinegar potato chips. Horse was at his master's side in a shot. One ear was up; one was down.

Linus greeted his dog while munching happily on a chip. "There's no sign of Brendan, " he said. "The Iroquois must have captured him."

Horse stared at the bag of chips. He licked his lips in anticipation.

"Don't worry, Horse. I'm sure Brendan will be fine. The Iroquois often adopted their prisoners into the tribe."

But the hound wasn't interested in Brendan's life story. His eyes were fixed upon the bag of chips.

"Sorry, Horse, no human food for you," Grandpere said, thrusting his hand into his coat pocket, "but I do have some tasty dog biscuits you might like."

Back in the tall grass, watching the goings-on, was Young Bear. He was getting hungry. He could almost taste those chips. His stomach was beginning to rumble. His mouth was watering. He had to remind himself he was a disciplined warrior. His grandfather had told him that the Iroquois subsisted on fish and vegetables. He pondered that. There may be fish in the Humber, but that was a long way off. Nor were there any fields of squash or corn around. He didn't like fish and vegetables anyway. Young Bear would bet many beaver pelts that kind of 17th century diet wouldn't even be good for a young warrior.

How he longed to be back in the 21st century where the food was plentiful, salted, and deep-fried in pork fat.

He swallowed his pride and decided to turn himself in.

The boy-warrior emerged sheepishly from the tall grass.

"Maybe being an Iroquois warrior wasn't such a great idea," he admitted, as his grandfather offered him some chips.

"It was not an easy life back then for the indigenous people," his grandfather said. "It became even more difficult for them when the Europeans arrived."

Brendan realized he might have made a mistake. He now began to wonder if he was really suited for the life of Young Bear.

Maybe he needed more training.

He had to think about this.

But first the potato chips.

CHAPTER TWO

1784

Escape from the Mohawk Valley

"Loyal she began and Loyal she remains"
Motto of the Province of Ontario

"IT'S TAKEN ME EIGHTY YEARS, BRENDAN, BUT I'VE FINALLY FIG-
URED OUT HOW TO BOIL THE PERFECT EGG."

Linus and his grandson had started their day with a full
breakfast. Now they were driving east along the Loyalist
Highway on the north shore of the St. Lawrence River in the
comfort of their air-conditioned sedan. They were heading towards the Williamstown Fall Fair.

"You're sure a good cook, Grandpa. What's your secret
formula?"

"I boil the egg until the lid rattles, quickly turn off the stove
and then let it sit for fifteen minutes," Linus explained. "That's
the secret."

"That was a great breakfast," Brendan said. *"Was I ever
hungry!"*

"What do you usually have in the morning?"

"Mostly pepperoni and cheese sandwiches."

Linus visibly flinched. "Once we get to the fair, you'll see first
hand where bacon and eggs come from," he said.

"I *know* where bacon and eggs come from, Grandpa."

Sometimes his grandfather forgot that Brendan was getting
up in years. The boy was now nine.

20

Linus had wanted to take his grandson to an Ontario fall fair for a long time, and he knew that Williamstown was special. It would do the world of good for a city kid like Brendan to appreciate locally grown fresh food.

"We'll see chickens, pigs and cows and maybe buy some fruit and vegetables that are right off the farm," Linus said. "It's wonderful that we still have people making their living in agriculture."

"Why do we have to go all the way to Williamstown, Grandpa? Aren't there any fall fairs closer to where we live?"

"There are," Linus said, "but the one at Williamstown is the oldest. It's over two hundred years old."

"How did I know you would find out which one was the oldest?" Brendan asked, giving his grandfather a quick grin. He would have given Linus a pat on the back had he not been driving.

After arriving at the park, Linus and Brendan soon discovered how much an Ontario fall fair had to offer.

They sampled homemade pies, listened to old time fiddlers, admired prize winning pigs and watched a demonstration of sheep shearing. Brendan rode a pony and even had his face painted.

At one demonstration, a burly Glengarry County dairy farmer was showing children how to milk a goat. There were five or six girls, but not one boy lined up to give it a try.

"Why not have a go, Brendan? Have you ever milked a goat?"

"Not really," he answered, looking at the palms of his hands. "Can I take a rain check on that, Grandpa?"

"You're not going to let the girls get the better of you, are you?"

Brendan gave no reply, but stood watching their attempts at milking. One after another they came up empty. The big farmer gave each girl a polite smile.

Linus put his hand on the boy's shoulder. "Fortune never favoured the faint of heart, my boy."

Brendan took a deep breath and decided to face his fears.

Sir William Johnson, 1715-1774
Painted by John Wollaston in 1750.
Williamstown, Ontario, Johnstown, Ontario, Johnstown, New York and Fort
Johnson, New York are all named after him.

"I'll do it," he announced. He approached the stool, sat down and with everyone watching, began his work. The milk flowed like a river. The boy was a natural.

The farmer was ready to hire Brendan full time.

As the milk pail was quickly filling up, the boy glanced over to his grandfather with a concerned look on his face and asked, "Should I stop now?"

Linus shrugged. "That's a good question," he answered. He had no idea. He was a city boy too.

Then the big farmer came to the rescue with some wise words of advice. "You'd better ask the goat," he said.

Linus chuckled. "You can see for yourself just how much there is for us to learn here." They continued their leisurely stroll through the old fairgrounds.

"Here's another good question," Linus said. "Ever wonder how Williamstown was named?"

"Was it named after some guy named William?"

"It's actually a very interesting story," his grandfather said. "Let's sit down for a moment. I'd like to tell you about it."

They found a bench in the shade and Linus began his tale.

"I wonder how many people here today know that this town was named after Sir William Johnson."

"I bet not many," Brendan said. "Who was he?"

"Johnson was an Irishman, born in 1715. He immigrated to New York State as a young man and was given the chance of managing his uncle's large estate in the Mohawk Valley. A very enterprising young fellow by nature, he immediately began to trade with the Iroquois, who also lived in the valley."

"He was probably a fur trader," Brendan suggested.

"William traded in all sorts of goods," replied Linus, "but the important thing was that he was determined to be fair in all his dealings with the Six Nations. Even as a young man, he was mature enough to understand that all trade is based on trust."

"That's pretty good."

"Not all traders were honest with the Iroquois in those frontier days, Brendan. While many tried to put one over on them if they could, Johnson respected them. The Iroquois rewarded

William's friendship by adopting him into their tribe."

"Was he *really* adopted by the Iroquois?" the nine-year-old asked, still very much interested in resuming his life as an Iroquois warrior himself.

"Yes, he was. Johnson and his family always remained close to the Iroquois," Linus said. "With many successful commercial activities on the go, William became a very wealthy man. In 1749, he built Fort Johnson, a great stone house in the Mohawk Valley that still stands today. His growing influence amongst the Six Nations people was brought to the attention of the Governor of New York State, who appointed him Colonel of the Iroquois Confederacy."

"Was that like a war chief?" asked Brendan, admiring Johnson more and more.

"That's a good way to put it. Johnson actually became one in 1755. At the height of the Seven Years War, lacking any formal military training, he was given command of an army of provincial troops and Iroquois warriors. It was most unusual for the British to have a man lead one of their armies into battle who had never been a soldier."

"Then why did they do it?"

"I think they recognized a natural leader when they saw one and Johnson proved them right. His army defeated the French in a critical battle at Crown Point in New York State, and he was knighted for his victory."

"So did he move here and they named the town after him or something?"

"The town *is* named after him, but Sir William Johnson never set foot here," answered Linus.

"Well, there must be *some* reason they named it after him," persisted the boy.

"There was," his grandfather agreed. "One very hot day in 1774, Sir William gave a four-hour speech at a Six Nation conference.

After concluding it, he keeled over and was dead at the age of fifty-nine."

"*Dead?*" Brendan asked, taken by surprise with that ending. "They didn't name the place after him just because he was dead, did they?"

"There's more to the story of course," Linus went on. "Sir William's only son, on the death of his father, immediately inherited 200,000 acres of land. Think of the size of that inheritance! The Johnson Estate was by far the largest landholding in the Mohawk Valley."

"*Two hundred thousand acres!*" the boy exclaimed. He wasn't sure how much land that was, but it sure sounded *huge*.

"William's son also inherited a great deal of responsibility."

"What was the son's name?"

"Sir John Johnson."

"Sir John Johnson?" repeated Brendan. "That's not very original."

"After the death of his father, Sir John became very concerned about the state of affairs between the British government and the colonists," Linus continued. "King George had been very unpopular and the colonies complained bitterly about the taxes he had imposed on them to pay off the debt following the Seven Years War. The despised Stamp Tax of 1765 incited rioting which soon escalated into open rebellion."

"I don't know that much about the American Revolution," the fifth-grade pupil said. "All I know is that George Washington never told a lie."

"The rebels were led by some very prominent men such as Washington, Benjamin Franklin, John Adams and Thomas Jefferson," Linus said. "You know, I've often wondered why such great men as that, couldn't have peacefully negotiated a good case for independence with their British counterparts instead of resorting to eight years of warfare."

"Do you mean they were wrong to want their independence?" Brendan asked, thinking that independence was something worth fighting for.

Linus scratched his head, giving that question some thought. "No, not wrong," he answered. "The Thirteen Colonies had matured and certainly needed their own constitution. Nevertheless, a large number of American colonists, many critical of the King, still preferred to remain under the crown. There's no question the politics was handled badly by the leaders of both sides."

"So whose side are you on, anyway?"

"I'm only asking why the colonists couldn't be granted full independence and still remain connected to the crown."

"Could that have happened?"

"I don't know. I wasn't living back then."

"Are you sure about that?" asked Brendan, giving his grandfather a gentle pat on the back.

"But can you imagine how history might have changed, had both sides sat down and worked out some practical solutions to their differences?"

"It probably would have."

"Like his father, Sir John Johnson was loyal to the crown," Linus went on. "In 1776, he was forced to escape to Canada after his Mohawk Valley property was confiscated by the rebels. Following Mohawk friends, Sir John, along with two hundred and fifty of his Scottish tenants, trekked through the Adirondack Mountains, finally arriving near present day Cornwall, Ontario. The arduous nineteen-day journey, with little food or shelter, was made even more difficult as the group was forced to travel by seldom used back routes to avoid Washington's scouts."

Brendan considered their plight. "I still think the colonists deserved their independence, but I don't think people should lose their homes just because other people don't agree with them."

Linus agreed. "With the loss of his great estate, Sir John Johnson had found out how difficult life could be for those branded as 'Tories'," he said. "He fought back from a base in Montreal by raising a regiment named 'The Royal Yorkers'. This military unit was made up of men who had fled the Mohawk Valley. Joining forces with the Mohawks under their war chief, Joseph Brant, they raided the valley and destroyed rebel barns and mills."

"You mean they fought the people that used to be their neighbours?"

"It must have been horrible to go to war against your neighbour and fight him in hand-to-hand combat"

Brendan shuddered. "They really did that?"

"It was a long and brutal civil war. The bitterness would remain with both sides for generations."

"I never knew it was that bad," said the boy.

"After the redcoats were defeated by the Colonial Army at the Battle of Saratoga in 1777, the French entered the war on the American side. The British formally recognized the United States of America as an independent country with the signing of the Treaty of Versailles in 1783. That was followed by a Loyalist exodus to Canada."

"I still don't understand why this place is named after Sir William Johnson if he never lived here," Brendan said.

"Sir John Johnson settled the Royal Yorkers along here with their families in 1784 and he named the town after his father," Linus said.

"So that's why."

"Sir John helped to get the town started by building a great manor house, sawmill and a gristmill," Linus said. "He also gave the townspeople twelve acres of land to be used for an agricultural fair and it's been going strong ever since."

"That's a pretty good story, Grandpa. Now I know why you said this fall fair was the oldest."

"I wonder how many people know that the first settlements

along the north shore of Lake Ontario began in 1784, with men, women, boys and girls from New York State, who had left their farms in the Mohawk Valley? In 1791, this settled area along the St. Lawrence was sufficiently populated to become a province. It has been known by several names over the years—Canada West, Upper Canada—but we know it as Ontario."

"What about the Iroquois?" the boy asked, always personally interested in that great race of warriors. "So what happened to them?"

Linus was always sensitive about giving bad news to Brendan. "I'm afraid that European conflicts such as the Seven Years War and the American Revolution dreadfully reduced the Iroquois by war and disease," he answered. "The Six Nations Confederacy, having survived for more than three hundred years, had now broken apart. The Oneida and the Tuscarora had supported the rebel cause; the ancestral lands of the Iroquois in the State of New York now became part of the new Republic."

Brendan was saddened to hear this. "Where did the Iroquois go?" he asked. "Did they settle here too?"

"Joseph Brant settled his Loyalist warriors on land along the Grand River," answered his grandfather.

"I just wondered because one of my ancestors settled his regiment somewhere around here too," the boy said in a matter of fact way.

"I never heard about an ancestor of yours being a Loyalist. Who was he?"

"Well, he never liked publicity, so nobody knows too much about him," Brendan answered, sounding suspiciously evasive.

"What was his name?" Linus persisted, very skeptical of the authenticity of Brendan's Loyalist ancestor.

"Sir Brendan Brendanson," answered the boy. "He led his regiment up here to a place they called Brendanstown, and they lived in peace happily ever after."

"How could they live in peace when the American Revolution wasn't over?"

"It wasn't? I thought you said the treaty was signed and everything and the colonists won."

"They did," answered Linus. "That was the first part of the American Revolution. The second part hadn't started yet."

"The second part?" asked Brendan, with disbelief. "I never heard of a second part."

"Well, it's true. They all fought again—Loyalists, Iroquois, redcoats and the American Army—even Sir John Johnson was involved. You may have heard the second part referred to by a different name."

"I have?"

"Yes. The War of 1812"

CHAPTER THREE

1 8 1 3

⚜

The Capture of Johnny McGinnis

"There's a deepened faith in the autumn glow,
When October's sun is sinking low,"
—M.J. Shiels, *Autumn Moods*

LINUS WAS SO EXCITED THAT MORNING HE DECIDED TO MAKE HIMSELF ANOTHER PIECE OF TOAST.

He had just received important information from his researcher in England and he couldn't wait to tell his grandson.

When Brendan arrived, the boy wondered what all the fuss was about. He knew that his grandfather had been tracing his family tree, but he was acting as if he had won the lottery.

"I have news about my great-great-great-grandfather," Linus announced, standing in the kitchen in front of his toaster and counting out the number of 'greats' on his fingers. "His name was John McGinnis and I just found out he was captured and taken prisoner. This is *wonderful* news."

"How much coffee have you had today, Grandpa?" the boy asked, thinking that a letter announcing the capture of a relative was not something to brag about.

"Only one cup," Linus said, as he fumbled with the twister on his loaf of bread. "I just found out he was captured on October 5, 1813. Do you know what that means?"

"Was he a highwayman or something like that?"

"October 5, 1813, is one of the most famous dates in Canadian history," Linus said, holding up one of his documents. "That means he fought in the Battle of the Thames."

"He did?"

"That was a tragic Canadian story. That was the day that Tecumseh was killed."

"He was an Indian warrior, wasn't he?"

"Tecumseh was the great Shawnee warrior who made one last, brave attempt to unite the western tribes," replied his grandfather. "It all ended for him at the Battle of the Thames."

"So Johnny fought with Tecumseh?" asked Brendan. "Is that what you mean?"

"Yes, John McGinnis fought in that battle as a private with the 41st Regiment. It's very interesting to read about him. The letter says he was born in Armagh, Ireland, in 1762."

"*In 1762?*" exclaimed the boy. "That's sure a long time ago."

"That would make him an old man of over fifty years of age when he was captured."

"We should call him 'Pops'," Brendan suggested.

"It also meant he was only fifteen years old when he first enlisted."

"Was he a drummer boy or something like that?"

"It says here that he enlisted in Ireland with the 32nd Regiment as a private in 1777."

"That's really young to join the army, isn't it?"

"It sure is," agreed his grandfather. "He was paid eight guineas to sign up, which was a lot of money then."

Brendan grinned. "Eight guinea pigs?"

"A guinea was a *coin*, Brendan, not a pig," Linus said, shaking his head. "Eight guineas would be a year's salary for an unskilled labourer. That was a very good wage back in 1777." Linus opened his atlas to a map of Ireland to explain more of the story. "When Johnny first joined, his regiment was stationed in Dublin, Ireland, but in 1783, when it was ordered to Gibraltar,

Johnny resigned from the army and returned home. It seems he was employed as a weaver in Ireland for a long time and then for some reason he decided to enlist again in 1798."

"I wonder why he changed his mind about being in the army."

"Maybe he had a hard time supporting his family as a weaver," his grandfather suggested. "Times were difficult in Ireland back then. It doesn't mention his wife, but he had two boys: William and John."

"But somehow he ended up in the War of 1812," Brendan said.

"My researcher says in his letter that a battalion of the 41st Regiment of Foot was being raised in 1798 for a long tour of duty in Upper Canada. That assignment must have appealed to him because Johnny signed up with the regiment at Cork, Ireland as a private. They sailed on the transport *Asia* to Canada the following year."

"What happened to his sons?" asked Brendan. "Did he leave them behind?"

"In those days, families often traveled with the army," answered Linus. "Johnny was allowed to take his two sons with him. It mentions that he was in charge of one of the guns on the ship. Maybe his sons had been given some minor duties too, although I'm sure they all wished they had stayed home. The *Asia* had a terrible ocean voyage."

"What happened?"

"There had been an epidemic of smallpox on board. Some contaminated blankets had been brought onto the ship at Cork and the disease spread. They couldn't contain the outbreak and thirty-four people died on the crossing."

"Couldn't anybody save them?"

"They didn't have the medical knowledge we have today," Linus said quietly, "When the *Asia* finally docked in Quebec on

October 20, 1799, Johnny must have been very thankful that he and his two boys had all survived the crossing. From Quebec they continued on to Kingston."

Linus moved his finger in a circling motion on the map of Ontario. "Now the men of the 41st would have to get used to a new way of life in Upper Canada and their new posting."

"But at least there weren't any wars going on, were there?"

"There had been no wars, but a long period of bitterness between the United States and Britain had festered since the end of the American Revolution. Another trouble spot was in the Old Northwest, where American settlers were pushing hard for additional land and the native tribes were pushing back. It seemed to be only a matter of time before war would break out. You can tell that this story wasn't going to have a happy ending."

"I bet it was Tecumseh who was leading the Indians," Brendan said.

"Yes, Tecumseh was very active during this time," Linus replied. "He was primarily traveling throughout the Northwest in a quest to establish a confederacy of all the western tribes."

"I guess he wanted them all to join up to fight the settlers."

"Yes, the big issue for them was the ownership of their land."

"It sounds like there's going to be a lot of Indian attacks."

"The Old Northwest was like a coiled spring," Linus said. "I'm sure that Johnny and the other redcoats had no idea how serious the situation was."

"You mean that they didn't know the War of 1812 was around the corner?"

"Remember this was in 1799. Johnny and the rest of the redcoats of the 41st had just arrived in Upper Canada and wouldn't have been aware of all the forces at play in their new home. They would have been more concerned about the bad news they had just received from Britain."

"What bad news was that?"

Tecumseh

The Battle of the Thomas on October 5, 1813 ended the life of Tecumseh, the great Shawnee warrior, who had tried one last time to unite the western tribes.

"Britain was now at war with Napoleon. The British Army would be stretched to the limit for the next fifteen years."

"Gee, Grandpa, thanks for getting Johnny so depressed and he's hardly off the ship yet."

"It didn't turn out too badly for them at first. The Old Northwest might be a powder keg, but there were still many years of uninterrupted peace after his arrival in Canada."

"So what did Johnny do if there was no fighting going on?"

"The redcoats were always building things. They built block-houses, forts, military roads, canals and long flat bottomed boats called bateaux which they used for transporting men and supplies."

"But, I mean what do you think he did for *fun*?"

"Being from Ireland, I think he would have enjoyed traditional folk music," Linus answered. "There would have been many talented Irish fiddlers in the 41st regiment."

"Do you think Johnny played the fiddle?"

Linus didn't think so. "I see him instead as sitting back, listening to the music and smoking his clay pipe. That's how I think he liked to relax."

"I bet they didn't have that much fun back then."

"Probably because their regiment always had to be prepared for battle," Linus agreed. "They never knew when the call might come. There was one very serious diplomatic incident which almost brought the United States and Britain to war in 1807. Britain was desperately short of sailors in her war with Napoleon and was determined to apprehend any man who jumped ship. On June 22, 1807, HMS *Leopard* attacked the U.S. frigate *Chesapeake* and the crew seized several alleged deserters on board. One they hanged."

"Were they allowed to do that?"

"No, that was a reckless thing to do. Everyone wondered if that would cause a war."

"Why would they wonder about that?" Brendan said with a shrug of his shoulders. "Nobody's ever heard of the War of 1807."

Linus smiled patiently. "Well, it *was* a little early, but war was coming nonetheless. The hostility between Britain and the United States was escalating, and the situation in the Northwest was not improving."

"That's where Tecumseh was."

"Yes, he and his brother had built a great village on the Tippecanoe River. While the great Shawnee was away on a mission, the forces of William Harrison, the Governor of the Indiana Territory, attacked Tippecanoe with one thousand riflemen and burned it to the ground."

Brendan shook his head. "You're right about this story not having a happy ending."

"Events happened very quickly after Tippecanoe. Tecumseh immediately crossed the border with four hundred followers to fight beside the British."

"Is that when the War of 1812 started?"

"Yes," answered Linus. "The 41st Regiment had just completed its twelve-year posting and was about to return home. However, if Johnny thought he was going to be seeing Ireland any time soon, he was sadly mistaken. War with the United States was declared and the 41st would have to stay and fight. General Brock, who was in charge of the military defenses of Upper Canada, intended to use that regiment as his core fighting unit."

"What happened to Johnny's sons? Were they going to fight too?"

"His sons had returned to Ireland in 1807 to enlist in the 58th Regiment. They were both part of Wellington's army in the campaign against the French."

"You mean the war against Napoleon?"

"That's the one."

"I guess the last thing the redcoats needed was a war with the United States at the same time."

"They had their hands full," Linus agreed. "Johnny never saw Ireland again. His brave regiment was in almost every major battle in the War of 1812."

"Was Johnny in all those battles?"

"There may have been others, but we only have a record of

his being in two. This letter I received from England states that Johnny took part in the raid on the American naval depot at Black Rock, New York, on July 11, 1813."

"What happened there?"

"A company of the 41st crossed the Niagara River below Squaw Island and destroyed the blockhouses. Much needed flour, salt and pork were seized and loaded onto their boats. Just as they were leaving, American reinforcements arrived and opened fire. Johnny was on the last boat and was wounded in the left shoulder."

"I guess that kept him out of action for a while."

"Yes, but as soon as his wound healed, Johnny was sent to Fort Detroit to join the rest of his regiment. This was a critical area of the war. Detroit was a key fort, captured by Brock only a year before. It was garrisoned by the 41st Regiment, under Colonel Henry Proctor."

"Is that where Tecumseh was?"

"Tecumseh was using Fort Detroit as his base. He had been sent by Proctor to make frequent raids deep into Ohio and the Michigan Territory. However, all raiding stopped abruptly late in 1813 when Proctor received some very bad news."

"What was it?"

"Word was received that an American fleet, under Commodore Perry, had defeated the British fleet, under Captain Barclay, on Lake Erie. This was a *huge* loss. It meant the supply line to Fort Detroit was severed. The fort was now totally isolated. Colonel Proctor was forced to make a difficult decision. Would he stay and fight or would he evacuate the fort?"

"I guess it would depend on how big the army was that was going to attack him," Brendan suggested.

"Don't forget he had lost his supply line," Linus reminded him. "Even the smallest army can beat you if you run out of food and ammunition."

Brendan reconsidered his strategy. "Maybe they *should* try to get away," he said.

"The Army of the North West, commanded by Governor Harrison, was advancing to Detroit. Colonel Proctor came to the conclusion that he had no choice but to evacuate the fort. Tecumseh was totally against the decision, but finally agreed to accompany the 41st along with his followers and their families up the Thames. They knew they couldn't out run them. At some point they would have to make a stand against the American army. Harrison had thirty-five hundred men, which included a strong regiment of one thousand Kentucky Mounted Riflemen."

"Was that the cavalry?"

"Yes," Linus said. "It was made up of tough mounted frontiersmen; heavily armed veterans who could fight on any terrain. Harrison's army crossed into Canada and it didn't take them long to catch up to Tecumseh and the redcoats."

"They could smell blood," Brendan said.

"It was a sad ending," Linus said. "The Battle of the Thames took place on an early October day on the banks of the Thames River, near present day Chatham. After enduring a ten-day march, Proctor's rag tag army was in bad shape. They had gone without food for two days, lacked ammunition and supplies and were outnumbered three to one. Morale was poor."

Brendan shook his head sadly. "They're going to lose," he said, knowing how badly the story was going to end.

"In spite of this, Johnny and the rest of the 41st formed a long line across the field. Tecumseh and his warriors took up the right on the edge of a great swamp and prepared to receive the enemy."

"I would have been scared if I was one of those guys," Brendan said. "I wouldn't want to have to face a cavalry charge, that's for sure."

"What must have been going through Johnny's mind as he

gazed across that field and saw more than one thousand mounted riflemen in blue hunting jackets forming up?" Linus asked.

Brendan shivered at the thought. "My heart would be pounding, that's all I know," he answered.

"This would be no time for a veteran like Johnny to show fear," said Linus. "I'd like to think that as the cavalry began their charge, the two younger redcoats on either side of him heard old Johnny say quietly in his Irish brogue 'Steady on, boys'."

" 'Steady on'," Brendan repeated quietly to himself as he imagined a thousand blue jackets galloping boldly towards him.

"The Battle of the Thames was a one-sided affair," Linus said. "After one volley by the 41st, it was all over. Some accounts say that over six hundred redcoats and officers were killed, wounded or fell into the hands of the enemy. Johnny was immediately captured. Proctor got away, but Tecumseh and many of the native allies were killed."

"It sounds like Proctor's army was pulverized," the boy said sadly.

"The stand-up volley system of the redcoats might have worked in Europe, but not here," Linus said, sounding very displeased with the redcoats' tactics. "I'm afraid the 41st needed to be faster and use less conventional tactics against this type of enemy."

Brendan knew exactly what was wrong with the British strategy. "They should have fought more like ninjas."

"Yes, their red coats made them easy targets. The 41st should never have dressed like that in the wilderness of Upper Canada."

"And the important ones should never have worn white wigs," Brendan added for good measure.

"Nonetheless, we owe the men who fought that day a big debt."

"At least Johnny survived," Brendan said, "even though he

was taken prisoner."

"When the war was over, Johnny was released from a prisoner of war camp in Ohio, returned to Upper Canada and retired on an army pension of a shilling a day," Linus said.

"The sad part was that Tecumseh was killed."

"His body was never found," Linus said. "It was the end of his dream of a 'Great Indian Alliance'. Tecumseh has gone down in Canadian history as a great warrior and a great man."

"What became of Colonel Proctor?"

"History has never viewed Proctor in a favourable light after his defeat at the Thames," answered Linus, "although this might be unfair to him."

Brendan shrugged. "Why would it be unfair?" he asked. "He lost the battle, didn't he?"

"It wasn't his fault the British fleet had been defeated on Lake Erie a month earlier." Linus answered. "That had been a bitter blow to Proctor. He suddenly found himself in a very precarious position. I think he was right to leave Detroit, but the retreat was extremely difficult. He had to keep his alliance with Tecumseh intact. There were many native dependents to be evacuated. I'm beginning to think that perhaps Henry Proctor did the very best he could under trying circumstances."

"Maybe you're right," Brendan admitted, after giving it some thought. "I guess it was a tough spot to be in." The boy then stood and drew himself up to his full height. "Don't worry, General," he said, in his best parade square voice. "We will regroup."

He then threw Linus a crisp salute and added, "This war can still be won."

CHAPTER FOUR

1814

The Story of the Great Anchor

And of a beautiful island with limestone cliffs

"IT'S WONDERFUL TO READ ABOUT CANADIAN HISTORY, BRENDAN, BUT THERE'S NOTHING BETTER THAN SEEING IT BEFORE YOUR VERY EYES," HIS GRANDFATHER SAID.

They were both staring at the Great Anchor of Upper Canada in Anchor Park, in the old village of Holland Landing, Ontario.

Never had Brendan seen an anchor that size before. "It's *huge*," he said. "It must weigh a ton."

"Two tons to be exact," corrected Linus. "That's why it's called 'The Great Anchor'."

Brendan was admiring all the names that had been carved into the shank of the anchor over the years. He also noticed a series of numbers: 35-3-0 etched into the arm. "What do those numbers mean?"

"That's the anchor's weight in hundredweights, quarter-weights and pounds."

"That sounds really heavy," replied Brendan, who really didn't know too much about the old kind of measurement.

Linus pointed to another inscription on the anchor. "This is the official stamp of the naval dockyard in Chatham, England, where it was forged early in the 1800's."

"That's where it was made?" the nine-year-old asked, taking a closer look.

"Yes, it was shipped from England when the War of 1812 broke out."

"But how did it end up here?"

"It's a very interesting story how that happened," Linus said, running his hand along the cold metal. "The Great Anchor was taken off a ship in Quebec City, sent to Kingston by barge and then on to Toronto. Legend has it that it arrived in Muddy York, as Toronto was then known, on the very day that General Isaac Brock was killed at Queenston Heights."

"And then what happened to it?"

"It remained in York for a while, but I think we're getting ahead of our story. Do you remember what I told you about the opening days of the War of 1812?"

"You told me all about Tecumseh and Brock and Johnny McGinnis and some of the battles they were in."

"And that General Brock was the commanding officer in charge of the defense of Upper Canada?"

"Sure—I remember all that."

"Brock was expecting the invasion of a large American army at some weak point along the border and he knew he didn't have enough redcoats to hold them off. He felt most vulnerable on his right flank."

"What was he going to do about it?"

"The United States held two key western forts which Brock wanted."

"What forts?"

"Detroit and Michilimackinac."

Brendan thought that second name was a mouthful. "Well, you told me all about the fort at Detroit, but I've never even heard of Michili...what?"

"Michili-mack-in-aw," Linus said, pronouncing the name very slowly.

"Where's that place?"

MACKINAOK, FROM ROUND ISLAND.[4]

Fort Michilimackinac, as it must have looked to Captain Edward Collier of the HMS Niagara on June 2, 1815. It was built by the British in 1781 on a beautiful island with limestone cliffs.

"It's 400 miles from Detroit at the juncture of Lake Huron and Lake Michigan," Linus answered, "Michilimackinac was a famous fur trading post. The original fort, on the mainland, had been built by the French in 1715, but after Quebec fell, was surrendered to the British. The British thought that location was not well protected so they decided to build a new fort."

"Somewhere else?"

"In 1781, they decided to build offshore, on a beautiful island with limestone cliffs. They held it until it was awarded to the United States after the American Revolution. When the War of 1812 broke out, the American army had a small garrison stationed there."

"So it wasn't a very big fort, you mean?"

"No, it wasn't very big, but it was one of the most important forts in North America. If Brock could get his hands on it, he would immediately gain considerable influence in the whole region."

"So it was a pretty important fort to get?"

"Because of its strategic position, it was the centre of the fur trade," Linus said. "It's had a wonderful history. The good thing is that the old fort still exists. It's an historical site today."

"Even after all these years?"

"It's located in the State of Michigan."

"Sounds like it was a long way away from everything, back then, I mean," the boy said.

"It was very remote," Linus agreed. "The men serving at Michilimackinac thought they were at the end of the world."

"It must have been a hard place to get to."

Linus nodded in agreement. "Only a very good pilot could get a ship in and out of there."

"So what happened when war was declared?"

"Brock immediately dispatched Captain Charles Roberts, who commanded the small outpost on St. Joseph Island on Lake Huron, to Michilimackinac, which was forty-five miles away. Together with a force of Sioux, Ojibway, Ottawa and Menominee, Roberts and his redcoats slipped onto the island fort without being seen and captured it without firing a shot."

"*Without firing a shot?*" asked Brendan. "That wasn't much of a battle."

"It turned out to be one of the most important battles in the War of 1812," Linus said.

"Then how come the American soldiers didn't fight back?"

"They hadn't received word that war had been declared," answered Linus. "The garrison was completely surprised."

"They should have had *somebody* on guard, though. It *was* a fort, remember."

"It was a great moral victory for Brock," Linus said. "Michilimackinac guarded the fur trade and he needed native warriors in his front lines to help in the defense of Upper Canada. Hoisting the Union Jack atop Michilimackinac was a critical factor in gaining the support of the First Nations."

"Did the warriors agree to help Brock?"

"They did," his grandfather answered. "Now that Roberts had captured Michilimackinac, many of the western tribes threw in their lot with the redcoats."

"Maybe they figured the redcoats would win the war now that they had won that fort," the boy suggested.

"Not only that, Brendan, but a month after taking Michilimackinac, Brock and Tecumseh captured Detroit as well. Everything was going as planned for the redcoats. Brock was now in possession of the two forts that he needed."

"Detroit was the fort that Colonel Proctor had to give up, wasn't it?"

"Yes, they *did* lose Detroit. It fell about a year later, but the important thing was that the redcoats held onto Michilimackinac for the remainder of the war. Losing that island fort would prove to be very costly to the Americans."

"It meant they wouldn't win the War of 1812—is that what you mean?"

"That's right, because without Michilimackinac, they would never be able to support an occupying army in Upper Canada."

"Then they must have tried pretty hard to get that fort back."

"They came very close to recapturing it a couple of times."

"What happened?"

"In July of 1814, the Americans landed an invasion force on the island."

"But they didn't capture it?"

"No, although the British and Native forces were very much outnumbered, they held the high ground and drove the attackers from the island."

"That's pretty good."

"But the Americans never gave up. They knew how important it was to win it back."

"So what did they do next?"

"On August 14, 1814, the Royal Navy's last remaining ship on the Upper Lake's, the schooner *Nancy*, was sunk in the Nottawasaga River by a small American fleet. Captain Worsley and his crew were safe, but the gallant *Nancy* was lost. That meant that American ships could now sail without fear of being attacked. Two American schooners, the *Tigress* and the *Scorpion* remained on Lake Huron and set up a blockade on Michilimackinac."

"What does that mean?"

"A blockade is a military strategy. The two American ships were positioned not only to intercept essential supplies going into Michilimackinac, but also to prevent brigades of Nor' Westers from taking their pelts to Montreal. This could have an important bearing on the outcome of the war. You see, Brendan, Canada's economy at that time was dependent on the fur trade, so you can imagine what the economic consequences would be if the voyageurs hadn't been able to get their furs through."

Brendan always loved to hear about the voyageurs. How he admired those adventurers! With visions of brigades of Nor' Westers swirling in his head, it occurred to him that he would look very smart with a toque on his head, a red sash around his waist and wearing a pair of deerskin leggings.

"Actually, I wouldn't mind being a voyageur," he confided to his grandfather, ignoring for the moment his loyalty to the Iroquois, who had adopted him in 1615. "I think it would be a great job."

"I'm sure you'd make a very good Nor' Wester, Brendan."

The boy saw himself as one of those daring young men in canoes. "Call me Jean-Brendan Batice," said the young would-be Quebecer.

"You *do* look like a young voyageur," Linus observed.

"I just need a canoe," Jean-Brendan said.

"I think I have an old paddle in the attic," Linus said. "We can look for it later. Right now I want to tell you why the American ships never intercepted any voyageurs."

"I bet it was because the voyageurs were too fast for them."

"Actually, the reason was the decisiveness of Lieutenant Miller Worsley, who was the Captain of the *Nancy*. He, along with his crew, a company of Royal Newfoundland Fencibles, and several hundred native warriors, silently paddled their canoes toward one of the schooners which were blockading the fort. After a short exchange of gunfire, Worsley's men boarded the *Tigress* and captured her in a short battle."

"Good," said Brendan. "That's one ship out of the way."

"But that's not all," Linus said. "Worsley left the Stars and Stripes flying on the *Tigress*, and waited patiently for the *Scorpion* to make her appearance. As soon as he saw her approaching, he allowed the *Tigress* to drift toward it. The captain of the *Scorpion* didn't suspect an ambush. He thought the *Tigress* was still in American hands. Within minutes, the second ship was boarded and she too, was Worsley's." Linus took a deep breath. "Those naval captains of 1812 were certainly bold men."

"That's a *great* story, Grandpa."

"Michilimackinac was relieved, but it was *still* isolated," Linus went on. "The British had learned how critical control of the Upper Lakes had become. Having almost lost their key fort, they were determined never to let that happen again."

"How were they going to do that?"

"In November of 1814, the British Admiralty assigned Edward Collier, captain of HMS *Niagara* to establish a new naval base at Penetanguishene on Georgian Bay."

Linus loved the old naval stories of the Napoleonic era. He gazed off into the distance. "I've often wondered what it would be like to walk in the shoes of a man like Edward Collier," he said.

"Because of the great captain's uniforms they wore back then?" Brendan asked.

"I was thinking more of the responsibility that he had," Linus explained.

"So that new base was going to protect Michilimackinac somehow?" Brendan asked, taking great pains to pronounce the name of the fort correctly. "Is that what you mean?"

"Yes, the base would link York with the old Northwest and protect the fort. Captain Collier's first order of business was the construction of a forty-four-gun frigate at the new dockyard and to arrange transport of men, cannon, equipment and supplies from the town of York up the newly-built Penetanguishene Road."

"I bet Captain Collier sent for the Great Anchor," suggested Brendan.

"He did indeed," Linus said. "In the early months of 1815, the Great Anchor was placed on a sleigh by two teamsters and pulled up Yonge Street by twelve oxen to the new dockyard at Penetanguishene. Can you imagine the effort it took them to do that?"

"That would be really hard," said the boy. "Look how heavy it is."

"It never made it to Penetanguishene, of course. By the time the anchor reached Soldiers Bay, near the village of Holland Landing, the two teamsters finally heard the news that the war was over."

"You mean they were the last to know?"

"The Treaty of Ghent had been signed on Christmas Eve of 1814," explained Linus. "The War of 1812 officially ended in a draw, but it took months before the news reached the men who were doing the actual fighting. The story goes that the teamsters were so happy to be told the war had ended, the two of them dropped the anchor in a field and headed to the village pub to celebrate."

"And I bet they're still celebrating," Brendan said, with a grin. "I would be if I didn't have to drag the anchor anymore."

"Well, I don't know what happened to the two teamsters, but the anchor sat in the field for almost sixty years."

"*Sixty years?* Then what happened to it?"

"Then an enterprising fellow named John McKay bought it from the farmer who owned the land. McKay intended to bring it to Toronto as a tourist attraction. Rather than let it go to Toronto, the good townsfolk of Holland Landing decided to keep it. In 1870, they purchased the anchor from McKay and delivered it to this location. Anchor Park was built around it."

"So the anchor was never actually in any battles in the War of 1812?"

"It never even got on board," Linus said. "The forty-four-gun frigate was never completed. Construction on it was stopped in February of 1815, when the war ended."

"To think the anchor's still here after all these years," Brendan said.

Linus stood back and looked admiringly at it. "That's the important thing. The Great Anchor remains with us today as one of our most enduring symbols of the War of 1812."

EPILOGUE

On June 2, 1815, a young voyageur was at the dockside looking for Captain Collier of the Royal Navy.

"Captain Collier?" he inquired, approaching a grandfatherly looking man in a splendid naval uniform. The officer had been supervising a party of seamen who were loading supplies onto a gunboat. He turned toward the young Quebecer and offered his hand.

"You're Jean-Brendan Batice, are you not?" the captain replied. "I've been looking for you."

"How may I help you?"

"HMS *Niagara* leaves in the morning on an important mission, my boy, and I want you with me."

"To which port of call, sir?"

"First to Detroit," the captain answered, "and then on to Michilimackinac. We must hand the old fort back I'm afraid, and our garrison must be relocated."

"I'm sorry to hear that."

"I am too—Treaty of Ghent and all that, you see."

"What do you want me to do, Captain?" Batice asked.

"We have a long way to go and the voyage through the straits to Michilimackinac is treacherous, as you well know," explained Collier. "There's fog, mist, rocks, reefs and an endless number of little islands. I need a good pilot with me who can navigate those waters. You'll be well paid, of course."

The young voyageur answered with a salute.

They shook hands once again.

A partnership was sealed; the *Niagara* set sail the next morning on a long voyage.

On July 18, 1815, the little island that saved a country was formally handed over to Colonel Butler of the United States Army.

1 8 2 1

Isabella's Lamp

"We thank thee for the sacrifice
Of daring men of old,
For faith to cross unchartered seas,
For dreams to make men bold;
For saintly men and pioneers,
For all who served their age,
And left for us who follow on
A sacred heritage."
—Mary S. Edgar, 1927

THERE HAD BEEN A POWER FAILURE AT LINUS' HOUSE. This happened during one of his grandson's visits.

Both Linus and Brendan sat helplessly in the dark for an hour. Horse, the very sensible basset hound, simply climbed onto the chesterfield, snuggled into the afghan and slept through the whole thing.

"I want to be ready the next time this happens," Linus said. "As soon as the lights are back on, I'm going to look for my old oil lamp and repair it. I think it's been pushed to the back of one of my kitchen shelves."

"I wish we had it now," the boy said, experiencing life without electricity for the first time. "This is boring. We can't *do* anything."

"We just have to be patient," Linus said.

"The worst part is that I can't even watch TV," grumbled the boy.

When the power was eventually restored and the lights went on, the first thing that Linus did was to locate his old lamp. "This is what our pioneers used before we had electricity, Brendan. It wouldn't hurt us to be more self sufficient and go back to how we did things in the past. We're too pampered today."

"I can go without light and I can go without heat," the nine-year-old announced dramatically, "but I can't give up my favourite television shows."

"None of us likes to give up our comforts," his grandfather agreed, "And we all have them, don't we?"

"I guess mine would be TV and yours would be coffee," Brendan said, noticing another half-empty mug on the table.

"I should cut down," agreed Linus. "If Isabella Hughes was alive today, I doubt she'd be impressed how dependent we are on things like coffee and television. She was the lady that owned this lamp."

"It looks really old."

"I'm told it's from the 1870's," his grandfather said.

"How'd you get it?"

"Before the war, business took me frequently between Toronto and Ottawa. I always stopped in the little village of Innisville at lunchtime for a sandwich. A lady named Mrs. McLaren ran a general store on the main street. She was a tall, middle-aged woman who always wore a white apron. *Everything* was sold in that store: newspapers, pots, pans, pails, boots, work-gloves and groceries. There were even overalls for sale hanging from the ceiling. On the glass counter, she had several jars of penny candies filled with jelly beans, licorice pipes and gum."

"I like that place already," Brendan said, with visions of jars of candies swirling in his imagination.

"Behind the counter there was an old pot-bellied stove, and

the floor was the creakiest I've ever walked on." Linus thought back to that simpler era. "I loved that old country store."

"Like a convenience store today," his grandson suggested, "except for the creaky floors, I guess."

"And I became a very good customer," Linus said.

Isabella Hughes (1809-1911) and her son Robert, who took over his father's blacksmith shop at the age of 15 and carried on the business for another fifty years. Photo circa 1863.

"Just like you are still at the convenience store, Grandpa. Isn't that where you buy all your coffee?"

"Well...some coffee, but I remember Mrs. McLaren sold coffee too."

"Did she sell you the lamp?" Brendan asked. "Is that how you got it?"

"The lamp had been in the home of Isabella Hughes, which was the old stone house next door to the store and is still standing today, by the way. Mrs. McLaren was related to Isabella by marriage and she acquired the lamp when the old house was later put up for sale. I bought the lamp from her. "

He carefully handed it to Brendan. "You take hold of this while I tell you about Isabella. She had a very interesting life. She was a pioneer."

"A pioneer?" was all Brendan could say. He was concentrating on taking the lamp from his grandfather. He didn't want to drop it. He'd had some breakage issues in his past.

"Mrs. Hughes was born Isabella Tomlinson in Glasgow, Scotland, in 1809," Linus said. "At that time, Glasgow was in the grip of a depression and thousands of men who had been put out of work by the Industrial Revolution considered moving to Canada."

"Did they all want to become pioneers?"

"They were very unsuited for pioneer life, Brendan. Those lowland Scots were weavers and factory workers. They knew *nothing* about farming or life in the bush."

"I think the frontier would have been exciting back then," Brendan said. "I'd love to go into the forest with a knife and gun and fight bears and stuff like that."

Like most nine-year-olds, the boy preferred adventure to reality.

Linus tried to explain what it was really like. "You'd be in for a rude awakening if you thought that all you had to do to live off the land was to charge into the bush wearing your buck-skin jacket and coonskin cap. They were taking on a difficult life. Isabella's mother and father had no idea how challenging it would be."

"You make it sound like they shouldn't go, Grandpa."

"I'm sure it was the father's decision. Anyway, Isabella was eleven years old when she was told that her family was leaving Scotland."

"Were they happy about that?" Brendan asked. "I would have been."

Linus furrowed his brow. "A man like John Tomlinson doesn't pick up and leave his country with his wife and seven children for the wilderness, unless he has a very good reason."

"It *still* sounds exciting to me."

"All I can say, Brendan, is that the situation must have been very bad in Glasgow because on May 22, 1821, John and his wife Jean, along with their children boarded the *Commerce* for a long, perilous journey to an unknown world. A Glasgow emigration society had arranged for a one hundred acre lot in the frontier of Upper Canada to be waiting for them."

"I wish I lived back then," the boy said, ignoring that only moments before he had complained about the absence of so many of his modern comforts.

"You might think otherwise if you had to cross the Atlantic in a cramped wooden sailing ship," Linus said. "Those old square riggers were extremely unhealthy."

"How can a ship be unhealthy?"

"Lack of sanitation for one thing," his grandfather replied. "That's how diseases spread. The elderly and the very young were the most vulnerable. Three deaths occurred on the *Commerce* during that single voyage."

"Just from diseases on a ship?" Brendan asked. He hadn't expected that.

"Don't you remember that I told you about Johnny McGinnis'
Atlantic crossing on the *Asia* in 1799? Thirty-four people died
on that voyage."

"I forgot about that. Some disease was brought on board in
blankets or something like that."

"It was smallpox," Linus said quietly. "Diseases spread very
easily on board those ships. Isabella's baby sister was one of the
three people who died on the *Commerce*."

Brendan's heart sank.

Linus put his hand on his grandson's shoulder. "Can you
imagine the grief that poor Scottish family felt, as they stood on
the deck listening to Captain Coverdale read the burial service?
They knew now there would be no turning back."

Brendan had a lump in his throat. There was already one death
in the family and it didn't sound like any of the Tomlinsons
would ever see Scotland again.

"Each person had their responsibilities on board," Linus
continued. "Isabella was in charge of baking oat cakes for her
family."

"Oat cakes?" the boy asked, turning his nose up. He preferred
his food deep-fried. "Did they have them every day?"

"There were no restaurants or snack bars on board the
Commerce. Families had to bring their own food with them."

"Then I guess they ate a lot of oat cakes."

"They probably *survived* on them for forty-one days," Linus
said. "That's how long they'd been at sea. Their ship finally
docked at Quebec City on June 20, 1821."

"Then where did they go?" Brendan was now becoming more
concerned about their welfare.

"All four hundred passengers from the *Commerce* were going
to Lanark County. They boarded sturdy barges called 'Durham
Boats' to take them up the turbulent St. Lawrence River. The
men used twenty-foot long poles to push the boats forward.

When rapids proved too difficult, they tied ropes to oxen on the shore to help pull the boats. It was heavy going. It took them over a week, but they finally arrived in Brockville."

"Is that where they settled?"

"Brockville was just a stopping place," said Linus. "The group now began the long trek north from there. Wagons were used to carry provisions and the children. Their leaders followed the same trail established the year before by the first emigration group. It took them through swamps and bush and across meadows and creeks. They fought off black flies, bugs, wasps and mosquitoes. At night they slept in fields or barns. Finally, the group reached the little village of New Lanark on August 4, 1821."

"It doesn't sound very comfortable," said the boy who was beginning to appreciate his own bed.

"John Tomlinson and his two eldest sons headed into the bush to take up their one hundred acres on the first concession line of Ramsay Township. Isabella, her mother and the other children remained in New Lanark while the men prepared the home. Three months later, enough bush had been cleared to build a log shanty. Isabella's father then sent for the rest of the family."

"That's a pretty good story," Brendan said, thinking that was the end of it. "Maybe now we should check and make sure your T.V.'s working."

"But first I want to tell you more about the Tomlinsons," Linus said. "I was never able to find out anything more about them until 1837."

"We're only up to 1837?"

"That's right. The records of 1837 show the Tomlinsons had cleared, ploughed and sown twenty acres of land."

"I guess that's a lot," Brendan sighed.

"By then, Isabella's older brother, Jonathan, had acquired one hundred acres of his own," continued Linus. "His property was alongside the lot owned by Patrick Hughes, who had recently arrived from Ireland. Patrick's son, Robert, was a young blacksmith and well liked in the community. Isabella and Robert became a twosome and were married in November of 1837."

"Did they build their own log house?"

"They did," agreed Linus. "The newlyweds moved to Innisville and rented a little shack from James Ennis, while their permanent log house was being constructed. However, sometimes nothing goes right when you are starting a new life. A fire broke out in the chimney on New Year's Eve, 1838, and they were forced to move into the unfinished log house. They were fortunate that the fireplace was completed, half the floor was laid and the cellar was full of hay."

"Their first child was born a month later. Isabella and Robert named her Isabella."

"The same name as the mom?" Brendan asked. "Couldn't they think up a different name?"

"Then the boys were born. There were William, Jonathan, John and Robert."

"*Hey—wait a minute,*" Brendan interrupted. "Aren't John and Jonathan the same name?"

Linus scratched his head. "That *is* confusing, isn't it?" he asked. "I wonder why Isabella and Robert would give their third child essentially the same name they gave to their second?"

"Maybe they forgot," the boy said.

"If it had been up to me, Brendan, I would have named those boys 'Obadiah' and 'Plantagenet'. That way, no one would get them mixed up."

"I've never even heard of those names before," the boy said.

"Isabella and Robert had eight children in all," Linus continued. "By the early 1850's, with a growing family and a prospering blacksmith business, Robert and Isabella decided to have a stone house built. They were encouraged by the strong work ethic of their boys. One son Jonathan, took up carriage-making, the three others became blacksmiths."

"*Three blacksmiths!*" Brendan exclaimed. "I bet they played a lot of horseshoes in that family."

"They sure did," agreed Linus. "Remember, in pioneer days people didn't have any money."

"I don't have any money."

"You may not think so, Brendan, but we have more of *everything* than the pioneers had. It was a different era then. They relied on their harvests and trades and they placed great importance on reading."

"They had to because they didn't have television back then."

"Isabella would be disappointed if she knew how much time boys and girls today spend watching television."

"What's wrong with that?" the boy asked.

Linus paused to recall a story that Mrs. McLaren had told him. One Sunday, Isabella noticed her teenage granddaughter reading *Ivanhoe* in the parlour of the old home. Isabella, speaking softly in her Scots burr, reminded the girl that 'it would serve a young person better to be reading the Bible on a Sunday'. When you consider *Ivanhoe* is a classic piece of English literature, you can imagine what Isabella would have thought of television."

"She probably wouldn't like it," admitted the boy.

"Pioneer life certainly didn't do her any harm, though," Linus said. "She lived to be one hundred and two years of age and when she died in 1911, she had spent almost seventy-five years of her life in that old home."

"That's a long time," Brendan said.

"Isabella had visited the nearby towns of Almonte and Carleton Place, but it wasn't until she was more than ninety years of age that she finally saw the big city. She took the train from Perth to her daughter Jane's home in Toronto. Traveling alone, she carried with her an overnight bag and her feather tick."

"What's a feather tick?"

"It's a feather mattress. What an unwieldy thing for an elderly lady to have to carry all the way to Toronto, but it seems that even Isabella—that strict, hard-working, determined, little Scots woman—had her comforts."

"See, Grandpa? Everybody has them."

"Human nature doesn't change," Linus said, "but I certainly admire Isabella and all those early pioneers. They built our country. I think you and I could learn from them."

"What could we possibly learn from *them?*" asked the boy, with a shrug of his shoulders. "They lived a long time ago and you just said things were really different then."

"I'm thinking," said his grandfather, slowly stroking his chin, "that you and I should learn to live with fewer modern conveniences. Don't you think we take too many things for granted today?"

Brendan's eyes glazed over. "Probably," he mumbled.

His grandfather hoped that Brendan could learn something about pioneer life that would help build his character. "We should turn back the clock," he said.

The boy wasn't so sure about this. "How are we supposed to do that?" he asked.

"Well, one thing we can do is put Isabella's old lamp in working order so we'll be ready for the next blackout," Linus suggested. "All we need to do is buy some wick and I know just the place."

So Linus and Brendan headed downtown later that day to the oldest hardware store in the city to buy some wick.

When they entered the store, the two of them immediately thought they had gone back into time. It was like an old country general store of yesteryear. Every bit of interior was jammed with hardware.

"This old store really reminds me of Mrs. McLaren's," said Linus excitedly. "Even the floor creaks. And look what's on the counter!"

A big jar of penny candies sat there. They both could recognize jelly beans from a mile away. This was too good to be true.

Linus reached into his pocket and handed his grandson a five-dollar bill. "You buy the wick, Brendan. It shouldn't be more than five dollars. I want to look around." Then, as an afterthought, he said, "If there's any change, treat yourself to some penny candies."

In the meantime, while Linus sorted through a big barrel of three-quarter inch nails, his grandson approached the shopkeeper.

"I'd like to buy some wick for a coal oil lamp," the boy asked. He was a little unsure how to order it.

"Lamp wick?" The storekeeper asked in a hearty voice. "Sure—I have some."

He lifted a large coil of a wick from under the counter.

"How much do you want, son?" the man asked, holding a pair of scissors in his hand.

Brendan thought for a moment. He mentally measured the height of the lamp and very wisely doubled that to be on the safe side. He considered himself to be a smart shopper. "This much," he said, holding his hands apart.

The shopkeeper cut off a couple of feet of wick and handed it to the boy. "That will be eleven cents," he said.

"Eleven cents?" Brendan asked, surprised at how little the shopkeeper wanted for it. He handed him his five-dollar bill.

"And here's your change," the man said.

To Brendan's huge delight, he received $4.89 cents in change, more money than he ever had in his whole life. And he immediately remembered his grandfather telling him he could buy penny candies with the change if he wanted. He carefully put the wick in his pocket.

"Anything else?" asked the shopkeeper.

The boy looked at all the money in his hand. Then he looked at the jar of penny candy on the counter. Then he looked again at all his money. Then he thought about the pioneers.

Then he bought the whole jar.

CHAPTER SIX

1864

The Shooting of Frank Lynch

"He shall have dominion also from sea to sea
And from the river unto the ends of the earth."

Psalm 72:8

It was July the first and Linus was basking in the morning sun.

Horse, the famous basset hound, was stretched out beside him, dreaming happy thoughts of past heroics.

Brendan, who was Linus' nine-year-old grandson, burst upon the scene with a cheerful, "Good morning, Grandpa."

"Happy Dominion Day to you."

"Actually, it's Canada Day," replied the boy.

"You're right," admitted Linus, "but to me, it's Dominion Day. That name reminds me this country extends from sea to sea; from the Atlantic to the Pacific and to the Arctic." He paused and added, "We should be very thankful we live in Canada shouldn't we, Brendan?"

"We sure should," he agreed, removing a bag of salt and vinegar potato chips from his schoolbag. "Do you have any pop?"

"There's some in the fridge, but have an orange instead. I bought some really juicy ones this morning."

"I'll just have a pop, Grandpa. I don't want to spoil my junk food."

"Well, maybe I'll have a second cup of coffee," Linus said.

"Then I have a little tale to tell you about how Canada became a country."

"You mean about the Fathers of Confederation and stuff like that?" Brendan asked. "We took that in school."

"Yes," Linus said, leaning forward in his chair. "The Fathers of Confederation and stuff like that, but I bet you've never heard of a man named Frank Lynch."

"So who's Frank Lynch, Grandpa?"

"An ordinary Lanark County farmer," answered his grandfather, having forgotten about his second cup of coffee. "His family came to Canada from Killarney, Ireland, in the early 1820's and settled in Ramsey Township. Early in 1841, Frank's father, Pat, bought the lot beside my grandfather's property on the fourth line. My grandparents knew the Lynch family well. They became neighbours just one month before the Act of Union."

"I've never even heard of the Act of Union," the boy said.

"The Act of Union joined Upper and Lower Canada politically in 1841," his grandfather explained. "That was our first step toward responsible government."

"So how does Frank Lynch get into this story?"

"Well, Patrick Lynch had four strapping boys. There were Tom, Dan, John, and Frank. They were a very hard working family. You had to be on that kind of land. The soil in that part of Ramsay was not the best to farm."

"Were they poor?"

"I would call their farm sub marginal. It was very hard to make a decent living on it."

Brendan had finished his orange drink and was now crushing the can. "Are you sure this has to do with Confederation, Grandpa?"

"I think it helps with the time line," Linus said. "There had been a lot of discussion about unifying all the self-governing colonies since the Act of Union. This included Ontario, Quebec, Nova Scotia, New Brunswick, Prince Edward Island and

Newfoundland. It was argued that each of them would benefit economically and politically by union. It seemed a good idea, but nothing ever came of it."

"Weren't they interested in joining up to be a country?"

The Right Hon. Sir John A. Macdonald, 1815-1891
Father of Confederation and Canada's First Prime Minister

"The colonies had very little in common, Brendan. For example, by the 1850's there was still more trade between the Maritimes and the New England states than between the Maritimes and the other colonies, so you can see that Confederation wasn't a pressing issue."

"When did they change their mind about joining up to become Canada?" asked Brendan. He was trying to assist his grandfather to get to the point. Secretly he thought the story of Confederation was boring. He wondered if he could get Frank Lynch back into it. "And what about Frank Lynch and his brothers?" he asked. "I bet they got into a lot of fights."

"Frank Lynch got into a big fight in 1861."

"Who started it?" asked the boy. "I bet it was Frank."

"I'm talking about the American Civil War."

"The American Civil War?"

"There were two large armies," Linus said. "The blue army in the North and the gray army in the South."

"I think I know about the South, Grandpa. They spoke very slowly and they all dressed like Colonel Sanders."

His grandfather smiled at the comparison. "That's true," he said, "many of them owned plantations."

"Didn't they fight the war because of the slave trade?"

"Yes, the causes of the Civil War involved political, economic and moral issues of the slave trade. There was little compromise between the North and the South. The North was abolitionist."

"That means they were against it—right?"

"That's right," agreed Linus. "The North was against it and the South was not. The Canadian colonies at first were quite friendly to the North. Canada had abolished slavery a generation before so was very sympathetic with the North's cause."

"Is that the moral of the story?"

"My story has to do with Frank Lynch," explained Linus. "To a farmer like Frank, the war was an opportunity. He was not making much money on the farm and the Union Army might pay a man up to $800.00 just to sign up. That was really good money. Frank was a tough country lad and figured he could hold his own against any 'johnny reb'. So he crossed the border and enlisted in a northern regiment. He wasn't the only Canadian. There were thousands."

"There were?"

"Of the Canadians who fought in the Civil War, most enlisted with the North," Linus said. "The North was closer, but some joined the South too. It certainly wasn't a smart thing for any of them to do."

"Why not, Grandpa?"

"There's a very good reason for that," his grandfather answered, "but first I'm going to have that second cup of coffee."

"May I have another pop too?" Brendan said, holding up his crushed can.

"Sure, help yourself," Linus said, pouring himself a refill. "Now—about Frank Lynch." He took a sip and continued. "Immediately after Frank joined up, there occurred a very serious international incident."

"What happened?"

"The U.S.S. *San Jacinto*, commanded by Captain Wilkes, stopped a British mail packet called the *Trente*, after it had left Havana. Armed with sabres and muskets, the American captain and his crew boarded the *Trente*, seized two very senior Confederate diplomats, brought them both on board the *San Jacinto* and threw them into the brig. The *Trente* sailed on to England without them."

"Could they just do that?"

"Absolutely not," Linus said. "If there is anything that can start a war between two seafaring countries faster than interference on the high seas, I don't know what it is. That was an act of piracy of the highest order and Britain demanded an apology."

"Were they going to fight about it?"

"Britain certainly didn't want to," Linus said, "but the Union didn't mind stepping on Britain's toes. They'd been unfriendly with Britain long before the *Trente* Incident. Britain and the United States hadn't warmed to each other since 1776."

"You mean since they won their independence."

"Yes, they'd been bickering back and forth ever since. They even went to war about it in 1812. There was only one brief moment that any sort of friendship was ever shown between the two countries in all those years."

"When was that?"

"It occurred during the tour of the young Prince of Wales to America in 1860. The American public had warmed to the Prince, but once the American Civil War began, the old hostilities between Britain and the United States resurfaced."

"I didn't think Britain had anything to do with the Civil War," Brendan said, wondering how to get his grandfather telling about Frank Lynch again. "But I know Frank Lynch did. So what happened to him?"

"We're getting to that," Linus said. "But you're right about what you just said about Britain. Britain hadn't anything to do with the Civil War—at least on the surface."

"What do you mean—on the surface?"

"You see, Queen Victoria had declared Britain neutral. That meant they were not taking sides, but that wasn't how the North understood it. The North couldn't understand how a law-abiding country like Britain could accept the Confederacy as a legitimate country, when it was obviously a rebellion that had to be crushed. Why was Britain giving them recognition by declaring its neutrality, if not sympathetic to them?"

"Maybe Britain was secretly rooting for the South to win," the boy suggested.

"That's exactly what the Union thought too," agreed Linus. "They had suspected all along that Britain had been quietly helping the South behind the scenes. That's why they had no intention of apologizing for boarding the *Trente*. Nor did Britain expect one. Britain knew that the Union army could easily march a few divisions into Canada and end the British presence in North America once and for all. With such a small population, we were not in any position to stop them."

"Why not?" asked the boy. "Didn't we have enough soldiers?"

"Britain immediately sent reinforcements to Canada. That brought our total strength up to eighteen thousand redcoats. That was the highest number of soldiers the British army ever had in Canada, but we needed more. We called up our militia. That was a few thousand more, but the North had a million."

"Which included Frank Lynch, I guess," Brendan said.

"Imagine what thoughts were going through Frank Lynch's mind now? He had only been in the Northern army for several months. Could the rumours of a war with Britain be true? He was now dreading that his regiment might be ordered to invade Canada."

"I bet he never thought about *that* when he joined up."

"The sad part was that Canada needed recruits and so many of our young men were fighting for the Union. If the Union Army marched north, Frank would have to take up arms against his father and brothers." Linus looked his grandson with a penetrating gaze. "Brendan, don't ever think of enlisting in some other country's army."

"Don't worry," he promised. "I won't."

"Money isn't everything," his grandfather said, making sure he got his point across.

"But they didn't invade Canada, did they?" the boy asked, trying to get his grandfather back to the story.

"You're right. A month after the abduction, the diplomats were released by the Union and the immediate crisis was over. The tension had lessened, but the bitterness remained. There was no apology."

"Did the North board any more British ships after that?"

"No," Linus answered, "but that didn't end the naval problems between the Union and Britain. Do you want to hear about some more?"

Brendan brightened up. "I sure would," he answered. This was more like it.

"As the Civil War raged on," Linus continued, "the Confederacy arranged to have several ships built for them in England. It appeared that they were simply ordinary merchant ships, but the true purpose was concealed. They were ships of *war*."

"I *told* you Britain was rooting for the South, Grandpa."

Linus nodded. "If the British had really been neutral, they would never have allowed Confederate warships to be built in her shipyards. The deadliest ship of them all was called the *Alabama*."

"The *Alabama*?" asked the boy, pronouncing the name in his best southern drawl. "Was that a battleship?"

"Not really a battleship. The *Alabama* was basically a sailing ship, but it also had a very powerful engine. She was fast and had an experienced captain and crew. During her two-year career, the *Alabama* captured many Union merchant ships and took plenty of prisoners. As far as the Union was concerned, this was a deliberate act of piracy and Britain was responsible."

"I bet it captured a lot of treasure too," Brendan said, rubbing his hands together.

"Millions of dollars worth," Linus answered. "The *Alabama* always avoided being caught by finding safe harbours in out of the way tropical islands from Bermuda to Singapore. She finally ran out of luck when a Union warship located her off the coast of France. In a desperate sea battle, the legendary raider was finally sunk."

"I guess the Union was happy about that."

"But they were very unhappy with Britain. They were determined that Britain must pay."

"So what happened?"

"Britain's involvement in these events and the growing unfriendliness of the North made everyone in the Canadian colonies very nervous. We looked south across the border and saw huge armies, railways, ironclad ships and observation balloons, all of which were being used in their great struggle. We didn't have any of that kind of military hardware. It was obvious we would be in a stronger position to defend ourselves if we were united."

"So Canada became a country after all that?"

"Representatives from all the colonies met at Charlottetown in 1864 and again in Quebec the same year. Meanwhile, the American Civil War raged on."

To Brendan, it was Frank who was central to his grandfather's story. "So what happened to Frank Lynch, anyway?" the nine-year-old asked, wondering how the Ontario farm boy faired in combat.

"Frank had managed for the longest time to stay out of trouble," Linus answered, "but in the spring of 1864 he found himself in the infantry of Grant's Army of the Potomac as it crossed through a dangerous area of Virginia known as 'The Wilderness'. It was there that Grant's army met the Southern army commanded by Robert E. Lee and a great battle took place which lasted two days. There were many casualties on both sides. One was Frank."

"Oh, no," Brendan groaned. "What happened to him?"

"A Confederate sharpshooter took dead aim at Frank and the musket ball tore through his upper left side."

Brendan instinctively clutched his chest with his hands. "Was he killed?"

"He was very lucky to survive," answered Linus. "That kind of wound was usually fatal. Civil War army surgeons called them 'double dusters', but Frank miraculously recovered. He returned to Lanark County and farmed for another thirty-five years."

"At least we have a happy ending to this story, Grandpa," said Brendan cheerfully.

Linus agreed. "A happy ending for Frank Lynch, but the question is whether we have a happy ending for Canada too. We now have to look at our relationship with that powerful neighbour to the south. Robert E. Lee had surrendered in 1865 to the Union Army. In turn, The Union Army looked north and wondered if this might be the time to knock Britain down a peg or two."

"They sure didn't like Britain."

"You can't blame them. With all that the *Alabama* had done, the United States' resentment ran deep."

"It was Britain's fault, that's for sure," Brendan said.

"As the Civil War came to an end, the Americans were certainly wary about anything happening north of their border. And there was a lot of political activity going on. Sir John A. Macdonald had been the driving force in making Confederation a reality. Self-defense was one of his selling points. The four colonies of New Brunswick, Nova Scotia, Quebec and Ontario formally declared their decision to unite to become The Dominion of Canada in 1867 and that grand man, Sir John A., became our first prime minister."

"That's pretty good but what did the United States think about that?"

"They only saw the Union Jack still flying up here and they weren't happy about that. But they didn't do anything—they just waited."

"What were they waiting for?"

"They hadn't decided whether to accept the new Dominion as a friend or a foe."

CHAPTER SEVEN

1 8 7 0

❦

The Secret Mission of John Rose

"Constant and True"
Motto of the Clan Rose

LINUS HAD FINISHED READING HIS MORNING PAPER. He folded it up, rested his chin on his hand and sat staring at his coffee mug. Something he had read in the paper he had not liked. There had been a report of an increase in bullying in local schools.

Horse, unflappable basset hound that he was, simply ignored all bad news and curled up in the hallway. He didn't read the papers, listen to the radio nor did he watch television.

Then Brendan arrived.

Before his grandson could utter a word, Linus showed him the paper. "Is there *bullying* going on in your school?"

"I haven't seen any," Brendan replied.

Linus gave that answer some thought. "Say, isn't that exactly the answer the school bully would give the principal?"

The boy responded with his best tough guy look. "Oh, yeah? Then I want to see you at four o'clock sharp outside the schoolyard," and then he added in his most sinister voice, " . . . *alone.*"

Linus shook his head and smiled. "You're a fake, Brendan. I know you're not a bully."

The boy's mood turned serious. "There *is* one kid at school who doesn't like me."

"Is he a bully?"

"I don't know," Brendan shrugged. "I get along with most of the kids except him."

Linus looked at Brenda over his glasses. "Who is he?"

"You don't know him, Grandpa."

"But does this boy have a name?"

"Let's just call him Kid X."

"What did he do to make you think he doesn't like you?"

"He made fun of me a couple of times in front of some of my friends."

"How did you handle that?"

"I made fun of him back."

Linus removed his glasses and rubbed his eyes. "How diplomatic of you," he sighed. "It would appear that both of you owe each other an apology."

Brendan looked away. "I'd rather have a root canal," he said, having heard his grandfather use that same expression while preparing his last income tax return.

Linus stood and cleared the table. "I should tell you my story of the most expensive apology in Canadian history. You might find it interesting."

"You even have a story for that?" the boy asked. Seemingly, his grandfather never ran out.

"It's the story of John Rose," Linus said, "one of Canada's greatest diplomats. It's a shame so few have heard of him today."

"I've never heard of him," the boy said, as he watched his grandfather get up from the table to walk over to his bookcase.

"Let's take a look at this map of Scotland," Linus said. He returned to the kitchen table and opened his big atlas.

"John Rose was a Scot, born in 1820. The Rose clan lived near Inverness and was well known for its diplomacy. They were always able to avoid the violent feuds that plagued so many of the other Highland clans."

"How did they do that?"

"The Rose family didn't ally themselves too closely with any one faction."

"If John Rose got along with everybody in Scotland so well, why did he end up having to come to Canada?"

"The area of Scotland, where the Rose family lived, was in the grip of famine," Linus replied. "Young John came to Canada with his parents when he was sixteen. He'd been well educated in Scotland and was now making a very good living in Montreal as a tutor. But he was generous too. In 1837, his cousin Alexander Rose and his wife and children, also recent Highland immigrants, began farming in the Scottish community of Glengarry, Ontario. John gave Alexander and his wife Lillias a cow to help get them started."

"A *cow*?" Brendan exclaimed. "I never heard of anybody giving someone a cow before."

"That's because you live in an apartment in the city and don't appreciate how important cows are," Linus said. "A cow would have been an excellent gift. It might have made the difference between success and failure for a young pioneer family."

The boy thought that over. "Maybe it *would* have been a good gift," he admitted, "back then, I mean."

"Alexander's children named the cow 'John Rose' in honour of the donor," added Linus. "They were certainly very thankful to receive it."

"Imagine what my Mom would say if *my* cousin sent me something like that," the boy said. "We're not allowed pets in our building."

"It would be different if you lived on a farm," Linus said.

"I guess so."

"Getting back to the story—John Rose was a very good student."

"The *cow* was?" the boy asked with a grin.

Linus raised an eyebrow. "No," he sighed, "the *person* was a good student, not the *cow*. John Rose, the *person*, returned to school to obtain a degree in law and by the early 1850's had one of the largest commercial practices in Montreal. He also became closely acquainted with another young Scottish lawyer by the name of John A. Macdonald. You know who he was."

"I know he was our first Prime Minister," Brendan said. "You're always talking about him."

"He's the Father of Confederation."

"And was he a friend of John Rose?"

"They were very close friends," answered Linus, "The story goes that John Rose and Sir John A., as young men, visited the United States together and for fun disguised themselves as strolling musicians. John A. played a musical instrument and John Rose dressed up as a dancing bear. Obviously neither of them was very shy."

"A dancing bear!" Brendan laughed, "It would have been even better if he had ridden a unicycle and juggled."

"I only mentioned it to show how close their friendship was," Linus said. "They were friends in politics too. After running successfully for parliament, John Rose joined the Macdonald-Cartier cabinet in 1857."

"What did he have to do there?"

"For one thing, in his role as Minister of Public Works in 1860, Rose was the man responsible for the first Royal Visit to Canada of the eighteen-year-old heir to the British throne."

"Now *that* would be a good job to get."

"Sir John A. Macdonald had assigned Rose the daunting task of travel arrangements for the young Prince of Wales and his huge entourage. Rose performed the job with his usual efficiency and thus began a lifelong friendship with the future King of England."

Sir John Rose, Bart, 1820-1888
"The man the English-speaking world turned to when critical diplomacy was
required. His task was to ensure Canada was not lost."

"I don't know anybody like that," said Brendan, whose only
friend in high places was the blackboard monitor.

"The Prince followed up the Canadian portion of the visit
with his first trip to the United States," Linus continued. "He

was surprisingly well received in the young republic, which was good news for the British Foreign Office. After years of hostility between the two countries since the American Revolution and the War of 1812, it looked as if the relationship might finally be improving. However, the good feelings did not last."

"Why not?"

"By the time the American Civil War ended with General Lee's surrender, there were very hard feelings in the United States about Britain's involvement in the war."

"I bet it was because of the *Alabama*," the boy said.

"It was indeed. The United States claimed that Britain had undermined their war effort by allowing the *Alabama* and some other Confederate warships to be built in their shipyards."

"I remember you told me those ships caused a lot of damage," Brendan said. "I think it was Britain's fault."

"According to Union spies," Linus went on, "Britain had been well aware of what was going on, but she refused to admit to any wrongdoing. Britain was once again becoming the United States' number one enemy. Despite the hostility between the politicians, many diplomats from both sides were very concerned about the deteriorating Anglo-American relationship. They felt that both sides must swallow their pride, sit down and resolve their differences with the signing of a treaty."

"Did they think a treaty was going to solve all their problems?"

"It didn't matter anyway because it was never signed. In 1870, a very influential American Senator, Charles Sumner, gave a famous speech condemning the treaty. He argued that it did not address the considerable damages owing to the United States caused by the *Alabama*."

"It's pretty obvious that Britain should give them something to make up for it," the boy said. "That would be fair."

"Senator Sumner said that only the acquisition of Canada would be fair compensation."

Brendan was stunned to hear that. *"He wanted Canada?"* he cried out. *"Was he off his rocker?"*

"Senator Sumner was deadly serious," Linus answered. "He reminded everyone that the piracy committed by the *Alabama* had destroyed the U.S. Merchant Marine and had also doubled the duration of the Civil War."

"But that doesn't give him the right to take Canada."

"Try telling that to an outraged American public," answered the grandfather. "They hadn't forgotten how much damage the *Alabama* had caused. Even *you* said that Britain was responsible."

"We should call that guy 'Senator X'," Brendan said bitterly.

"After the Senator's speech, the treaty was thrown onto the scrapheap. Britain and the United States were now locked in a fatal impasse. National pride made it impossible for either side to give in."

"I don't like that Senator, that's for sure," Brendan said.

"Britain realized she'd made a huge mistake," his grandfather said. "She had put herself in a very precarious position. Why in the world did she declare herself neutral and then turn around and allow one of the warring parties to use her shipyards? What if the shoe was on the other foot?"

"What do you mean?"

"The European balance of power was already shifting. Both a newly-united Germany and an aggressive Russia were threatening their neighbours. Britain could soon be drawn into a conflict."

"The balance of power—what's that?"

"In those days European countries were always forming military alliances and when one alliance strengthened, the other felt threatened. It was an old system created to preserve peace, but it always seemed to cause the opposite. Britain's problem now was that in the event of war, the United States would certainly assist *any* alliance that was opposed to Britain."

"I bet Britain wished they'd never heard of the *Alabama*."

"Suppose German and Russian battleships were able to operate freely out of American ports? Think of the damage they would do to Britain's navy."

"Britain would lose for sure," Brendan said.

Linus thought so too. "Britain's only hope was to acknowledge her mistake and repair the damage somehow. Otherwise, Sumner would press America's claim for Canada."

Brendan scratched his head. "I *still* can't believe that guy thought he could get away with it."

"This is where John Rose came in," Linus said. "Here was a man who understood the importance of treaties and knew that negotiations must be reopened. Sir John A. had thought so highly of him that he had promoted Rose to the position of Canada's second Minister of Finance two years before. Rose had held that post before recently retiring to accept a partnership in a London merchant bank."

"He sure had a lot of good jobs."

Linus agreed. "Not only did John Rose begin a new life as a banker, but he also took on another very important task."

"What was that?"

"He became Sir John A.'s eyes and ears in London."

"His eyes and ears?"

"That meant Rose agreed to serve the Canadian Prime Minister as his personal representative in London in addition to working at his bank."

"I wish I owned a bank," the cash-strapped nine-year-old said, thinking of all the pizza he could buy.

"John Rose had become very well connected," added his grandfather.

"So why isn't he famous?"

"It's too bad he isn't known today, but he preferred to work behind the scenes. Rose had formed a close friendship with one of the leading American statesmen of the day; a man named

Caleb Cushing. They often discussed U.S.-British politics. Cushing introduced Rose to Hamilton Fish, who was President Grant's Secretary of State. All three men became great friends and amongst themselves came to the conclusion that what the two countries needed was a mediator."

"What's a mediator?" asked the boy.

"Someone who can help get the two sides together," answered Linus. "It was critical that Britain and the United States renew the negotiations that could possibly lead to a treaty."

"Did John Rose volunteer to be the mediator? Is that what happened?"

"Yes, the British Foreign Office heard about these informal talks and they asked John Rose if he would do it."

"Did they really think John Rose could change the American's minds about the *Alabama*?"

"Rose was in a unique position. He was a Scot who lived in London, England. He'd been the Canadian Finance Minister. He was trusted at the highest levels of both the US State Department and the British Foreign Office. Remember too that he was a life-long friend of both the Canadian Prime Minister *and* the Prince of Wales. Last, but not least, he was married to an American."

"It sure sounds like he had a good resume."

"John Rose was the man the English-speaking world turned to when critical diplomacy was required. It would be his task to ensure Canada was not lost," Linus said.

"Don't forget he had his own bank," the boy reminded his grandfather, zeroing in on yet another Rose attribute.

"Actually, that's a good point Brendan, because the United States had piled up huge debts during the Civil War. As a matter of fact, President Grant at that time was very interested in refinancing his war debt at better interest rates. Perhaps John Rose could do something about that. "

"I bet John Rose would have been happy to lend him some

money," Brendan said.

Linus smiled. "At good rates, I'm sure; for a reasonable fee, of course," he said. "Now that he had something to bargain with, Rose sailed for America on Christmas Eve in 1870. The trip was not publicized by either government; in fact, Rose merely said his visit to the States was for private reasons."

"Did he meet with Senator X?" asked Brendan. "His house would be the first place I'd go to."

"John Rose not only had dinner with Senator X, but he also met with newspaper publishers, editors, economists and other politicians. He understood the importance of public relations to get the message out. Rose told everyone from the start that he was open to any suggestions other than the annexation of Canada and the response was very positive.

"The main thing is that he talked them out of wanting Canada," Brendan said. "He must have been pretty good at his job."

"Yes, he was a very good diplomat," Linus agreed. "John Rose understood international affairs. He was an experienced negotiator, very persuasive and he had an endless amount of tact, discretion and charm. In only three weeks his secret mission paid off. U.S. public opinion had softened and President Ulysses S. Grant agreed to talk. This led directly to the signing of the Treaty of Washington, which ushered in a new era of friendship between the two countries. And you know something?"

"What?"

"That friendship has lasted to this day," Linus said. "It was also a great personal achievement for John Rose. He was knighted for his work."

"That's pretty good."

"Would you like to know what the main compensation was to the United States?"

"I know they never got Canada," Brendan said. "That's all I care about."

"Britain gave the United States fifteen million dollars in gold," said Linus, "and an apology."

"That's sure a lot of gold! Britain must have been rich."

"Countries can always find a spare $15 million in gold if they need it."

"They can?" Brendan asked, not realizing there was so much gold lying around.

"If they don't have it," said Linus casually, "they just borrow it."

"It's that easy?" The boy was amazed at the simplicity of it all.

"Many countries find it easy to borrow money," Linus said, "but just like in the schoolyard, Brendan, the offering of an apology is always the hard part."

1 8 7 8

Black Pete's Last Fight

"What memories must these rivers know,
While murmuring on their winding way
Toward the sea; with even flow;
Perhaps 'tis of a by-gone day."
—M.J.Shiels, *The Mississippi*

LINUS SANK BACK INTO HIS WICKER CHAIR WITH A FARAWAY LOOK IN HIS EYE. Nine-year-old Brendan recognized that look instantly. And then he heard the magic words that began, "That reminds me..."

Those three words meant there was probably a story about the Ottawa Valley to be told. The boy always loved his grandfather's stories of the Valley. Even Horse, Linus' trusty basset hound and retired frisbee champion, woke from his morning nap.

"What are you being reminded about, Grandpa?"

"I was thinking about my own grandfather and the stories he told me about the old days in the lumber camps."

"Do you need some paper?" Brendan asked, knowing his grandfather liked to draw maps while he was telling a story.

"I want to show you where the log jams and the rapids were," Linus said, removing his fountain pen from his top pocket.

Brendan raced to his schoolbag and returned with some foolscap.

Linus then sketched out the landmarks on the paper and began his story. "In the 1800's, the Ottawa Valley was the major supplier of lumber to the shipyards of Britain."

"It must have been an important place back then, Grandpa."

"It sure was, Brendan. I wish sometimes I could go back in time and experience those days. Grandfather used to tell me of long trips he'd taken on rafts of square timber and of the great characters he'd met along the river. The men he spoke of always seemed larger than life to me."

"I'd love to be a lumberjack," said the boy. "I'd be like Paul Bunyan crashing through the forest and riding down the rapids on a log."

"But Paul Bunyan was a *fictitious* character," his grandfather said. "Someone just made him up; but the Ottawa Valley river drivers and lumberjacks and fighting foremen were not imaginary. They *really* lived."

Linus wanted his grandson to know that *real* men lived those lives. Their stories were true and if he didn't tell him about them, who would? "It's *ridiculous* that the only lumberjack anyone has ever heard of today never even existed."

"Don't forget his blue ox, Grandpa."

"That whole Paul Bunyan and his blue ox story makes absolutely no sense to me," Linus grumbled, shaking his head. "But think of all the rafts of square timber that ran down the Ottawa River in a hundred years. Think of the great stands of white pine, the excitement of the spring drives and the bitter rivalries between the lumber companies. Think of all that history, yet if you ask anyone living today how many real river drivers or lumberjacks they could name, they wouldn't even be able to come up with *one*."

"They probably just don't remember them, Grandpa."

"Forgotten, like a dream," Linus said, looking sadly into the distance. "I wonder what my grandfather would have thought about that."

"Was your grandfather a lumberjack?"

"Jim Shiels was employed by McLaughlin Brothers, an old Arnprior lumber company, as a *scalar.*"

"What's a scalar?"

"He was the man who graded and measured the logs. You see, the logs were cut during the winter and stacked alongside the big water routes—like the Mississippi or the Madawaska; or further north, the Petawawa or the Bonnechere. In the spring, they were dumped into the rivers and began their journey to the Ottawa."

"And what happened to them when they got there?"

"That's where the logs would be identified by each lumber company's mark. The scalar or culler would take over the process at that point. That's what my grandfather did for McLaughlin. He was known to be a good judge of timber."

Linus remembered his grandfather as a hard worker but a man difficult to get to know. "He spent over forty years working in the bush."

"*Forty years!*" Brendan repeated. "That's a long time."

"I wish now that I had questioned him more about his life," Linus said. "He left his family in Carleton Place each fall and headed into the bush for the winter. He wouldn't return home until after the spring drive. He never talked too much about it, but would only say that life was hard in the shanties. On more than one occasion he mentioned how tough the men were." He smiled at Brendan and stroked his chin, "Men had to be tough to bunk all winter with a couple of hundred lumberjacks while living on a diet of pork and beans seven days a week."

The boy nodded in agreement.

"Wintering in the bush was dangerous for the lumbermen. They had to contend with frostbite and rheumatism and some very bad axe wounds. Many were injured while loading lumber. My grandfather knew men who'd been crushed."

Brendan was quickly changing his mind about being a lumberjack. "Ouch!" he blurted out, with a pained look on his face. "What about the river drivers? Were their jobs any easier?"

"The spring drives were exciting, but a man had to know what he was doing to last on the river," Linus continued. "Each man had to prove himself. Of course, the most respected river drivers were always the Quebecers."

"Why were the Quebecers so good?"

"It always seemed to me that life on the river was in their blood," Linus said. "Maybe it was because they were the grandsons of the voyageurs."

Brendan's eyes lit up. *"Ah—the voyageurs!"* he said to himself. The boy had been a great admirer of the men of the north for a long time. There was a day when he had aspirations of donning the toque and red sash of the voyageur too. This started him thinking. No reason why he couldn't make a good river driver as well. He was light enough on his feet and would be very nimble on the logs. Not only that, he thought himself a hard worker as well, especially when he was in the right mood.

Meanwhile, Linus studied his map. He then drew a long river that ran from Algonquin Park into the Ottawa. "There was one Quebecer with whom my grandfather worked by the name of Poulin. He was one of the bravest and hardest working of the river drivers, short of stature, light on his feet and very popular with the gang. One spring drive on the Petawawa River, Poulin and another man were on a boat rounding up loose logs. My grandfather and some other men were working on the riverbank some distance away when they heard a yell and looked up to see a tragedy in the making."

"What happened?"

"Poulin's boat mate had fallen overboard into the river and every man in the gang knew he couldn't swim."

Brendan grimaced. "Did he drown?"

"Poulin hung desperately over the side of the boat, his eyes fixed upon the spot where he had seen his boatmate go under. Against all odds, the little Quebecer stabbed blindly into the black water until his fingers touched fabric, seized the man's collar, and with his great strength, hauled him back into the boat."

"That man was really lucky, wasn't he?" Brendan asked, "If it wasn't for Poulin, he would have drowned."

"Poulin was lucky too," Linus said. "He couldn't swim either."

Brendan was amazed that the rivermen took such chances. "I'd want to be able to swim if I had a job like that," he said, "that's for sure."

"It was a shameful fact of the lumber business in the 1800's that so few of the men could swim," Linus said. "For most of the men in the gang, it was the only work they could find in the winter and spring."

"I'm sure glad I wasn't living back then," Brendan said.

"The river drivers were tough, but their bosses were even tougher," Linus said. "We can be very glad we don't have to make a living today under those conditions. Back then, it seemed that the foremen always felt they had to prove they were better than their men. It was their pride, I suppose. There was a story my grandfather told of an incident that happened on the *Rocher Capitaine* about a boss like that."

"The *Rocher Capitaine*?" asked the boy, "What's that?"

"It was a stretch of rapids on the Ottawa," Linus replied, "It's long gone now, but my grandfather always referred to it as 'The Russian Captain'."

"Why?"

"It was a nickname for it the men used back then."

"That's pretty good."

"The Russian Captain was one of the most treacherous spots along the Ottawa. A well known fighting foreman by the name of Jim Thompson asked his men to run the boats down it."

"Did they do it?"

"They refused and Thompson called them cowards. When they still wouldn't get in the boats, he rode the rapids alone."

"That would have been dangerous, I bet."

"Yes, it was a foolish thing for Thompson to do."

Then with a broad stroke of his pen, Linus drew yet another river with great bends and loops that also wound its way to join up with the Ottawa. He marked an 'X' at its headwaters and said. "This brings me to the story my grandfather told me of one lumberjack who stood out from all the rest. This man lived before my time so I never met him, but I recall as a boy seeing an old photograph taken of him beside my grandfather in a lumber camp about 1889 or 1890. The two men were great friends."

"Who was he, Grandpa?"

"My grandfather called him 'Black Pete'," Linus said. "His real name was Peter McIlquham and he was a foreman for the McLaren Lumber Company. In fact, my grandfather said he was the toughest fighting foreman in the Ottawa Valley. He and his family were very well known in Lanark County. They were all scrappers. Any kid in those days would be as thrilled to meet Black Pete in the flesh as you would be to meet a famous sports figure today."

"Now that's what I call a great nickname," said the boy who loved nicknames.

"However, in the spring of 1878, everything began to change for the fighting foremen," Linus continued. "Job prospects for men like Peter McIlquham became scarce."

"Why—what happened?"

"That was the year the Caldwell Lumber Company of Lanark acquired timber limits on one side of the Mississippi River." He drew closer to his grandson and added in a low voice, "That's when all the problems started."

"What difference did that make?"

A rare photograph of the old timberslide at the High Falls on the Mississippi River in Lanark County, Ontario that caused the McLaren-Caldwell lumber feud in 1878.

"The McLaren Lumber Company of Perth had long held limits on the opposite side. Peter McLaren's outfit owned a large timber slide on the river that they used to pass their logs around the High Falls. They had to use a slide to get their logs to the Ottawa River."

"Do you mean a slide like we have in our playground?"

asked the boy. "Is that what they used?"

"This one was *huge*. It was more like a long water slide, but made of wood. It cost McLaren a fortune to build it. I can certainly understand him not wanting anyone else using it, but I can also understand Caldwell not wanting to build one of his own."

"Is that the same Mississippi River I've read about in *Tom Sawyer* and *Huckleberry Finn*?" asked the nine-year-old.

"Not at all," answered Linus. "This is a much smaller Mississippi River and runs into the Ottawa. We don't know for sure how the river got that name. It might have been a surveyor's error, because the Algonquins never called it that. Anyway, the name Mississippi stuck and the river has been called that ever since."

"Did Boyd Caldwell use the slide without permission?" Brendan asked "Is that what caused the problem?"

"Boyd Caldwell offered to pay McLaren to use it on the spring drive, but McLaren refused. McLaren said his slide was private property. The last thing he wanted was a rival lumberman making use of expensive improvements he had made to the river."

"So what did Caldwell do now?"

"He shot back that the slide was on crown land and was therefore public property. If McLaren's slide was the only way Caldwell could get his logs out of the bush and around the High Falls to his sawmill at Carleton Place, then he would use it with or *without* permission."

"Trouble's brewing!" Brendan exclaimed, rubbing his hands together and smiling in anticipation of the conflict to come.

Linus agreed. "Now began a long and bitter feud between the two lumbermen."

"So what happened next?"

"McLaren's initial move was to successfully obtain a court injunction from a sympathetic judge, which temporarily gave him exclusive use of the river. He also decided that if Caldwell chose to ignore the injunction, he would send his best man up to the slide to enforce it. Who do you think that was?"

"Was it Black Pete?"

"Yes, it was Black Pete who was sent up to McLaren's Depot on the Mississippi with 'Keep Off the River' signs," Linus said. "He would be an imposing physical presence. McLaren had often used Pete's muscles as weapons."

"Was there a lot of fighting back then?"

"Yes, there was. It seems uncivilized to us now, but that was the way lumber disputes were settled in those days. There was no provincial police force out in the bush. The lumbermen simply took the law into their own hands. It was an era of constant struggles between rival companies for the use of the flood-waters or a dam or slide. The firm that won the driving rights to the river was often determined by the toughness of their foreman."

"And we know McLaren had a *really* tough foreman," the boy said.

"Boyd Caldwell knew he had to respond. The future of his lumber company was at stake. He and his partners now had a tough decision to make. The coal oil lamps would be flickering late into the night in the Caldwell offices." Linus looked at Brendan over his glasses, "What do you suppose Caldwell would do now?"

"Send his own foreman to fight Black Pete?" the boy suggested.

"That's *exactly* what he decided to do," answered Linus. "Boyd Caldwell would find someone as tough as Black Pete to bring his drive down the Mississippi and he knew just the man."

"Who was it?" Brendan asked eagerly, wondering who Caldwell would choose.

"Caldwell hired Larry Frost from Pontiac County," Linus answered.

"Was he a fighting foreman too?"

"Larry Frost was one of the most ruthless brawlers in the

Valley."

"He was?"

"Oh, yes. He was well known for the work he did for certain lumber companies. He'd been on the Caldwell payroll before."

"Imagine what Black Pete must have thought when he heard who was coming to fight him," Brendan said.

"Pete certainly knew of Larry Frost's reputation. He was well aware that Caldwell had chosen a man whose stock-in-trade was going one-on-one with the best a rival lumber camp had to offer. When it came to bare-knuckle fighting with some kicking thrown into the mix, Larry Frost was your man. "

"It sounds like Caldwell made a good choice."

"He immediately sent Larry Frost up to McLaren's Depot to have a word with Pete."

"And did they fight?"

"Picture the scene, Brendan," Linus said, gazing dramatically into the distance. "It was just before the spring break-up. Here were the two toughest men in the Ottawa Valley. They alone would determine whose logs would be driven down to the Ottawa. Imagine Black Pete standing on one side of the river. He was a menacing figure—strong and experienced. He was a loyal company man and would give no quarter. Waiting for him on the other side was Larry Frost—tall and quick with his hands and feet. And make no mistake—that man was quick."

"He was?"

"I've often heard old river drivers talk about the day Larry Frost kicked so high from a standing position that he left the heel marks of his caulked boots on the ceiling of a Lanark tavern."

"On the ceiling?" Brendan asked, thinking that was far fetched. "For real?"

Linus nodded. "And you can be sure Larry intended to leave a pair of heel marks on Pete's face too, before he was through."

Then did they fight?" the nine-year-old asked once again.

Linus was very coy in his response. "I can almost see Black Pete glancing warily across the river at the figure of Larry Frost and getting ready for combat."

"But what happened?" persisted Brendan, reaching over to grab the arm of his grandfather's wicker chair. He was getting impatient.

Linus shook his head. "Nothing," he answered. "Absolutely nothing."

Brendan was astonished. "That's how the story ends?" he asked, wanting more action from those two. "Are you sure about that?"

"We don't know how close they came to blows," Linus said. "To be quite honest, no one even knows for sure if they actually stood on opposite sides of the river."

"Were you just making that up?"

"Well, I guess I like to imagine them on the opposite sides staring one another down," said Linus. "Maybe it wasn't like that at all."

"Let's pretend it *was*, Grandpa."

"We only know for sure they never fought."

But Brendan's disappointment was obvious. "That would have been such a *great* fight," he sighed.

"Caldwell had abruptly changed his mind," Linus said. "Notice had been rushed from his office that Larry Frost was to withdraw and to wave the McLaren drive through."

"Just when things were getting interesting," Brendan said wistfully.

"Larry Frost would never get a chance to use his fists and feet on Black Pete. He was told to return home."

"Why did Caldwell change his mind so fast?"

"He decided to fight McLaren in court, not on the river."

"In court?" Brendan repeated. "Imagine how mad Larry Frost must have been when he heard that."

"He must have cussed a bunch," laughed Linus.

"So who really won in the end, Grandpa—McLaren or Caldwell?"

"Caldwell appealed the injunction," Linus explained, "and sued McLaren for damages for being unable to bring his logs out. With a stroke of a pen, the era of the 'fighting foreman' was over."

"That was fast," Brendan said, shaking his head at that turn of events.

"It became a famous court case," Linus said.

Brendan considered this for a few moments. "I think Caldwell was smart," he said. "I guess fighting wouldn't have proven anything anyway."

Linus sighed and said in a low voice, "To be honest, I'm just a little disappointed that we don't know who would have won that fight." He glanced at the boy and asked, "Aren't you?"

"I guess it *would* have made the story more exciting."

"I can only tell you that my grandfather knew both these men personally, and he told me that Black Pete was the better man," Linus said. "That was his opinion." Linus placed his hand on the map. "But there's more to this story."

"There is?"

"There's a lot more," his grandfather replied. "Caldwell's lawsuit caused a chain reaction of national events. First of all, the Ontario premier Oliver Mowat, decided that Caldwell was in the right and should have access to the McLaren slide. Mowat then enacted legislation that said the lumber companies from then on were legally required to share the rivers and the structures that were built on them. In exchange, they would be entitled to charge a reasonable user's fee. The new law was called the Rivers and Streams Bill. It was a controversial law and not everyone agreed with it."

"What was wrong with it?"

"Sir John A. Macdonald, our Prime Minister, believed the

improvements were on private property and was very much opposed to it. He had the power to disallow the law federally and did so. In response, Oliver Mowat simply went back to the Ontario legislature and passed the law provincially once again."

"Could he do that? Just pass the law over again?"

"Not only that, but Macdonald disallowed it again."

Brendan groaned. "That could go on forever."

"Who would have thought an old wooden timber slide in the backwoods of Lanark County, would be at the heart of a federal-provincial constitutional crisis?" Linus asked.

"Not me—that's for sure," the nine-year-old said.

"It became the big political issue of the day. The outcome would affect property rights on two hundred and thirty-four rivers in Ontario. There was a lot at stake. The Prime Minister and the Ontario Premier were each determined to be the last man standing."

"Just like Black Pete and Larry Frost," the boy said.

"That's right. Sir John A. and Oliver were like fighting foremen when it came to the politics of the timber trade. The issue went back and forth until it was finally resolved in 1884."

"Is that when they all stopped arguing about it?"

"The highest court in Canada at the time—the Privy Council in London, England—ruled in Caldwell's favour."

"So Caldwell won," Brendan said, "That's pretty good."

"It meant that Mowat's Rivers and Streams bill became the law of the land."

"I guess Boyd Caldwell was happy."

"He certainly was," agreed Linus. "He celebrated by inviting everyone back to his place for pancakes."

"Really, Grandpa?"

Linus laughed. "With lots of maple syrup too, I'll wager to bet," he said. "Those old lumbering stories make a man hungry. I'd like some pancakes right now. How about you?"

"Would I ever... but first—" Brendan broke off, and then added in a secretive manner, "I know how we can find out who would have won that fight."

Linus was baffled by that statement. "What are you talking about? You can't change something that happened a hundred and thirty years ago!"

The boy smiled and raced to his schoolbag.

Linus watched as Brendan dug deep into the bag and pulled out crayons, pencils, gum, paper bags, an elastic band, and half a leftover sandwich. He finally came up with two horse chestnuts dangling on shoestrings.

"Conkers?" Linus asked. "I don't believe it. I haven't played conkers in over 70 years! I used to boil them in vinegar."

"I dipped these in varnish," the boy said, handing a conker to his grandfather. "So who do you want to be?"

"You choose."

"I'll be Black Pete,"

"Then I'll be Larry Frost," Linus said. "Now we'll finally find out who won."

So one last time Black Pete glanced warily across the river at the figure of Larry Frost and readied himself for combat.

CHAPTER NINE

1 8 8 5

The Empire Builders

As soon as the words were out of his mouth, Brendan wondered if he had said too much.

He had casually mentioned to his grandfather that he was going to the public library to research a Canadian history project.

"What's the topic?" asked Linus.

"The building of the railway and the opening of the West," Brendan answered. "I have to write a composition about it."

Linus' eyes lit up. "I can help you," he said very quickly. "You don't have to go to the public library. I have *all* the books you could ever want about the history of the Canadian West."

"I don't know about that, Grandpa," the boy said with some

hesitation. He always liked his grandfather's stories, but when it came to helping with schoolwork, Brendan secretly thought his grandfather might be too out of date to help.

However, Linus considered this a wonderful opportunity. "I can finally help you with something at school," he said happily. "*I love Canadian history.* I was beginning to think they didn't teach it any more." Without waiting for a response, he went immediately to his big bookcase and returned with a stack of books which he deposited with a thud on the kitchen table. "Let's begin," he said, feasting his eyes on all the Canadian history in front of him. Linus had been waiting a long time for this moment.

Brendan sat down quietly across from him. He removed some paper out of his schoolbag and was ready to take notes.

"When we think of the history of the West," his grandfather began, rubbing his hands together, "we must begin by asking ourselves a very important question. What has been the biggest challenge facing the West since Confederation?"

The nine-year-old had no idea.

"It's the same problem the West has today," Linus hinted.

"Gophers?"

Linus gave a deep sigh. "No, it was isolation, Brendan, isolation—that's *always* been their problem," he said. "The West needed to move people and wheat over great distances. A railway would allow them to do that."

"I think my teacher said that the railway made Canada."

"*All teachers* say that," Linus said, warming to the subject. He then leaned forward and added in a low voice, "but which railway are they referring to?"

Brendan hadn't heard his teacher mention any railway other than the Canadian Pacific Railway. What in the world was Linus talking about? Had his grandfather got his story mixed up?

Linus buried his head in one of the books. "It's true that Canada had promised British Columbia a railway that would link them with the East. That had been the primary condition of British Columbia's agreeing to join Confederation in 1871. Sir John A. Macdonald's 'National Policy' was created to open the West, but it would take *years* before his promise would be kept. So we know it couldn't have been the Canadian Pacific Railway that did it."

"It wasn't?"

Linus pursed his lips and nodded. "It was *another* railway."

A frown line appeared immediately on Brendan's forehead. "*Another* railway?"

"It was the St. Paul, Minneapolis and Manitoba Railway that opened the West," Linus said.

That didn't sound right to Brendan. "I'm pretty sure my teacher is thinking about the *Canadian Pacific Railway* for this project, Grandpa," the fifth-grader said, and he couldn't help but adding, "I don't think she wants us to write about some other railway nobody's ever heard of."

Linus peered at his grandson. "Had there not been a St. Paul, Minneapolis and Manitoba Railway, it is very doubtful that the Canadian Pacific Railway would have ever been completed."

"Are you sure about that?" asked Brendan, worrying about the embarrassment he would suffer as the only kid in his class who wrote about the wrong railway.

His grandfather leaned back in his wicker chair clasping his hands behind his head. "You'll have to put it in your own words of course, but by the time we're finished, my boy, you'll be able to tell your teacher all about this obscure American railway; how it started up in 1857 as a link between Minnesota and the West Coast, lost tons of money, was put into receivership; yet went on to become the *gateway* to the Canadian West."

Linus had spoken those stirring words as if he was running for parliament, but the boy wasn't as moved.

"I sure hope my teacher has heard about this *other* railway," he said. If not, he could see his mid term average going into receivership too.

"The Canadian Pacific Railway wasn't even completed until 1885," Linus said, rounding into form on his favourite topic. "Thousands of settlers had taken up land in the West long before then. How do you think they got there?"

Brendan hadn't given much thought to that. Hadn't they just hopped on covered wagons heading west? "I'm not exactly sure," he admitted.

"Do you remember the story of Isabella Hughes?"

"She owned the old lamp you have."

"Her son, Jonathan, was a carriage maker, and with a growing family in Innisville, Ontario, was very interested in the opportunities in the West. In May of 1878 he traveled by train from Perth to Toronto and then on to Chicago. From Chicago he took a train to St. Paul. The trip from Perth to St. Paul alone had taken him three days. Then he had a back breaking fifty-eight hour wagon trip from St. Paul to Winnipeg. That wouldn't be very pleasant, would it?"

"Not unless he got to ride shotgun," Brendan put in, knowing a thing or two about western travel.

"Jonathan returned home. Even though that route was the easiest and fastest way to get to Manitoba, can you blame him for deciding against putting his wife and family through such an ordeal?"

"I guess not," said the boy, thinking of all the comfortable drives he had taken in his grandfather's eight-cylinder sedan.

"That wagon route was the only way to go out to the Canadian West in 1878," said Linus.

"A train between St. Paul and Winnipeg would have made that trip a lot easier, that's for sure," Brendan said.

"The operators of the St. Paul Railway thought so too," Linus said. "They had intended to go as far north as the Canadian border, but they had never been able to complete the line."

"Why not—was it hard to build?"

"Building railways is expensive. There were enormous costs in laying tracks to the border and maintaining rolling stock. The St. Paul simply ran out of money. The railway was in a total state of disrepair."

"I guess it's harder to build one than I thought."

"They had other problems as well. The economy was in recession. And to top it off, two years of locust attacks had made the land bordering the right of way useless for farming."

"No wonder they went broke."

"But four men turned that derelict line around. The St. Paul, Minneapolis and Manitoba Railway became one of the most important railways in North America, making the men rich beyond their wildest dreams."

"It did?" Brendan said. That comment got his attention. Not having any money of his own, the boy was always interested in hearing stories of men becoming rich beyond their wildest dreams.

"All four men were Canadians."

"But how did they end up making so much money?" asked Brendan. "Were they robber barons or something?"

"They *were* all hard-boiled capitalists, but they also understood the West. They willingly put up a lot of money to form a syndicate to buy the old St. Paul Railway. While it posed a big risk, shipping goods and people between St. Paul and Winnipeg had the potential for enormous profits. But there was more to it. If they could meet certain conditions, the new owners of the St. Paul Railway had the rights to two and a half million acres of land."

"That's a lot," agreed Brendan.

"One of the four men was Norman Kittson, a former fur trader born in Quebec," Linus went on. "He owned a company that ran steamboats down the Red River. Another was James Hill, originally from Guelph, Ontario. He was an amazing railway man. At one time, he had been a partner of Kittson's. In later

years, Hill became such a giant of the American West he was referred to by the nickname, 'The Empire Builder'. He went down
in history as the man who built the Great Northern Railway.
Amtrak's transcontinental route from Chicago to Seattle is still
called The Empire Builder to this day in honour of James Hill.

Donald Smith drives the last spike on the Candian Pacific Railway November 7,
1885, at Craigellachie, British Columbia. To Smith's right is Sandford Fleming
and to Fleming's right is William Van Horne.

The boy scribbled this information down in his journal as fast as
he could. His grandfather waited for him to write it all down.

"In my opinion, Brendan, all these men could be called Empire
Builders." Linus was pleased to notice out of the corner of his eye
that the boy had titled his composition, "The Empire Builders."

"Another of the partners was Donald Smith, who later became Lord Strathcona. At the time of the purchase of the St. Paul Railway, Smith was the Resident Governor and Land Commissioner of the Hudson Bay Company and a Member of Parliament. There is a very famous photograph taken of him sporting a white beard and top hat, hammering the last spike of the CPR in 1885."

"Wasn't it a *gold* spike that they used?"

"No, it was just a regular iron one," Linus said, "but I've read since that it took him two attempts before he made a direct hit on it. On his first swing, he only bent it."

"He only bent it?"

Linus had a twinkle in his eye. "It seems to me," he said, chuckling to himself, "that Lord Strathcona understood East and West better than he did up and down."

"I bet he would have hit it the first time if it had been a *gold* spike, Grandpa."

Linus resumed his list of the partners. "The fourth member of the quartet was George Stephen, an industrialist and president of the Bank of Montreal. He would take the leadership role."

Brendan wrote down all these names.

"It would take a couple of years of negotiating before the group actually gained control of the railway," Linus went on. "But once they did, the first order of business was to assign James Hill the task of pushing a route up to the Manitoba border. Then, to bring the whole project together, they began preparations to make the connection from the border to Winnipeg. That was a difficult hurdle, but they finally managed to obtain the running rights to a CPR branch line that ran from Winnipeg to the American border."

"Which meant the line was now complete," Brendan said.

"And the first train to St. Paul rattled down the tracks from Winnipeg to St. Paul in December of 1878."

Linus leaned back in his chair with a satisfied look on his face. "The West was open."

"I guess it did make it a lot easier for people to move to Manitoba," Brendan agreed, now understanding what his grandfather had meant about the importance of the St. Paul Railway.

"Jonathan Hughes was happy," Linus said. "In 1881 he brought his whole family out by rail and a son, Charles was born in Altamonte, Manitoba, just three months after their arrival."

"Then what was the Canadian Pacific Railway for, Grandpa? Why was it so important?"

"The only problem with the St. Paul route was that the traffic to and from the Canadian West went through the United States. What if the border was closed for some reason? The St. Paul route was a temporary fix to the problem. An all-Canadian route was needed and that's where the Canadian Pacific Railway comes in. Tracks would have to be laid right across Canada."

"That would be hard to do."

"Everybody knows the rest of the story. It was the Empire Builders who offered to build the CPR. They were fresh from their success in St. Paul and were looking for new challenges. They now had a huge amount of cash to invest, but more importantly, they *knew* how to build railways. The four men were awarded the contract by the Canadian Government to complete the transcontinental. Only a few miles of track had actually been laid when they took over, so you know how much work they had to do."

"Laying tracks must have been boring work, wasn't it?" Brendan asked. "It must have seemed like it would never end."

"Can you imagine how difficult it must have been to lay tracks north of Lake Superior?" Linus asked. "And think of putting a railway through the Rocky Mountains. The men working on that project were amazing. Some of the most dangerous assignments were given to men from China who handled the explosives. We owe those men a debt."

"It sounds like they had really hard jobs," the boy said.

"Building a railway is very expensive too," Linus said. "At one point the Empire Builders were very low on credit and everyone wondered if they would be able to continue. In order to raise more money for the CPR, they put up their St. Paul Railway stock as collateral."

Brendan wondered if his teacher knew that. "I'll put that in the story too," he said. "That sounds important."

"William Van Horne, who was hired as general manager, was another important person. He was as good a railway man as you could find. The Empire Builders were given ten years to complete the railway, but with Van Horne in charge of operations, they did it in five. Could anyone else have done that?"

"We should include Van Horne in our list of Empire Builders," the nine-year-old suggested, making a note of the fifth name.

"I don't think we should include him just now, Brendan. Let's confine the project only to the St. Paul Railway. Van Horne worked on the Canadian Pacific and it will get too confusing if we start talking about the history of the CPR line too."

"You're sure right about the St. Paul Railway opening up the West, Grandpa," the boy said, looking over his notes. "I bet we get a great mark on this."

Linus reached over and shook his grandson's hand. "I think we've aced it," he said with a proud smile on his face. It was a bonding moment for them both.

Their lunch of roast beef sandwiches tasted especially good after such a job well done.

"The Empire Builders" was handed in on Monday morning.

The following Saturday, Brendan dropped by his grandfather's house again.

Linus tried to hide it, but a look of anticipation was written all over his face. "Did you get our marks back yet, Brendan?" Secretly he'd been anxious for the results all week.

"We got them back yesterday."

"What did we get?" Linus asked, trying hard to contain his excitement.

"B minus, I think," the boy replied. "That's right. It *was* B minus. Do you have any pop?"

Linus turned pale. "*B minus?*" he groaned. "*That's all?*"

The boy immediately noticed his grandfather's disappointment and tried to boost his self-esteem. "A B minus is a good mark, Grandpa. Don't forget they mark pretty hard in Grade Five."

But Linus had his heart set on an A plus. He couldn't understand what had gone wrong. "You mean I couldn't do any better than a *B minus?*" he asked in a voice sounding very much as if his confidence had been shot to smithereens. "Look at all the Canadian history books I own, Brendan. See all the old maps I have on my walls. I'm a member of the local historical society." Then his voice sank to a whisper, "I'm a veteran."

Brendan didn't think that a B minus was anything to sneeze at. "There were lots of kids who didn't get as good a mark as you," he said, patting his grandfather on the back in a grown-up kind of way. "Don't worry, Grandpa. The *important* thing is to pass."

Linus sat down while his grandson went out to the kitchen for a pop.

"What else did your teacher say about it?" Linus asked, his voice fading badly.

"I think she wrote something down on the paper," the boy shouted from the kitchen, trying to remember the exact words she used.

Linus could hear pop fizzing into a glass. Then he heard the fridge door shut. "She said it was '*not comprehensive*'," Brendan called out, "What does that word mean, Grandpa?"

But Grandpa didn't answer.

He had gone to lie down.

CHAPTER TEN

1895

The Sage of Aru

"Philosophical Zealot or Simple Charlatan?"
Montreal Star, April 27,1898

LINUS HAD BEEN HAVING CAR TROUBLE ALL WEEK.

The very day he was scheduled to take it to the mechanic for repairs, he was called upon to keep his grandson company. Brendan was at home recovering from an appendectomy.

Linus immediately cancelled the trip to the mechanic and went directly to Brendan's home.

The nine-year-old, feeling better and wearing a dressing gown and slippers, greeted Linus at the door with a big smile.

"I thought you were going in to get your car fixed this morning?" Brendan asked, delighted to see his grandfather so early in the day.

Linus winked at the boy. "I was scheduled to go in for a front end alignment today, but do you think I really need one?" he said, patting his stomach. "Maybe I should just cut down on desserts instead?"

Brendan recognized the humour and laughed politely. He then ushered his grandfather into his apartment.

A deflated and sad looking soccer ball caught Linus' eye.

"Didn't I give that ball to you for your birthday, Brendan?"

"I lent it to this kid in my class," the boy answered, admitting to a modest error in judgment. "He promised to return it to me in good condition but look what happened."

"I wonder if we can get some air into it," Linus said, picking up the ball and poking it.

"He also borrowed my best friend's baseball glove and lost it."

Linus raised his eyebrow. "Did you know all this before you lent him the soccer ball?"

"I found that out later," the boy answered. "He said he was sorry."

"They always are," Linus said, shaking his head.

"It's getting so you just don't know who to trust these days," Brendan said, waxing philosophically. "What a fake that kid is."

"He probably doesn't pay his taxes either," Linus put in.

"I think he's too young to pay taxes, Grandpa."

"What's this world coming to?" Linus muttered. "This kid has a bit of snake oil salesman in him, I'd say."

"What's a snake oil salesman?"

"They were men in the late 1800's who sold fake liniment to the public, claiming it would cure all their ailments," Linus explained. "They had everyone convinced that oil from snakes was very good for you."

"Yuck!" Brendan stuck his tongue out at the thought of a spoonful of snake oil.

"These men, and there were women too, traveled from town to town selling colourful bottles of tonic, that according to them, relieved aches and pains, cured bunions and even restored hair."

"Not that you need that," the boy said, giving his hair-challenged grandfather an affectionate pat on the back.

"In those days, medicine could make you sick," Linus said. "Who knew what was in those bottles? Fortunately, we can now read all the ingredients."

"It sounds like someone should have put some skull and crossbones labels on those bottles," Brendan said.

"I remember one of those snake oil peddlers when I was a

boy growing up in Carleton Place, Ontario," said Linus. "A man claiming to be a doctor of some kind arrived in town in 1895 and began to manufacture patent medicines from a store opposite the old CPR station. His place was near my grandparents' house on Miguel Street. I asked them about him, but they didn't say too much. I suppose they thought the less said about him the better."

"I think it would be exciting to have a snake oil salesman as a neighbour," Brendan said, always seeing the bright side of things.

"I remember there was a long brick wall at the side of the store where he displayed his advertising. He had posted one big faded sign on it that read 'Stop that Cough for 10 cents'. I forget what the other signs said. He lived at the back of the store."

"Did you ever go in?"

"To be honest, I was a little afraid of him, so I never did," admitted Linus. "He had a great white beard and always looked so very serious. I often saw him at his doorway wearing a green silk robe and a little cap. He was an unforgettable character."

"Reminds me of Merlin," Brendan observed.

"It's very hard to forget a man like that," agreed Linus. "I'll always remember his eccentric personality of course, but there was something else about him that made an even bigger impression on me at that age."

"Like what?"

"His automobile was the first I ever saw. You would have loved it, Brendan. It was fire engine red and opened on the top and sides. It had lots of brass on it, great mudguard fenders and a large rubber bulbed horn. Being a young boy, I enjoyed hearing the sound of his horn, but better still, I loved the great explosive noises that came out of the engine."

"What was the man's name, Grandpa?"

"He called himself the 'Sage of Aru'," answered Linus, "but his real name was George Howard."

"The Sage of Aru?" Brendan repeated. "I never heard of a

name like that."

"Howard claimed the title originated in the Himalayas. He said he was the master of some pseudo-mystical, spiritual order called *Sat Bai Kooha*."

"Maybe he was a psychic or something like that," suggested Brendan.

"He might have been," agreed Linus. "In addition to selling medicine, he lectured, practiced hypnotism, wrote horoscopes, performed healing rituals and claimed to be able to cure nervous disorders. There was very little he couldn't do for you. The Sage of Aru was always looking for wealthy customers to whom he could offer his services."

"Imagine meeting someone like that," Brendan said, his eyes widening,

"Hold on to your wallet if you do," Linus cautioned.

"What do you mean?"

George S. Howard, of Carleton Place, Ontario, also known as "The Sage of Aru"

"I found out more about him many years later," Linus went on. "George Howard was actually an Englishman, who arrived in the United States in 1884. After a speaking engagement in Virginia, he came to the attention of a Mr. and Mrs. Specht, who were impressed by Howard's professed desire to help people live better lives. They thought the Sage of Aru was enlightened. He was certainly convincing."

"Did he ask them for money?"

"Oh, yes," his grandfather said. "Mr. Specht gave the Sage $5000.00. Before long, Dr. Howard had moved into Gunston Hall, the Specht's Virginia mansion on the Potomac River. Howard's dream was to turn the home into an elite college that would benefit humanity or so he said. Mrs. Specht began to fall under his spell and thought seriously of bequeathing the home to him. The Sage of Aru's influence over the couple was quite strong."

"I guess he had good communication skills and stuff like that," said Brendan, recognizing the Sage of Aru's greatest attribute.

"He had an endless line of patter," said Linus. "He even told people he had met his present wife at a reception given by Charles Dickens."

"Wasn't he the person who writes those books you read?"

"He's still my favourite author."

"So did the Sage of Aru end up owning that big mansion?" asked Brendan.

"Fortunately, no," replied Linus. "Mr. Specht and Dr. Howard finally had a falling out. It was serious enough for Specht to file a charge of false pretenses against Howard."

"Was he arrested?"

"He never was. To avoid standing trial, The Sage put on a show for the good citizens of Virginia."

"Like a benefit?"

"No, he performed a vanishing act," Linus said. "Howard fled Gunston Hall, just one step ahead of a pair of Pinkerton detectives who were after him and that's when he turned up in Carleton Place, Ontario."

"I'm just glad he didn't get their home," Brendan said.

"That would have been a shame," Linus said. "Gunston Hall was an historic American home. It had been built in 1755 for George Mason, who was one of the founding fathers of the United States. Mason had written the Virginia Declaration of Rights there in 1776. That was the document which became the foundation of the American Declaration of Independence. All the giants of American history, such as Washington, Jefferson, Franklin and LaFayette were guests at Gunston Hall at one time or another. That shows you how important the house was from an historical point of view."

"More important than the White House?"

"Not quite as important as the White House because the President lives there."

"Who lives in Gunston Hall now?"

"It was purchased by the State of Virginia in 1932 and is now an American national historic landmark."

"Imagine an important national landmark like that almost falling into the hands of the Sage of Aru," said the boy, rubbing his hands together.

"I'm sure the memory of the notorious Sage of Aru living in Gunston Hall has been long forgotten," Linus said. "I doubt if anyone in Virginia has ever heard of the man today."

"What ever became of him, anyway?"

"The *Montreal Star* wrote a long expose on him and he sued them for libel. The trial was held in Perth, Ontario, in 1898 with the Chief Justice presiding. The Sage lost his case, but gained a certain celebrity status just the same. I remember his being involved in another scandal in Carlton Place a little later on."

"What did he do then?"

"He had sold some oil paintings that turned out to be fakes.

The purchasers of the paintings successfully sued him and got their money back. He said he thought they were genuine."

"It sounds like he was always getting into trouble."

"He was not a young man either. His wife Adylia died in Carleton Place in 1920," Linus went on. "The Sage of Aru was then said to be 93 years of age and recovering from a fall down a flight of stairs. That's the last I ever heard of him."

Brendan listened to the story with great interest. It made him think. He began to imagine his dressing gown as a green silk robe.

"Wait here, Grandpa," he shouted, turning on his heels and scurrying off to his bedroom. Brendan was beginning to feel like his old self again.

Although the nine-year-old secretly wanted to become an Iroquois warrior, or maybe a voyageur or a river driver, he also fancied he had the makings of a good psychic.

Linus rubbed his eyes at the sight of Brendan when he reappeared.

"What the...?" Linus asked, quoting those immortal words penned by every dime novelist since *The Adventures of Buffalo Bill.*

Brendan had returned from his room wearing a towel wrapped around his head and sunglasses. The boy introduced himself as Madam Aru. Linus watched in fascination as Madam placed the deflated soccer ball on the coffee table and very dramatically peered into it, as if it were a crystal ball.

The young psychic entered into a trance of some kind. "I am Madam Aru and I am getting vibrations from beyond...and I believe you will be receiving some unexpected... money."

Madam Aru began mumbling strange words and phrases that Linus didn't understand.

Nonetheless, the grandfather was spellbound by the performance. "You can tell the future?"

"Oh, yes," the psychic droned on in a high-pitched monotone. "If you wish to know how to get this money there will be a small fee of one dollar."

"Only a dollar?" Linus thrust his hand into his pocket and handed Madam Aru one dollar. "This is money well spent," he said happily.

"Very good, very good," Aru said, a satisfied smile appearing on her face. "I see a winning lottery ticket. Would you like to know more?"

"I *sure* would, Madam Aru," Linus said, drawing his chair closer to the magical soccer ball.

Madam Aru peered into the future and frowned. "The image is fading. This is most regrettable," she announced, placing both hands on her forehead. Then a worried look came over her face. "This is a very difficult case. I must have more time. Of course, there *will* be another small fee of one dollar."

"Of course," Linus said, obediently handed over another dollar.

"I can now see the store where you will buy the winning ticket," Madam said at last, and then quickly added in her strange falsetto, "may I trouble you for another fee of one dollar—to provide you with the address, of course? I'm sure you will understand."

Linus glanced at her over his glasses. "Of *course*, I understand." He handed her a five dollar bill.

"Maybe it would be better if I kept the change. That way I could include the postal code," Madam suggested.

"*What?*" Linus cried, pointing an accusing finger at the seer. "*Keep the change? Include the postal code? You know what I think?*

"I beg your pardon," harrumphed the psychic, not liking her customer's tone of voice one bit.

"*I think you're a fraud, Aru—if that's your real name.*"

Now any self-respecting psychic would be highly insulted by such an accusation and this one was no exception. "*I'm a hard-working woman!*" Madam Aru angrily protested, defending her reputation from this unwarranted attack on her dignity. When she couldn't think of anything else to say, she leaned forward to stare down her accuser.

With those harsh words in the air and with so little distance between them, Linus bravely reached toward Madam's head, seized the towel and pulled.

What happened next is steeped in local legend. In the confusion that followed, people were yelling and bumping into one another.

Then someone shrieked, *"It's a man!"*

CHAPTER ELEVEN

1 8 9 8

Double Cross on Eldorado Creek

*"Most left the gold fields destitute and despondent.
There was no real romance"*
—Lewis McLauchlan, *letter to the author*

EVER SINCE HE WAS A SCHOOLBOY, LINUS HAD REGRETTED NOT BE-
ING BORN IN TIME TO GO ON THE KLONDIKE GOLD RUSH. His interest had been sparked long ago by Lewis McLauchlan, a man he
had met in his youth. Although a generation older than Linus,
the two became friends. Lewis had served with the North West
Mounted Police in the Yukon Territory during that frenzied year
of 1898.

*The son of a Scottish farmer, Lewis McLauchlan had been born in
Edinburgh in 1874 and left his job as a law clerk for a life of adventure in
the American West in 1893. A rancher by the name of Busby gave him
a job on his cattle ranch in Montana. Thirty years before, Busby himself
had prospected for gold in Alaska. Busby eventually left the north and
started ranching in Montana. When gold was discovered in the Yukon
in 1897, the rancher suggested to Lew that he go and try his luck.*

*With a pal, Lew headed north to Edmonton, but the two lads didn't
have the minimum year's provision to be allowed to go further. The
North West Mounted Police didn't want to be responsible for a lot
of greenhorns who had been lured to the Yukon by the gold bug. The
Mounties, however, were looking for some good men. Both young
cowboys from Montana were accepted as new recruits after achieving*

117 .

high scores on the musketry range at Fort Saskatchewan. Lewis' first commanding officer was Major Arthur Griesbach, well remembered in western lore as the first officer signed up after the Mounted Police were formed in 1873. Lew was posted to the detachment in Dawson.

After the gold rush ended, Lew stayed in the force and was transferred to the detachment in Whitehorse. Between assignments, he found time to do some mining. He had a small operation, but he never made much money out of it. Lew was more successful at police work, acquiring the reputation of one of the force's best man hunters. The NWMP later became the RCMP and when Lewis died at the age of 97, he had the distinction of being the last surviving member of the old North West Mounted Police.

How Linus admired Lew and his life of adventure. Lew was gone now and Linus often wished he could go back in time and head to the Klondike with his old friend. He often wondered whatever became of Busby's claim . . . could there still be an old oil soaked map hidden away somewhere . . . ?

One evening Linus hatched a plan. Brendan's birthday was coming up. What to give a nine-year-old grandson who had everything? How about a long lost gold claim in the Klondike goldfields?

Linus set to work. With his trusty fountain pen and an old piece of paper, he began to draw a map of the local neighbourhood. But instead of the usual place-names, Linus substituted the names of rapids, camps, mountains and rivers of the Klondike. He then aged the map; he singed it, steamed it, crumpled it and even his dog, Horse, slobbered over it until the document began to acquire a genuine look of antiquity. When that was completed, as a final touch, he left it outside for a couple of days pinned to a clothes peg so that the weather made it appear even more authentic. The most important landmark on the map was the spot where Linus intended to bury the treasure. He marked this spot with an 'X'. Next, he put together a treasure. He filled a plastic bag with hard candy, marbles, paperclips, a magnet, a couple of acorns, some coppers, a dime, a key chain, a small plastic dinosaur and other assorted odds and ends. One morning, while Horse slept and Brendan was at school, Linus set off to the ravine for the burial.

After a long walk, he found a perfect spot on a sandy area alongside the ravine's creek-bed. Here he dug a hole, placed the bag inside, packed it down and marked the old Busby claim with a pile of pebbles. It was a job well done.

On Saturday, Brendan dropped by his grandfather's house. He had hoped that his grandfather had remembered it was his birthday.

Linus hadn't forgotten. He greeted Brendan with a hearty "Happy birthday, my boy" and handed him the old manuscript. "Many happy returns."

"What's this, Grandpa? It looks kind of old to be a birthday card."

"It's much more valuable than that," his grandfather replied. "Do you remember I told you about my friend, Lewis McLauchlan, a man who had actually been in the Klondike Gold Rush?"

"I think you showed me a picture of him once," Brendan replied. "He was an old man with a cane and a long white beard."

Linus nodded. "Before he died, Lew gave me this map to an old gold claim in the Klondike. It was given to him by an old Montana rancher by the name of Busby. I think you're old enough now that I can share it with you."

Brendan was just a little too sharp to have a trick like that pulled on him. "Are you sure this is real?"

"Why do you ask? You don't think it's real?"

"There's something about this map that looks vaguely familiar."

Linus gave his grandson a little tap on the arm. "You're too smart for me," he admitted. "I guess you recognized your own neighborhood. I just changed the names."

Brendan grinned back at him. "Actually, I recognized the coffee stains," he said, patting his grandfather's back. "Just kidding."

"But there really *is* buried treasure," Linus said, in a conspiratorial tone. "I just hope I can trust you to share it."

"But can I trust you?" Brendan whispered back, in an even greater sinister tone.

"Maybe," said the old prospector, avoiding eye contact, "*or maybe not.*"

"But you're coming with me, right?"

"Of course, I am," replied Linus. "We'll go this afternoon."

Brendan loved playing the role of a grizzled prospector starting out on a treasure hunt. "I'm going to have to keep you in sight," he said to Linus, his eyes narrowing. Thoughts of untold riches waiting to be found were swirling in his head.

They agreed to become partners and decided to cut a deal before heading out. There was a lively discussion on how best to split the loot. Linus suggested that all the profits should be invested in long term, high yield Government of Canada bonds that would go towards Brendan's post secondary school education. Brendan suggested that all the profits be spent immediately on pizza and pop. No agreement was reached.

The next step was to make a list of the gear that they needed to take. They required a year's supply of provisions so they began to work on the type of list that a real Klondiker would make: flour, candles, picks, shovels, axes, medicine, compass, tents, sled, rope, extra socks and a coffee pot for Linus.

After that list was completed, they put it aside and made the real one: popsicle sticks and several chocolate bars.

And they both agreed they would wear plaid shirts.

Before they headed off to the goldfields in the afternoon, they studied their map once more.

"First we have to decide which trail to take," the older prospector said, indicating two routes into the wilderness marked on the map. "We can take either the White Pass Trail or the Chilkoot Trail.

I recommend we take the Chilkoot, which we can get to from Dyea. Once we've crossed it, we can go overland to Lake Bennett."

"Sounds good to me, Grandpa."

"I should warn you that a man needs to be in really good shape to climb the Chilkoot Pass. That will be the hardest part."

"Then why don't we just take the White Pass trail instead?"

"Because then we would have to go through Skagway, and I want to keep away from that place."

"What's the matter with it?"

"Skagway is too dangerous, Brendan. Even the Superintendent of the Mounted Police, Sam Steele has called it 'the roughest place in the world'. The town is ruled by a swindler who goes by the name of 'Soapy' Smith. My fear is that one of his henchmen will try to steal our map. It will be much safer for us to take the Chilkoot."

"Even though it's harder?"

"I know you can do it, Brendan. Before we're through, we'll be calling you the 'Klondike Kid'."

So Linus, Horse and the Klondike Kid headed down their street on the way to the ravine. When they next checked their map they found they were approaching Sheep Camp, a tent-city created by the real Klondikers who had stopped at the encampment back in '98 to cache their provisions.

Linus peered ahead. "I think we should spread out," he whispered.

"Are you worried about an ambush?" Brendan asked, glancing warily over his shoulder.

"It wouldn't surprise me if some desperado has already heard about our map," Linus said. "Word travels fast in these parts." He looked nervously from side to side. "There are lots of rough characters around who would love to get their hands on it."

"Is it really that valuable?"

"It sure is. Our claim is on the Eldorado Creek and *everybody* wants to stake the Eldorado."

Linus set the pace with Brendan following a discreet distance behind. Lastly came Horse, who had dropped back to make sure that no one was following them.

The trio soon came to a ravine. Linus put a hand on the boy's shoulder and pointed to the high ground on the ridge. "There it is!" he announced, with great reverence in his voice. "There's the dreaded Chilkoot Pass!"

Klondikers near the summit of the Chilkoot Pass in 1898.
For two years, until the White Pass and Yukon Railway was built, this was the favoured route to the goldfields. Note the sled to the right being hauled up the mountain pass by a tram line.

Brendan gazed at the spot where his grandfather was pointing.

He was trying to imagine a great mountain pass.

Linus had no trouble thinking of what that Pass must have been like in 1898. "If you use your imagination Brendan, you can almost see the long line of Klondikers carrying their packs over Chilkoot Pass," he said. "What a sight it must have been! And now you and I have to do it."

"It'll be easy."

"The Chilkoot summit is 3600 feet above sea level," his grandfather said. "Still think it's going to be easy?"

Brendan was full of youthful vitality. "They don't call me the Klondike Kid for nothing!" he boasted, "This is going to be fun."

The boy raced up the hill and waved to his grandfather when he reached the top. Then he ran back down. He wasn't even out of breath.

"Forty more times and then we'll head down to the creek," his grandfather said. "I'll wait here for you."

The Kid's jaw dropped. "Wait a minute—*forty more times?*" he groaned. "*What are you talking about?*"

"Don't forget that we're carrying a year's provisions," explained his grandfather. "You just carried only about fifty pounds with you on that trip which would have taken a Klondiker about six hours. We'll probably be here for another three months at least before you've finished."

Brendan scratched his head. "They really did this?" he asked. His initial excitement of the grand adventure was quickly diminishing.

"About twenty to thirty thousand of them made this trip," Linus answered, "but not in the summer. The Klondikers could only use the Chilkoot in winter when the rocks and boulders were covered in snow and ice. They cut about fifteen hundred steps into the ice to make a path up the side. Otherwise, they would never make it."

"It would have been really hard to do this back then," the boy sighed.

Linus agreed. "It was backbreaking work."

"Let's just pretend we crossed that mountain," Brendan said. "Where do we go from here?"

Linus opened the map and studied their location. "Well," he said, "if we've finished climbing the Chilkoot, the next hurdle will be at Lake Bennett. That was the location of the largest tent-city in the world. It's still about seven hundred and fifty miles away from Dawson but at least we don't have to lug our gear. That's where the Klondikers made their homemade boats."

"And I get to make my raft?"

"Did you remember to bring your popsicle sticks?"

"I sure did."

"It's hard to believe there were over seven thousand boats of all descriptions that set off from this lake. So get those popsicle sticks out and do your stuff."

With great dexterity, Brendan placed eight popsicle sticks on the ground and then took eight others which he wove over and under the first lot until he had made a raft.

"That's a very good looking raft you've made there, my boy," praised his grandfather. "You didn't even need glue."

"I've made a million of these, Grandpa," said the nine-year-old, as he was about to toss the raft in the water.

"*Wait!*" Linus shouted. "Don't throw it in yet. Remember it's still winter and the rivers are frozen. We have to wait for the spring break up."

"How long will *that* take?"

"Another month or two."

"*That long?*" the boy moaned. "We'll *never* get there at this rate."

"Don't be in such a rush, Brendan. When you were on the Trail of '98, you had to follow nature's timetable. Mark a number on your raft while we're waiting. The Mounted Police registered all the boats and gave each one a number. Then they listed all the passengers' names."

"What did they do that for?"

"There had been so many accidents in the canyons and rapids, the Mounties began to register the boats in order to keep track of everyone's whereabouts. Every twenty-five miles there would be a police check point."

The Klondike Kid shook his head impatiently. "This is going to take forever," he grumbled.

After a little break, Brendan tossed the raft in the creek.

"It's heading into the Miles Canyon," Linus said, excitedly. "Miles Canyon has dangerous whirlpools and one hundred foot granite walls. I hope our raft makes it through."

Brendan was brimming with confidence. "Don't worry," he said. "That's one of my best rafts."

He was right. The raft made it through the Canyon with flying colours. The next hurdle to get over was the deadly White Horse Rapids. It was in these rapids that the raft jammed up between some rocks. Brendan had to do some fancy navigating with a long stick before he freed it with a gentle nudge.

"That was sure good navigation work. Next stop is the great Yukon River and then Dawson," his grandfather said, giving the boy two thumbs up. "We're getting close to the *City of Gold!*"

"Did you hear that, Horse?" the boy asked the third companion, "Were getting closer to the *gold!* "

Horse felt the excitement building too.

The three partners walked along the bank of the creek bed, which flowed into the mighty Yukon River. The river trip went very smoothly. Linus stopped and opened up the old map again. He pointed to some houses that backed onto the ravine. *"This must be Dawson City!"* he cried. *"We've made it!"* Then, pointing to a semi detached residential red brick house, he said excitedly, *"Look! There's the Palace Grand Theatre."* Linus had read fabulous stories about these places. "The Palace was built by 'Arizona'

Charlie Meadows, one of the great trick shot artists of the Old West. Some of the legendary characters of the Gold Rush might be playing poker in there right now."

"Like who?"

"Like 'The Montana Kid' or maybe even 'Calamity' Jane," Linus said. "They both frequented the place. 'Klondike Kate' might even be dancing on stage right now—although I think it's more likely she's performing down the street at the Orpheum. It doesn't matter, anyway. You're too young to go into either one of them." Linus turned and pointed to another house on a ravine lot. "There's the Monte Carlo...right up there!"

"It is?" Brendan asked. He was very impressed by how much his grandfather knew about the nightlife of old Dawson City.

" 'Swiftwater Bill' is probably playing a little faro in there, right now," Linus continued. "I can almost hear him say, 'Raise 'er up as far as you want to go, boys'. Yessiree, Brendan, the Monte Carlo was really quite the place. I heard it said that 'Kid' Kelly one time played faro in the Monte Carlo all night and by morning he actually owned the place."

"He did?" the boy asked, although secretly he had no idea what the game of faro was. All he knew was that Dawson City must have been a great place to go if you were looking for adventure.

Linus knew what his grandson was thinking. He could see it in his eyes. He knew he had been overdoing it about the glamour of the casinos. "The Gold Rush may have seemed exciting, Brendan, but as Lewis often reminded me, very few miners could frequent those establishments. There might have been a couple of lucky claim owners who had gold nuggets to spend, but that was about it. Otherwise, Dawson was just a shack town. Almost fifty thousand gold seekers arrived that summer and most were down on their luck. Jobs were paying sixteen times the current wages, but there was nothing available for the average person to buy. Imagine how difficult it was to get supplies up to the Klondike before the rivers froze. That sort of inflationary economy doesn't last."

The boy, however, preferred to think of Dawson as an exciting Wild West town where everyone had a poke of gold dust in his pocket and adventure was around every corner. "Aw, don't take all the fun out of the Gold Rush, Grandpa," he complained.

"You have to accept reality," his grandfather said. "Don't forget that Dawson City had poor sanitation, too many people, very little food, and everything was expensive. Can you imagine paying five dollars for a cucumber?"

"A *cucumber?*" Brendan asked. "Who wants to buy cucumber? But how much was a slice of pizza?" That was the sort of history Brendan could become interested in.

"You could have made a fortune selling pizza in the Gold Rush, Brendan, if only they'd had pizza back then. But we have work to do now. We have to check out our claim."

"This is going to be the best part," the Klondike Kid said, as they followed the path that Linus had taken the week before. They marched relentlessly on toward the mother lode.

They soon arrived at the sandy beach where Linus had buried the treasure the previous week.

"*This is Eldorado!*" Linus sang out. "It's taken us six months to get here but we've made it! Millions of dollars in gold ore were taken from claims along this very creek in 1898."

"Now it's our turn," the boy said with a big grin.

This was the moment they had been waiting for. The pair approached the little mound of pebbles which Linus instantly recognized. He had marked his buried treasure well. Both of them began digging and Horse too, put his big paws in to help. The hound was flinging out so much sand that both Klondikers decided to let him finish the job. It wasn't long before Horse found something.

Linus and Brendan smiled in anticipation as the dog grabbed

hold of the plastic bag and pulled it from the ground.

"*There's the treasure, my boy,*" Linus cried out triumphantly. "*We've struck pay dirt!*"

Brendan had never felt such excitement. "*This is my lucky day!*" he shouted.

Then occurred one of the most unsuspecting, double crosses in the long, sordid history of the pursuit of gold.

Horse, holding the treasure firmly in his teeth, ran off with it.

The treasure hunters were stunned. This was an unbelievable betrayal. "*Come back, Horse!*" they yelled.

But Horse had other ideas. He gave a yelp and ran through the thicket and up the hill, all the while happily shaking the contents out of the bag. He hadn't had this much fun since he was a pup. This was the last thing that Brendan and Linus had expected. The hound was having the time of his life.

Cries of "*Come back here, you backstabbing, no-good, claim jumper!*" echoed throughout the ravine.

After he ran out of steam, Horse returned meekly to the scene of the crime with only a small fragment of plastic stuck to his front teeth. He cocked his head to one side as he looked at Linus. One ear was up; one down.

Linus shook his head and wagged an accusing finger at his dog. "How *could* you?" he asked.

Only a single dime was recovered.

This was the reality of the Gold Rush. Linus and Brendan now knew how the original Klondikers felt over a century before. The stampeders had started their adventure full of promise, but had ended it in utter disappointment. The great majority had to return home when their grub ran out.

"I've learnt a valuable lesson today," Linus admitted.

"That money doesn't grow on trees?"

"I was thinking if I ever went looking for gold in the Klondike again," his grandfather said, and here he cast a bitter glance at his discredited basset hound, "I would thoroughly check out the references of my business partners."

The nine-year-old then stooped over and gave the dog a warm pat. "Don't worry, Horse," he said sympathetically. "We had a great time today. I bet I'm the only kid in my class who went on the *Klondike Gold Rush* for his birthday."

Linus heard Brendan's comment to Horse and it was at that moment that he realized he'd had a wonderful time as well. If only in their imagination, they had experienced the spirit of the Klondike together.

CHAPTER TWELVE

1 9 0 2

The Order of the Midnight Sun

*"The Mounted Police and the hospitals made the Yukon a safe place to live,
but hardly glamourous."*
—Lewis McLauchlan, *letter to the author*

BRENDAN AND HIS GRANDFATHER WERE FAMISHED AFTER THEIR
TRIP TO THE KLONDIKE GOLDFIELDS.

As soon as they returned home, they headed straight to
Linus' kitchen to prepare roast beef sandwiches for lunch.

Horse, being on a strict diet, was not allowed to partake. Over
his objections, he was banished to the hallway, where a bowl of
tasty dog food awaited.

Brendan did the honours and brought the sandwiches out to
the dining room table while Linus followed, carrying his big
world atlas. He deposited the book on the table with a loud
thud and opened it to the map of Alaska.

Placing his hand over that huge state, he dragged his fingers
down the Yukon Territory and northern half of British Columbia.

"This area is where the goldfields of the Klondike were located. I've always been fascinated by its history." He looked
up at his grandson over his glasses and sighed, "All my life I
wished I could have been up there in 1898."

"You weren't even living then, Grandpa, so how could you
have gone? And don't forget how lucky you were that your
friend told you all about it."

"You're right, Brendan. I *am* lucky that I had a friend like Lewis McLauchlan. He was a wonderful source of information about the history of the north. He had many great stories. I remember his telling me one time of a strange incident during his stint up in the Klondike. He didn't go into much detail, but said it had involved a group of men who called themselves 'The Order of the Midnight Sun'."

That had a magical ring to it. The boy was all ears.

"Have you ever heard of The Order of the Midnight Sun?" asked his grandfather.

"I don't think so."

"What do you suppose it might have been with a name like that?"

The boy shrugged. "I don't know."

"Come on, Brendan. *Guess.*"

The boy stroked his chin, as he had seen his grandfather do many times. "Let me see," he said, very deliberately. "The Order of the Midnight Sun might have been a lost tribe of zombies and skeletons." He then scratched his head and went on, "Yes, that's what they were. They were created when the sun and the moon collided at midnight. They were a *very* warlike people and they carried hatchets and bows and arrows and stuff like that." The nine-year-old then dragged his fingers down the map of Alaska and the Yukon. "They lived around here."

"*Wait a minute!*" Linus piped up, waving his hands. "What in the world are you talking about? *Zombies and skeletons?* That sounds dreadful."

"Well, you said, *guess.*"

"Let me tell you the *real* story of the Order of the Midnight Sun, just as Lewis told it to me," Linus said, settling into his wicker chair. "It all began in 1725."

"*1725?*" the boy asked. "Is this going to be a *long* story?"

"It's not a long story, but it began a long time ago. That was the year that Czar Peter the Great of Russia, sent Vitus Bering out to explore the eastern limits of Siberia and seek out the riches of the New World. Bering continued his sea journey until he arrived at the coast of Alaska. No one from Russia had been that far before. Others, of course, followed."

"Were they explorers too?"

"You *could* call them that, Brendan, but it was the beautiful fur of the sea otter, not exploration, that was their real interest. In time, trading posts, forts, houses, and a church were built on the west coast and administered by the Russian American Company."

"Is this a story about Alaska or the Yukon?"

"It's a story about the strip of land that runs along the coast of Alaska and British Columbia," said Linus, pointing to that area on the map.

"Isn't that called the 'Alaskan Panhandle'?" Brendan asked. "I think we learned about that in school."

"Good for you, my boy," Linus said, giving his grandson a little tap on the knee. "Do you know its history?"

"I think Canada and the United States fought over it."

"They did in a diplomatic way. Lewis' story leads up to that boundary dispute. You see, for many years after they first arrived, the Russian traders operated without any European competition, but by the early 1800's, traders of the Hudson Bay Company had approached from the east. When contact was finally made, the usual disputes over territorial rights arose. In 1825, Great Britain and Russia met to resolve their differences. They concluded a treaty and agreed on a boundary."

"I thought that Alaska was part of the United States?" Brendan asked.

"Alaska didn't become part of the United States until 1867. The other important date to remember is 1871, when British Columbia joined Confederation. By 1898, instead of Russia and Britain sharing the boundary, it was the United States and

Canada. But the old 1825 boundary, drawn up long before a proper survey had been made, was now in dispute."

"So when *did* Canada and the United States fight over it?"

"Until the Gold Rush, nobody thought too much about the Alaskan Panhandle. It was only sparsely inhabited by native people who lived on fish and caribou meat. I remember Lewis telling me that until then, neither Canada, Great Britain nor the United States felt any urgency to resolve the boundary question. Only when gold was discovered had every square foot of land become important. Who owned the land where the gold was found? Who owned the routes into the Klondike? Who owned the key seaport of Skagway?"

"But didn't Canada own the Klondike?" asked the boy.

"We thought we did, but we also thought we owned the seaport of Skagway. It was the only entry point into the goldfields. Back in 1898 Canada needed Skagway to ship the gold out; however, by then it was almost entirely occupied by American miners. It's now part of the United States, of course."

"Maybe we should have sent in the Mounties."

"By then it was too late. Canada didn't have enough Mounties up there anyway. It was going to be very difficult for Canada to claim ownership of Skagwag if it went to court. It was basically American territory. The Canadian Government was finally waking up to the fact that the rest of the Yukon Territory might also meet a similar fate. The Yukon's population was now 80% American."

"Do you mean if the Americans had wanted to take over all the Yukon, there wouldn't have been much we could have done about it?"

"Probably very little we could do. The Commissioner of the Yukon back then, Major Walsh, thought the situation was bad. The Major was very worried that just a few bold Yanks could take possession of the whole Yukon Territory. The region was rapidly changing. The Canadian presence was weakening and the American presence was strengthening. A few conspirators could quickly overthrow the Yukon government. There was a very real possibility of that happening."

Dawson City, July 1899

In 1898, fifty thousand stampeders arrived in town in search for gold. Most left when their grub ran out.

"But it didn't," Brendan said, sounding very confident in his history, "I know for a fact that the Yukon is still part of Canada." And then, hesitating, he asked, "It is. Isn't it?"

"We can thank Clifford Sifton that it is," answered his grandfather.

"Who was he?"

"Sifton was the Minister of the Interior in the Canadian government. In 1898, he recruited two hundred additional men for the North West Mounted Police. My old friend Lewis McLauchlan was one of the men sent to Dawson at that time."

"So that's how he got the job with the Mounties," Brendan said. "I remember that part."

"Lewis enlisted at Fort Saskatchewan in 1898, but Sifton wasn't taking any chances on losing the territory. The government also sent two hundred soldiers to Dawson."

"Only two hundred?" repeated Brendan. "That's not very many."

"It was a lot back then," Linus said. "The unit was called the Yukon Field Force. They would provide a strong military presence in the Klondike."

"What has this got to do with the Order of the Midnight Sun, Grandpa? Were they the conspirators you were talking about?"

"We're getting to that, Brendan. The Mounted Police and the Yukon Field Force did such a good job in the Yukon, there seemed to be little danger of Canada losing sovereignty over the area. Then a strange thing happened."

"What strange thing?"

"In 1901, as the Gold Rush was coming to an end and the miners were drifting back home, a man approached a Mounted Police corporal in Dawson City with a strange tale of a conspiracy to loot the gold of the Yukon. This man called himself 'Shorty'."

"Shorty?" the boy repeated with a grin. "*Was he short?*"

"It was a nickname," Linus answered. "He was too scared to give his real name."

"Are you just making this up?" Brendan asked, giving his grandfather a sideways look.

"That's exactly what he called himself," Linus insisted. "Shorty told the corporal there was a group of American miners making plans to take over the Yukon. They had a long list of grievances. The rebel group was against claim limits per prospector. They were also against paying taxes for policing *and* mandatory periodic check ins with the North West Mounted Police."

"I could have told you it was going to be the miners," the boy said, nodding his head.

"How can you be so sure, may I ask?" asked his grandfather. "Are you a psychic?"

"Other than the police, *everyone* up there was a miner."

"You're probably right about that. And it's very likely Shorty was a miner too. Anyway, it turned out that Shorty had important news. He informed the police there was a rebellion in the works. Apparently, the perpetrators' first plan of attack was to rush the detachment at Whitehorse, then overpower the detachments along the Yukon River and finally take over the police barracks in Dawson."

"Sounds like an uprising!" exclaimed the boy, eyes widening.

"Not quite, Brendan. Shorty told the corporal that The Order of the Midnight Sun was led by only two men: Herbert Grehl and Fred Clark although there were other members in Skagway and Seattle."

"I *can't* believe the Mounties would let them get away with that," the boy said, being a firm believer in the rule of law.

"According to Shorty, The Midnight Sun member's ultimate goal was to establish a republic in the Yukon. You can imagine what the corporal must have thought when he heard Shorty's warning."

"He probably put on his gun belt and called out his deputies," Brendan said, standing up to practice his quick draw. "That's what I'd do." He pretended to take a shot at Horse, who was half asleep in the hallway. The very tired basset hound opened one eye and immediately closed it again.

"Or he might have wondered how reliable Shorty's information was," added Linus.

Brendan put away his imaginary six guns and considered that. "Maybe Shorty went to the police because he had a falling out with the other members of the gang."

"Possibly," Linus said, "he might very well have been an informer. Anyway, the corporal passed this information onto his senior officers. They, in turn, wanted to bring the man in for further questioning, but it was too late."

"Why? What happened to him?"

"The man couldn't be found."

"Where'd he go?"

"He'd fled to Skagway."

"So what did the Mounties do then?"

"They sent some constables to Dawson and braced for trouble."

"Then did the conspirators attack?"

"No. Nothing happened."

Brendan was very disappointed to hear that. "Is this *another* one of those stories where there's a big build up and then nothing happens?" he asked. He remembered his grandfather's story of the two Ottawa Valley lumberjacks who faced each other across the river back in the days of square timber.

Linus gave that question some thought. "There's no reason why there has to be fighting in every story."

"If there's no fighting in the story then it's probably true," Brendan sighed.

"Lewis' stories were always true," Linus replied, "When he told me that he helped break up the Order of the Midnight Sun, I believed him. I don't know what his exact involvement was— maybe he deported some or arrested some—I just don't know. All I do know is that there never was an armed rebellion in the Yukon. Nothing was ever heard of that shadowy group again."

The boy still looked disappointed. "It's just not as exciting when all the bad guys have either been sent home or locked up."

"Don't forget, Brendan, that the Gold Rush was coming to an end and the boundary dispute was finally being settled."

"Our teacher said that Canada lost that fight."

"Your teacher's right," agreed Linus. "In 1903 Canada and the United States formed a commission to resolve the boundary dispute. We never did get our seaport."

"But how come we lost if Lewis broke up the Order of the Midnight Sun?" asked the boy.

"We were simply outvoted. There were three Americans, two Canadians and an Englishman. The Englishman was Lord Alverstone, who was the British Chief Justice. In those days, Britain was still responsible for Canada's foreign affairs. We lost the Panhandle by one vote."

"*By one vote?*" exclaimed the boy. "How did we end up losing by *one* vote? That's what I want to know."

"Lord Alverstone cast the deciding vote in favour of the United States," Linus answered.

"*What was the matter with him?*" Brendan exclaimed. "How come he voted for the United States?" He didn't like Alverstone at all once he'd heard that. The nine-year-old begrudged the loss of even one square inch of Canadian soil—*especially by only one vote.* Secretly, he wanted Canada to be the biggest country in the whole world. How was that ever going to happen with people like Lord Alverstone around, he wondered? "Whose side was that guy on, anyway?"

"Lord Alverstone voted the way he thought was right," Linus answered.

"We should have asked for a recount," Brendan grumbled.

Linus understood the boy's disappointment. "Yes, it was a tough pill to swallow."

Brendan then pointed an accusing finger at Horse, who was half-asleep in the hallway. "Does Lord Alverstone remind you of anyone we know?"

Linus smiled at the comparison, remembering only too well how Horse stole the treasure of Eldorado Creek back in '98. "I can see the resemblance," he agreed. "But Brendan, did you really believe the Americans would hand over Skagway? It was too valuable. President Theodore Roosevelt had stated openly that if the vote hadn't gone his way, he would have used force if necessary to keep that port. Lord Alverstone was looking at the long term global picture—with a close eye on the balance of power in Europe. These issues are complex."

"There's that darn balance of power again," the boy said. "I don't see what that has to do with it."

"A potential conflict with Germany was looming," his grandfather said. "Remember how important the Treaty of Washington was to Britain. The Alaskan boundary dispute became part of British global diplomacy. Alverstone wanted no disputes with the United States while Europe was in an arms war. That was the certainly the bigger issue." Linus rubbed the back of his neck and added, "I'm afraid that Alverstone had decided Skagway was expendable."

That explanation wasn't good enough for Brendan. That was not how he would have voted. "It was just another double cross," the boy muttered, thinking that Lord Alverstone was a man not to be trusted. "It makes you wonder."

Meanwhile, down the hall, Horse, with one ear up and listening to all that had been said, was honoured to be compared to the Lord Chief Justice of Great Britain. The noble hound then slipped quietly into a deep sleep filled with dreams of buried treasure, roast beef sandwiches and a world without boundaries.

CHAPTER THIRTEEN

1907

The Flight of the 'Cygnet'

" *Whatever we discover,*
on Earth or out in space,
God grant that we may use it
to bless the human race."
—Fred Kaan, *The Earth, the Sky, the Ocean*[1]

"I HAVE TO HAND IN A PROJECT FOR THE SCIENCE FAIR, GRANDPA," ANNOUNCED BRENDAN ONE SATURDAY MORNING, "AND IT'S DUE IN TWO WEEKS."

His grandfather sat in his wicker chair working diligently on a crossword puzzle. "What's your topic?" he asked.

"I haven't thought of one yet," Brendan replied, "We're supposed to choose an inventor and explain his work."

"I'm sure you'll do very well," his grandfather answered, without looking up. He was preoccupied with fifteen across.

Brendan liked to pretend he didn't care about school, but secretly he was worried. "I'm not very good at science," he confided. "I only know that Isaac Newton invented the telephone."

Linus was astonished to hear such a thing coming from his very bright grandson. "Hello?" he said, putting his newspaper down and looking up at the boy. "Wasn't it Alexander Graham

Bell who invented the telephone?"

"*It was?*" Brendan asked. If that was true, he could envision a big red 'D' on the top of his assignment for sure.

"Of *course* it was," said Linus. "I think you need some brushing up on your inventors."

"I guess," the boy sighed.

"Why not do a project on Alexander Graham Bell, Brendan? That might be a good place to start."

"Some other kids in the class are already going to do something about the telephone," the Grade Five pupil said in a subdued voice. "I think they're going to make one out of soup tins and strings and stuff like that."

Linus looked hard at the boy. "But don't forget that Alexander Graham Bell worked on other experiments too—not just the telephone."

"He did?"

"Dr. Bell was a pioneer in the development of flight in Canada. He was experimenting with kites in Nova Scotia at the same time the Wright Brothers were working at Kittyhawk. Maybe you could do something along those lines."

Brendan shrugged. "I guess I hadn't thought about it too much."

"I think that the study of flight would make a very interesting science project. Remember how you always used to tell me you wanted to be able to fly like a bird?"

The nine-year-old frowned. "Not like a *bird*, Grandpa," he protested. "I meant like a *super hero*."

"Anyway, I *still* think you should consider it," Linus said. "You know, I met a man in Halifax during the war who would have been a great help on a project like this."

"How could he have helped?"

"Because he had worked for Alexander Graham Bell."

"Who was he, Grandpa?"

"I don't know his name. He was an elderly gentleman who happened to sit beside me on a park bench on my lunch hour one day. We struck up a casual conversation and discovered we had a mutual interest in photography. I used to take a lot of photographs back then with my old box camera."

"You still have it, don't you?"

"I still have *all* my old cameras." Linus answered. "I sent away for my first Kodak in 1930. It was a box camera issued by the company to commemorate their 50th anniversary. And you know something?"

"What?"

"It's *still* a good camera."

"You should get a digital," the boy suggested.

"A digital?" Linus asked, a little uncomfortable with the thought of buying one. "I don't know about that."

"They're pretty good."

"Anyway, the elderly gentlemen I spoke with told me that he was also an amateur photographer and had worked for Dr. Bell forty years before."

"Did he help Alexander Graham Bell invent the telephone?"

"This story happened in the years after Bell had invented the telephone," Linus answered. "Bell had been working on two projects at his summer home in Cape Breton, Nova Scotia at the time. He was trying to develop a breed of sheep that would produce several lambs at a birth and he was also developing a man-carrying kite."

"You mean he thought he could make a kite so big that it could actually carry a man?" Brendan asked, sounding very skeptical. "I've never heard of a kite *that* big."

"Bell knew that it was the wind on the surface areas of the kite that produced lift so he started to make kites with large surface areas."

"And it really worked?"

Linus nodded. "Bell's structures were actually quite sophisticated. He covered his kites with thousands of little pyramids attached together and made of silk. That was how he increased the surface area. The types of pyramids that Bell used were referred to as tetrahedral cells. His biggest kite was a couple of thousand pounds in weight and was made up of several thousand of these little cells. He named it the *Cygnet.* It was his first kite that could actually carry a man."

"Was it really able to lift Alexander Graham Bell off the ground?" Brendan asked.

Linus grinned. "Are you asking if Alexander Graham Bell ever took one of his kites for a spin?"

"Maybe," said the boy, thinking he was being asked a trick question.

"Other people who worked for him did that."

"Like that man you met?"

"The gentleman that I met told me that once Bell had finally built a kite that was strong enough to lift a man, he invited the press to watch a public demonstration. Bell always performed his flight experiments on water because it was safer than over land. This gentleman's job was to take the press out on a power boat, so that when the kite went up into the air, photographs could be taken of it. Unfortunately for the photographers who sat in the stern, the boat created so much spray that their film was ruined. The gentleman, who was in the bow, also took a photograph."

"But *his* turned out, I bet."

"Yes, it was the only one that could be developed. Then he surprised me by what he did next."

"What did he do?"

"The man reached into his topcoat pocket and pulled out the very photograph he had been talking about and showed it to me. He said he always carried it with him."

Alexander Graham Bell, 1847-1922
Bell gives his first public demonstration of tetrahedral kites at Columbia,
Virginia in 1904.

Brendan understood why. "That's because he was proud of it," the nine-year-old explained. While he carried no photos of man-carrying kites with him, Brendan had in his pocket a very interesting jagged stone he claimed was a tooth from a prehistoric flying reptile.

"I guess he was," Linus agreed, "I've often wondered if that photograph was of the flight of the *Cygnet*. I can't remember which of Bell's kites he told me it was. I've read since that on December 6, 1907, the *Cygnet* lifted a man about 160 feet in the air."

"And it stayed up?"

"About seven minutes," Linus answered. "It came down fast and hit the water hard. Fortunately the pilot, an American army officer named Selfridge, wasn't hurt."

"That's good."

"I should have paid more attention to his story," Linus said. "I didn't even get the man's name."

"Can't you look him up in old records or something?"

"I'd need to have a copy of that picture. It's too late to do anything about it now."

"If *I* ever meet someone in the park like that, I'm going to interview him and then write *everything* down," Brendan said.

"I remember that he and I had discussed wartime bombing," Linus said. "This conversation had taken place during the 'Blitz' and he commented that he'd always found it hard to accept that the airplane had become such a destructive force. This man had thought that the invention of the airplane would make the world a better place, not make it worse."

"I thought the airplane made it a better place," Brendan said.

"An inventor would have had to be very naïve if he thought that airplanes would only be used for peaceful purposes," Linus answered. "As soon as there were manned flights, weapons were brought on board."

"I bet the first pilot took up a pair of Colt 45s." Brendan said, drawing a pair of imaginary six shooters out of his holster.

"Of course, the airplane hasn't been the only good idea of man that has caused harm," Linus said. "There have been many inventions over the years that have been misused, haven't there? I bet you can think of an obvious one."

"You mean like the chainsaw?"

"Actually, I was thinking of the *automobile*," Linus said, tapping his grandson's knee. "I'm sure that Henry Ford and the other early car makers never thought of all the accidents there would be on the highways."

"I guess not," the boy said.

"It might be a good idea to do a science project about safety on the highways," suggested Linus. "You can't go wrong with a topic like that."

"No, Grandpa," Brendan announced, in a dramatic display of decisiveness, "I'm going to do my science project on kites— even though I've never flown one before."

"I think that's an excellent choice, Brendan."

"I'm going to buy one on my way home."

"You can always buy an inexpensive kite at the convenience store. I can help too, if you want. Why don't we meet up at the park tomorrow and see if we can get it up in the air. I'll bring my camera along."

"That's a good idea, Grandpa. You could take pictures of the kite in the air."

"And you can mount them on Bristol board. That might be a good way of illustrating the principal of lift."

"Maybe I can also get some information about flight in the library too," the fifth-grader said, showing rare enthusiasm for schoolwork.

"This could work out well, my boy."

"I can't wait for tomorrow."

"And don't worry. We'll find a good spot on a hill to fly it."

"With no trees," Brendan cautioned him.

So the boy ran off to buy his kite, promising to meet his grandfather at the park the next day. In the meantime, Linus too, had an important purchase to make.

Sunday turned out to be a perfect day for kite flying. Brendan had arrived at the park promptly with the kite he had bought at a local store. Linus was already there, having taken his dog, Horse, for a walk around the park.

"I want to make sure I get some good pictures of the kite," Linus said, showing his grandson a brand-new camera which he had purchased. "What do you think of *this*?"

"This is *historic*!" cried his delighted grandson, very impressed to see the new camera. "You can be just like the man you met during the war. I bet you'll carry a picture of *my* kite around with you just as long as that guy did. What was the name of that big kite again, Grandpa?"

"The *Cygnet*."

"What is a cygnet, anyway?"

"It's a young swan."

"Then I'm naming mine 'The Ugly Duckling'."

Thus, began the great science project on lift. The two rookie aviators found that getting the kite up in the air was not as easy as they thought. They were close several times, but the kite would not stay up. Each time Linus quickly had his camera ready, and each time he had to put it away.

Finally, the Duckling was in the air.

For a few brief seconds, Linus and Brendan gazed at it in triumph. Linus reached for his camera.

He lined up the shot, clicked the shutter several times, but there was no flash.

Then the gallant Duckling wobbled in the air. "*Oh, no!*" shouted Brendan.

They watched as the kite crashed to the ground.

"What happened to your camera?" Brendan asked, looking into the eyes of his despondent grandfather. "I didn't see the flash."

"The camera didn't work," Linus moaned. "I can't understand it."

Linus continued to press the shutter out of frustration. The camera was dead. They looked at each other in bewilderment.

"I'm sorry, Brendan."

"Maybe I shouldn't have said anything to you about getting a new camera," the boy said, swallowing his disappointment. "Maybe we should have stuck with your old one."

"It *should* have worked. I only bought it yesterday."

"What are we going to do now?" the boy asked, worried that his science project was doomed for failure.

"We're going right back to the store where I bought this thing and get it fixed or my money back," Linus said, his face filled with determination.

They drove immediately to the photo shop and were looked after by the same young lady who had sold Linus the camera the day before.

"Are you sure you put the film in correctly?" she asked, examining the camera at different angles.

"This is not my first camera, you know," Linus replied, rolling his eyes upwards, "I've been taking pictures since before you were born."

"I'll look at it in the darkroom," she said, ignoring his comment.

"She looks like she's only about sixteen," Linus whispered to Brendan after she had left. "She'll probably have to ask the manager for help."

Brendan nodded in agreement.

In a moment she returned. "How long did you say you have been taking pictures?" she asked.

"*Since 1930!*" piped up Brendan, with pride.

"Really?" she said, turning to Linus. "Well, you forgot to take the plastic seal off the batteries."

CHAPTER FOURTEEN

1912

The Voyage of the 'Nolturno'

BRENDAN WATCHED A GREAT COMMERCIAL FOR A COMPUTER GAME ON TELEVISION. He knew he must have it.

Only this was not the best time. He had less than five dollars in his strongbox. His mother had been no help. She simply told him it was too expensive.

Brendan was not about to quit without a fight. He decided to ask his grandfather.

The boy knew that Linus had not embraced the new technology. It would be safe to say that his grandfather was an old-fashioned man. He never bought on credit (he always paid in cash), he had a rotary phone (black), wrote letters in longhand (with a fountain pen) and always wore a necktie. Brendan thought he must even wear a rubber one in the shower.

But to the boy, the strangest thing was that his grandfather didn't even own a computer. He would rather read.

There was one encouraging sign. Linus had been given an answering machine on his last birthday and had been using it.

One morning, Brendan found his grandfather soaking up the warmth in his sunroom. Before entering, the boy mentally rehearsed his sales pitch once more. Listing all the positives which were sure to win his grandfather over, he approached him. As he inched closer, he was surprised to see his grandfather speaking into what looked very much like a hand-held device. Had he finally purchased a cell phone? If so, that was very good news indeed. Any man who used a cell phone would certainly be sufficiently up to date to appreciate the benefits a young boy would gain from using the latest high-speed computer game.

Then his heart sank.

Linus was not speaking into a cell phone. He was eating a carrot.

This was a setback to Brendan, but undaunted he began his pitch.

"You know all about the technology today that's changing the world, don't you, Grandpa?"

"I think you have me mixed up with someone else," Linus replied. "I don't know the difference between a computer and a wristwatch."

"Sure you do," Brendan reminded him. "You even have an answering machine now."

"Worst thing that ever happened to me," Linus grunted.

"I want to tell you about this computer game," Brendan went on, describing it in glorious detail. He spoke in glowing terms of the fun, the excitement, and the realism of the game. He concluded his speech with his all important selling point which never failed to persuade prospective investors. He explained to his grandfather there had never been a game to match this one for *educational* value. The people who worked in the game store all said the same thing. The boy was confident he had made a convincing presentation.

"How much is it, exactly?" Linus inquired, noticing his grandson had conveniently not volunteered the price.

"About two hundred dollars," Brendan answered, "Don't forget that includes the system and maybe a controller."

Linus almost choked on his carrot. "*Two hundred dollars? Plus tax!* I bought my first car for less than that."

That comment put the boy temporarily on the defensive. "My mom says she's broke," he said, and then added with a half smile, "so I was just wondering if you'd like to put some money into this with me."

"How in the world did you acquire such expensive tastes?" Linus asked, shaking his head in despair for the youth of to-day. "You're nine years old! You should be interested in comic books, marbles and collecting stamps. They're simple, inexpensive and fun."

"But those things are expensive now too," Brendan argued. "Don't forget, Grandpa, you told me that everything only cost a nickel when you were my age."

"Well, a nickel was *still* a lot of money if you only made ten nickels a month," Linus replied.

"Aw, those old games are kind of boring anyway, Grandpa. They have *great* games out for kids these days."

Linus didn't buy that argument at all. "That's exactly the problem, Brendan. Young people are big business now. Don't you know that companies hire child psychologists these days to get inside children's heads so they know how to convince them to buy their products?"

Once again, Brendan was put back on his heels but undaunted. "But they have great graphics out now and in 3-D too," he said, not giving a hoot how many child psychologists were hired by companies. "You should at least try playing one game with me sometime. We could compete against each other."

Linus was unmoved by the challenge.

"I'd *love* to play you," Brendan insisted, "Who's your favourite action hero?"

"Tom Mix."

"Oh," the boy said, never having heard of that action figure. "Well, it doesn't matter anyway, because you can create your own characters with the game I want. You can *personalize* them. There's no end to the kinds of things you can do."

"All the bells and whistles, I suppose," Linus said, in a tone that suggested he hated bells and whistles.

"You might be really good at video games, *if you'd try*," Brendan persisted, *"Think outside the box."*

Linus shook his head. "You sound like one of those psychologists that I was talking about," he said, "but aren't you a little young to be a psychologist? They're usually in their forties."

Brendan grinned. "I'm forty-two," he said, very quick on the uptake. "Just short."

"Just short of sales resistance you mean," Linus said. "Don't let our materialistic world push you around, my boy. Just because a product exists and it's advertised on television and looks exciting, doesn't mean you have to have it. It might not even be good for you."

The young consumer stared at him blankly. How could a computer game not be good for you, he wondered?

Linus recognized that look. "Can I tell you a little story?" he asked.

"I *knew* there was a story coming on," Brendan said, having some of the wind taken out of his sails. "I know you too well."

Linus smiled at him. "That you do," he said. "Do you remember last year when we went to Pioneer Village?"

"I remember," Brendan answered in a subdued voice. He also remembered that he had wished that his grandfather had taken him to the local games arcade instead.

"You went looking for some snacks as usual and I waited for you in the livery stable. I noticed that the blacksmith was deep in conversation with a very old man. After the old visitor had left, the blacksmith told me the man's story. It was quite interesting."

"It was?"

"The old man had told the blacksmith that he was born in Germany at the turn of the last century. He was about your age when his father suddenly died. His mother decided to bring her son to Canada so that the two of them could start a new life together. They had barely enough money to book passage on an old tramp freighter."

"But what does this have to do with buying a video game?"

"I'm getting to that," Linus said. "The boy and his mother packed all their worldly belongings and managed to get a ride to the port city of Rotterdam in Holland, where they boarded the Nolturno. On April 11, the freighter sailed for Halifax. One morning, after a couple of days at sea, the two of them were on deck when they saw a wonderful sight. A great luxury liner steamed out of the mists on a parallel course and easily passed them. It too, was America-bound. The mother put her arm around the boy's shoulder and told him how she wished she could have taken her son to Canada on a great ship like that."

"That sounds pretty good to me too," Brendan said cheerfully. "Where can I get a ticket?"

Linus continued. "The old man said that he and his mother stared for the longest time at the ship as it knifed its way through the seas in all its glory. They watched with fascination, as it dwindled to a speck and disappeared into the distance."

Brendan began to get the message. "You mean that all good things don't last very long?" he asked. "Is that the moral of the story?"

"Wait until I finish. Of course, the boy and his mother certainly would have loved the comfort of a lavish stateroom on a ship like that. That's only natural. Those world-class luxury liners had elaborate cabins, wonderful food and marvelous parties in ballrooms. "

"Cruise ships are *still* like that, Grandpa."

"But those old ocean liners were really *opulent*," Linus said. "The two of them must have compared the grand comforts of that great liner with the limited offerings of the *Nolturno* and were a little envious. I'm sure they thought about it for the rest of their passage."

"I would have too," the nine-year-old said. "That's for sure."

Linus' eyes met his grandson's. "When we see the nice things that other people have, it's natural to feel that we would like to have them too."

Brendan began to fidget with his top button.

"Otherwise we feel left out," Linus said. "Don't we?"

The boy squirmed. "Probably," he sighed, feeling an uncomfortable twinge of guilt, and knowing for sure that he could kiss that video game goodbye.

"There's an interesting end to this story, Brendan. The old man said it was the next day that he and his mother heard some news. Word about the great ship had spread quickly on board. And having heard it, both he and his mother were very glad they had crossed the ocean on the *Nolturno*. They would always remember the ship that had passed them on that cold April morning."

"Why?" Brendan asked suspiciously. "Was there something special about it?"

"The old man told the blacksmith that even after all those years he would never forget how he and his mother had squinted into the mist trying to make out the name of the ship across her stern. He could still hear his mother's voice as she slowly spelled it out for him: T-I-T-A-N-I-C."

CHAPTER FIFTEEN

1917

Victoria Cross Hill

"where I got my first taste of shell fire"
—words written in pencil in the author's copy of *'Only This'*

"WHAT'S YOUR FAVOURITE TREE, BRENDAN?" ASKED THE BOY'S GRANDFATHER.

Linus was putting on his comfortable shoes and looking forward to a leisurely walk.

His basset hound, well known in the community as "Horse", was waiting patiently in the hallway.

"Is that a trick question, Grandpa?" The boy knew that there was often something behind those kinds of questions.

"I'm going to go down to the park to look for a tree and you're certainly welcome to come along."

"What kind of a tree are you looking for?"

"I know *exactly* what it will look like," Linus answered. "It has to be in good shape, nice to look at and growing on a slope. Once I've found it, I'm going to give it a name."

"You're giving it a *name*?" Brendan repeated, noticing that his grandfather certainly seemed to have a lot of spare time on his hands recently.

"I'm going to call it 'The General Currie Tree'. I want to honour one of Canada's great generals. "

"You're naming a *tree* after him?" Brendan asked, puzzled by the whole idea. "I've never heard of anyone giving a name to a tree before."

"There are two Giant Sequoia trees in California, each more than two thousand years old, named for Civil War generals. It's a way Americans honour General Sherman and General Grant. They're sentimental about their history and I think we should be too."

"Couldn't they just make a statue of them or something? Why a tree, Grandpa?"

"It's a living tribute to someone. That's what makes it special."

"I guess it kind of makes sense."

"Have you ever heard of General Currie?"

"Not really."

"That's *exactly* why he needs my tree. Few Canadians today remember our World War One leaders. Did you know that General Currie was our first full Canadian-born general?"

"He was?"

"Yes, in the First War, General Currie was awarded the command of the whole Canadian Corps because of his leadership at the Battle of Vimy Ridge in 1917. He was the first Canadian to be given such a command."

"Vimy Ridge?" repeated the boy. "At school they showed us a picture of the statue that they put up for the soldiers. I think that was the one."

"It was built on Vimy Ridge in France to honour the memory of the Canadian soldiers," agreed Linus. "They should have put up another memorial for them at Hill 70."

"Did they name hills in those days too?"

"I think they gave that hill a number because it was important strategically," Linus said. "It was General Currie's army that captured it."

"And that's why you want to name a tree for the general?"

"That war cost 60,000 Canadians their lives," he said. "Another 170,000 were wounded."

"That's a lot," Brendan said in a low voice.

"It's important for us as a country that we remember their sacrifices."

"I don't know why there has to be wars all the time," the nine-year-old said.

"Neither do I, Brendan. We lost a generation of young men in the Great War. It wasn't long ago that there were still quite a few survivors of it living among us. They used to parade each year to their town's cenotaph on Remembrance Day. But now there's only a couple left. We have to find other ways to remember them now."

"We learned about that war in school, Grandpa. Our teacher said for a long time the war was a stalemate."

Linus shook his head in despair at the memory of it. "Those poor boys had it in their heads that they were signing up to play 'Cowboys and Indians'. The ironic part was that they were worried that the game would be over before they got there. It didn't take them long before they realized the seriousness of it. When those raw recruits made it to the front lines, they were thrown into a grinder."

"It must have been pretty bad."

"It seems the soldiers' lives were expendable."

"Our teacher said the soldiers lived in trenches at the front," Brendan said, "and they always had to keep their heads down because snipers were shooting at them. But I think the trenches must have been the worst part. They were filled with mud and lice and diseases and stuff, so they had to build dugouts. The soldiers who built them were called 'sappers'."

"There were *many* trenches that didn't have dugouts, Brendan. After it rained, the water remained in the trenches and the soldiers' feet would be wet for months. They didn't have the luxury of a change of clothing. I was once told by a man who fought at the front that his trench was like a canal."

"Our teacher said that a lot of soldiers got 'trench foot'," the boy said. "I think that was something that happened to their feet because they were wet all the time."

"That's right," Linus said. "Many of the men suffered from frostbite."

"It sure must have been bad at the front."

"Our boys did their duty," Linus said quietly.

"I'm just glad I wasn't living back then," the nine-year-old said.

"After General Currie took command of the Canadian Division, he was ordered to attack the German positions at the coal mining town of Lens, which was near Hill 70."

"Did he capture it?"

"A frontal attack on Lens worried him. Currie argued his case to High Command that it would make more sense strategically to take the hill located beside Lens, instead of the town itself. He wanted to be in possession of the high ground. He thought there might be fewer casualties."

"It sounds like he was a good general."

"I think he was respected by his men and superiors, but none of our First World War generals came out of the war with much admiration."

"Even though they won?"

"It was not a war anybody claimed to win. The Great War brought nothing but death and destruction and an uncertain future. When people realized how many lives it cost and all the misery it caused, they wanted to know who was responsible for it."

"You mean they had to blame somebody for it?" Brendan asked.

"I don't think General Currie was to blame for the high casualty rates in those battles," Linus said. "He was a good general and was certainly an important figure in Canadian history."

"So what happened in that battle? Was that hill really hard to capture?"

"General Currie tried to conceal from the enemy that Hill 70 was his main objective. The battle began August 15, 1917, with a heavy artillery barrage. Then the Canadians went over the top. You can imagine what a terrifying moment that would have been. The German defenders used machine-guns, hand grenades, rifles and gas on them, but the Canadians finally took possession. The Germans weren't finished, however. They counter attacked again and again, but were unable to regain the hill. When the battle was over, there were eight thousand Canadian casualties; the Germans suffered twenty thousand."

Brendan was taken aback by the sheer numbers. "I thought you said that General Currie was worried about casualties," he said, "It sure doesn't sound like it."

"I *know,*" Linus sighed, "but by the military standards of the day, he did more than most to prepare his men for battle. But you're right, Brendan. No matter how hard a general tried to keep his army out of trouble, when all was said and done, the soldiers of the Great War always ended up as cannon fodder. "

"That doesn't seem fair."

"The best you can say about it is that there was a lot of courage shown by the men on both sides."

Linus looked at Brendan over his glasses. "Did you know that Canadian soldiers won five Victoria Crosses in the battle for Hill 70?"

"Is that like the Purple Heart?"

"The Purple Heart is an American medal, Brendan. *The Victoria Cross* is the highest decoration awarded in Canada for courage."

He walked to his bookcase and carefully brought down a green hard covered book.

"I bought this book a couple of days ago," Linus said. "I found it at the bottom of a bin in an old second hand book store downtown. It's a veteran's memoirs of the First World War. James Pedley, a soldier who fought at Hill 70, wrote it."

Linus handed the book to Brendan, while he patted his shirt pocket looking for his reading glasses.

"It looks really old," said the boy.

"The name of the book is *Only This*," Linus said, picking up his glasses off the kitchen table where he had left them. "I have no idea what the title means."

Brendan stared at the book with great interest. "I know what it might mean."

Linus gave his grandson a disbelieving look. "You *do*?"

"I think so. I remember there was a picture in a book at school of the trenches and rows of white crosses and all you could see was mud." Brendan pursed his lips and looked at the ceiling to help him recall the details. "The background was yellow because of the mustard gas and stuff like that. Maybe he just wanted to tell his story about what it was like in the war, but he didn't want to make too big deal out of it."

"That's a very good suggestion," Linus said, very proud of his grandson's insight. "I hadn't thought of that."

The boy was examining one of the pages intently. "Did you notice that somebody has written something on the page, Grandpa?"

"No, I hadn't," Linus answered, very surprised to hear that. "Where?"

"It's written in pencil along the sides," Brendan said. "Somebody has underlined parts of the story of Hill 70 with a pencil."

Linus removed his glasses and brought the book closer to his face. "You're right. Someone *has* written something in the margins." He then began to slowly read the notes aloud.

> *"This spot is where I got my first taste of shell fire. The identical battery position behind the crassier with the ruined houses on the left (see map 106)."*

He turned the page and read another notation written in pencil.

"This was a dirty place just before and after Hill 70"

Linus examined the writing with awe. *"Isn't this something?"* Linus exclaimed. "Some old 'sweat' in that battle owned this book before me. It wouldn't surprise me if he knew the author. Maybe they were in the same regiment."

"That makes this book really special."

"Does it ever!" Linus exclaimed. "Let's look up the map on page 106."

He quickly turned to page 106 and pointed, "See here? He's marked an 'X' just outside Lens and beside it he's written *'Shellfire'*."

"And over here he's written, *'Gas'*," Brendan noticed.

"It's too bad he didn't write in more detail," Linus said, excitedly. "This is history coming to life before our very eyes!"

"This would make a *great* movie!" Brendan said, with rising excitement in his voice. "Imagine if the 'X' stood for pirate treasure or something like that. A couple of boys find an old book in a trunk in a store just like you did and they look inside. Of course, it's not really a book—it's a *treasure map!* They buy it for a quarter, take it back to their clubhouse, decipher it and go and look for the treasure."

Linus was holding the book up to the light to see the soldier's writing better. "This is real *history*, my boy, not a movie. The man who owned this book was one of General Currie's soldiers. This is the personal war story of that man and we're holding it in our hands."

"And it's in his own *handwriting* too!" the boy exclaimed. *"That makes it even better."*

"We have to really take care of this book."

"Maybe put it in a museum," Brendan suggested.

General Sir Arthur Currie 1875-1933,
After the capture of Hill 70, General Currie (pointing) and General MacBrien
prepare for the next battle, September 1917.

Both of them gazed at it with reverence.

The nine-year-old clenched his jaw. He had now made a firm decision. "I'm going to help you find that tree, Grandpa," he announced. "It will be like having a real general living in our park."

"Let's choose a healthy one," Linus said. "We don't want to find out later that some efficient park employee has painted a big red 'X' on it. You know what that means, don't you?"

"It means that General Currie could end up as a sofa."

"The tree also has to be on a little hill to represent Hill 70."

"And we have to make an inscription so people will know that it's a tribute to our general," Brendan suggested.

"Something small, so it's not too noticeable," cautioned Linus. "Remember it's a public park after all."

"Can I write it?" asked Brendan. "But you tell me what to say."

After the inscription was completed, Brendan, Linus and Horse set off for the park to choose their favourite tree.

They chose well.

Somewhere in one of Canada's parks there stands a very stately looking jack pine, growing on a gentle slope.

There is a flat rock embedded in the ground in front of it.

On the surface of the rock written in Brendan's neatest handwriting are the words:

"The General Currie Tree
On Active Service"

CHAPTER SIXTEEN

1 9 1 8

I Flew with Roy Brown

"Per Ardua ad Astra"
(Through Struggles to the Stars)
Motto of the Royal Canadian Air Force
and the Royal Air Force

"Shake the hand that shook the hand of the last living World War One fighter pilot," Linus said. He stood at the doorway smiling. His nine-year-old grandson reached out to shake his hand. Meanwhile, Horse, Linus' trusty basset hound and occasional squirrel-chaser, stirred from his afternoon nap.

"That's pretty good," Brendan said. It sounded to him as if his grandfather should be congratulated, but he wondered why he used such roundabout expressions to say such simple things.

"I met Harry Botterill yesterday," Linus explained. "He's one hundred and four years of age."

"That's how old he is?" Brendan asked. He was immediately struck by the fact Harry Botterill was even older than his best friend's aunt. He had never heard of anyone being older than she was. "My best friend's aunt is ninety-five," he added. "She eats a lot of yogurt."

"Harry's in a nursing home now," Linus said. "He was at a presentation that I attended yesterday at Sunnybrook Hospital in honour of our old war heroes. That's where I met him. His claim to fame is that he shot down a German observation balloon in the First World War. Do you know what that was?"

"Was it a spy balloon or something like that?"

"That's exactly what it was," Linus replied. "The balloons were filled with hydrogen and tethered to the ground by a wire cable. An observer, perched high in a basket and with a good pair of binoculars, could watch what was happening along the Western Front and pass along reports to his superiors."

"That's all he did—shoot down a balloon?" Brendan asked. "Wouldn't that be kind of an easy target?"

"Not really. It was often harder to shoot down a balloon than a plane," Linus said, "Those balloons were very well protected on the ground by machine guns. An aircraft would have to fly very low to get a good shot at one and don't forget those old biplanes were really slow. It took a lot of courage to attack a balloon."

"So Harry was a war hero—right?"

"He was indeed," Linus said, "and when you consider that the life expectancy of a pilot in the First World War was six weeks, isn't it amazing that Harry is still going strong at one hundred and four?" Linus removed his pen from his shirt pocket. "I think we need a map," he said. "Do you have some paper?"

His grandson immediately recognized that Linus' face was assuming that familiar far off look which appeared just before he began one of his stories. "I'll get some," Brendan said and he raced off to his schoolbag. He always carried the supplies for his grandfather's expeditions into the past.

"Just one sheet," Linus said. The story would need a little diagram of the Western Front showing where the various armies were positioned during the spring offensive of 1918.

"I hope young people never forget the sacrifices that Canadians made in the First World War. We should be very proud of them," his grandfather said, gathering Brendan and Horse around him. He quickly drew an outline of the Somme River with a few broad strokes of his fountain pen. "This is where the aerial battles took place. Of all those early pilots, there's only one left—Harry Botterill."

Linus then rubbed his chin and added, "You know, those old World War One pilots were my heroes when I was your age. I never had the opportunity of meeting Bishop or Barker or Collishaw, but I'm grateful that I met both Botterill and Brown."

"Who's Brown?"

"You've never heard of Roy Brown?"

"No."

"He was a fighter pilot—was one of the best," Linus said, and then added in a casual manner, "I flew with him."

"*You flew with him*?" Brendan asked, very surprised to hear that. He was trying to picture his grandfather in a helmet and goggles with a white, silk scarf streaming in the wind. "How did that happen?" he asked. "Were *you* a pilot, Grandpa?"

"No," admitted Linus. "I wasn't a pilot, but I did fly with Brown. I'll have to explain how that happened." His thoughts went back to a summer day long ago when he was Brendan's age and living in Chatham, Ontario. "I was in the Boy Scouts and I won a prize for earning the most badges in the troop," he said, "And guess what the prize was?"

"I don't know," the boy shrugged his shoulders. "Another badge?"

"I won an airplane ride," Linus answered. "Remember that this was in the late 1920's. There were very few people who had flown in an airplane in those days."

"*Boy!*" Brendan gave a shout. "That would have been great back then—not as much now because I've already been on a plane a couple of times."

"You can imagine how excited I was," Linus said. "Roy Brown was the name of the man who ran the flying school on the outskirts of town. I was told to ask for him. The only problem was that it was a long way to go on my own, so I asked my pal, Charlie Patterson, a fellow Scout, to go with me. The following Saturday, Charlie and I hitchhiked out to the old airfield. I introduced myself to Captain Brown and I asked him if he would mind taking Charlie up with us."

"Did he say that Charlie could fly too?"

Linus thought back to that wonderful day so many years age. "He was very gracious about it. He simply waved both of us on board and up we went. We circled the town and the river and farms and fields and roads."

"That must have been exciting," said the boy.

It was *incredible* to see everything from the air. Charlie and I couldn't stop pointing at all the landmarks we recognized and I remember how we yelled to each other into the wind. We landed about fifteen minutes later and neither of us could believe what we had just done. *What a day! We had flown!* We immediately both wanted to become pilots. "

"Were you ever lucky!"

"But it was even more special to us because we had flown with Captain Brown."

"What was so special about that?"

"He was the man who had shot down the Red Baron."

"Who?"

"The Red Baron."

"The Red Baron?" Brendan looked puzzled. "Was he a super hero or something?"

"He was Germany's greatest air ace of the First World War," Linus explained. "His real name was Baron Manfred Von Richtoffen, and during the war, he and his red triplane were famous. You see, by the spring of 1918, the Red Baron had shot down eighty Allied planes."

"Boy, he must have been a good shot."

"No other pilot had shot down as many planes as that man had," explained Linus, "but when he took off on April 21, 1918, he was flying on borrowed time."

Captain Arthur Roy Brown, DSC. 1893-1944
Born in Carleton Place, Ontario, he learned to fly at the Wright Flying School, in
Dayton, Ohio and gained international fame for shooting down the "Red Baron"
on April 21, 1918.

"What do you mean?"

Linus pointed to the Somme River on his map. "Captain Brown was leading his squadron right about here. A young

Canadian flyer, Wilfred May, was in his first combat mission of the war. He spotted a lone enemy aircraft and foolishly broke from the formation to attack it. As luck would have it, May's guns jammed and the enemy aircraft escaped. Then the worst happened. May noticed a lone red triplane fighter, bearing a black cross on its side, flying above him."

"That must have been the Red Baron."

"Yes it was," Linus said. "When May saw who was attacking him, he swallowed hard and his heart began to pound. He knew he was in an awful spot. He dodged to get out of the line of fire. The triplane stayed with him. He swooped low over the Somme. The triplane was still on him. When he heard the sound of his plane being hit, May figured his time was up."

Brendan's heart was pounding too.

"Just as the Red Baron was about to finish him off, a third plane appeared."

"Was that Captain Brown?"

"It was Brown in his Sopwith Camel," Linus said. "He fired a burst of bullets into the red plane. The pilot slumped in his cockpit and his plane crashed into a field near an Australian artillery battery."

"Was the Red Baron killed?"

"Richtoffen died in his plane," his grandfather said quietly. "It was all over for him. The soldiers on the ground raced to the crash site to claim parts of his plane as souvenirs."

Linus marked a little 'X' on a spot inside the Allied lines where the famous crash occurred.

Brendan was very quiet.

His grandfather concluded his story. "There have been many debates over the years as to whether it was Brown's bullets or Australian ground troops that actually caused the Baron's death. Roy Brown was fairly sure he had killed him. He certainly never felt very good about it, even though in doing so, he had saved May's life."

"But the Red Baron was kind of a bad guy though, wasn't he?" Brendan asked, trying to justify the shooting.

"He actually wasn't a bad guy at all," Linus answered, "and that's always the tragedy of war. In fact, the Red Baron and Captain Brown were much alike in many respects: they were about the same age and each had a high sense of duty and love of country. And, of course, each loved to fly."

"So they were both heroes—right?"

"That's a good way to put it."

"Did Captain Brown tell you and Charlie all about shooting down the Red Baron?"

"Captain Brown wasn't the type of person to ever want to talk about something like that, nor did it even occur to us to ask. We were only interested in the airplane ride. Think about it, Brendan. Would you want to be world-famous for killing a man?"

"Not me—that's for sure," the boy said, now that his grandfather had put it like that.

"That was the last thing Roy Brown wanted too," Linus said. "He was a serious and quiet person who was horrified by the barbarity of war. Unfortunately, for years afterwards, reporters continually hounded him about shooting down the Red Baron, while he was trying his best to put it out of his mind."

"I guess that would be hard to do if everybody kept reminding you," Brendan said, having for the first time considered the burden of fame.

"I've always been glad I didn't ask," Linus said. "It was a perfect day. Not very many Canadians had ever flown back then. Charlie and I boasted about it for a long time afterwards. We were so proud of ourselves."

"I would have been proud of that too," Brendan said.

Linus gave his grandson a shoulder hug. "But I was prouder still to have flown with Roy Brown."

1920

J' Avance

"Remember that time is money"
Benjamin Franklin

BRENDAN'S GRANDFATHER KNEW THAT WHAT HE WAS ABOUT TO
SAY MIGHT BE THE MOST IMPORTANT FINANCIAL ADVICE THE BOY
WOULD EVER RECEIVE.

Linus had learned years before that only a young person can best take advantage of the principle of compound interest, yet few were aware of it.

As he sat in his wicker chair watching Brendan play with an electronic device, he wondered how he could teach his grandson to reinvest the interest earned on his savings. How could he best explain that it's not how much money you save each month, it's how long you have the money working for you?

"Let's say Little Johnny has a paper route," he said to Brendan, trying to get his attention. "He puts away a fixed amount each month and continues that habit for a certain period of time. Are you with me so far?"

The nine-year-old, who despised math with a passion, nodded his head, but really wasn't listening. His eyes were open but he had tuned out. His grandfather recognized that look immediately. The tranquil expression on the boy's face reminded Linus of the sleeping iguana they had seen on their last trip to the local zoo.

"Little Billy has a larger paper route," Linus went on. "After a while, he notices that Little Johnny has been saving his money and he wants to do the same thing. Little Billy, having a larger route, puts away a larger amount than Little Johnny. Are you still with me?"

One of Brendan's multiple-sets of eyelids blinked.

"Who would have saved the most money in, say, five years time?" Linus asked. "Little Johnny or Little Billy?"

Linus was hopeful that his grandson would grasp the importance of what he had just said.

"May I ask a question?" the boy said, having awoken from his lethargy.

"Sure," replied Linus, happily anticipating Brendan might want an example of this compounding principal with real numbers that he could sink his teeth into. "What's your question?"

"Why are all the people in your stories little?"

With a heavy sigh, Linus put his dreams of his grandson's financial independence on hold. "Little Johnny saved the most," he said, bringing the lesson to a close, "because his money was invested for a longer period of time. It just takes discipline."

"Actually, I won't need much money when I grow up," Brendan announced. "I'm going to live on the beach."

"Live on the beach?" Linus asked, puzzled by the boy's logic. "How will you be able to afford that?"

"I won't need any clothes," the boy answered.

"Well, you'll still have to learn to manage your money even living on the beach," his grandfather said, "I opened my first bank account with the old Bank of Ottawa in Carleton Place. It was an imposing looking building on Beckwith Street across from Hughes Drug Store."

"I've never even heard of the Bank of Ottawa before."

"They always referred to themselves as the lumberman's bank," Linus replied. "A group of Ottawa Valley lumbermen started the bank in 1874. They opened the Carleton Place branch in 1883.

*Bank of Ottawa, Five Dollar Bill, November 2,1880 The lumberman's bank issued
a series of banknotes with colourful illustrations of rafts, saw mills and river
drivers on spring drives.*

Their corporate seal was a hand holding a woodsman's axe."

"*A woodsman's axe!*" Brendan exclaimed. This was more like it. He loved his grandfather's old yarns about lumberjacks, river drivers and the days of square timber.

"And its corporate motto was *J'Avance*," added Linus.

"What does that mean?"

"To advance; to go forward. Isn't that a great motto?"

"*J'Avance*," Brendan repeated, spearing the air with an imaginary rapier.

"The manager of the bank in Carleton Place was John Adams Bangs," Linus said. "I remember Mr. Bangs as a well dressed, friendly man and very knowledgeable about investing. He'd been the manager there for more than twenty years. Because I was his youngest customer, he took the time to explain compound interest to me. He taught me the secret to a good standard of living was to learn to save part of my salary and reinvest the income. There's an old saying which says, a penny saved—"

"—keeps the doctor away," interrupted Brendan.

"Something along those lines," Linus laughed. "Anyway, after I left school, Mr. Bangs convinced me to apply for a job with the bank," he said. "I worked in the Toronto main branch until the war broke out. The Bank of Ottawa had long before merged with the Bank of Nova Scotia of course, but I still have fond memories of the old lumberman's bank as a boy."

"That's my kind of bank too," the boy announced.

"The Bank of Ottawa was a popular bank back then, but it wasn't limited to just branches in the Ottawa Valley like Carleton Place. It had expanded westward to Edmonton, Regina and even Vancouver. However, after the First World War, the Bank of Ottawa knew it must expand even further or die."

"Did they die? Is that why they're not around any more?"

"They amalgamated with the Bank of Nova Scotia in 1919."

"But I guess you always remember that great emblem and

the motto too."

"Actually, what I remember best were their banknotes."

"Their banknotes?"

"In those days each bank printed their own bills."

"*They did?*" Brendan asked, very surprised to hear the banks got away with that. "I wish I owned a bank back then." After giving that idea some serious thought, he added, "I'd print at least a trillion dollars every day. I'd be rich."

Linus shivered at the thought of the effects his grandson's disastrous inflationary policy would have had on Canada's economy. "Banks were very responsible about issuing banknotes back then. They didn't print any bills unless every dollar was backed up by gold bullion."

"I *knew* there was a catch to it," spoke the boy who owned no gold.

"The Bank of Ottawa was owned by lumber companies so they issued a series of banknotes with colourful illustrations of rafts, sawmills and lumberjacks on spring drives."

Brendan's eyes widened. "Imagine if they had a picture on their dollar bill of 'Black Pete' and Larry Frost staring down each other across that old timber slide," he said. "If I had money that looked like that, I'd save it for sure."

"That's exactly what I'm getting at, Brendan. Saving your money is an important habit to get into."

"I should start saving up lumberjack money."

"There's very few of those old notes around today. They're collector's items."

"But collecting is the same thing as saving, isn't it?"

"There is a slight difference."

"I bet the only difference is that old lumberjack money is probably just harder to find."

"That's because after the amalgamation, the old Bank of Ottawa notes were phased out. A few years later, *none* of the banks were allowed to issue their own notes."

"Why did they have to stop?" Brendan asked.

"In 1935, the Government of Canada created the Bank of Canada as our country's central bank and it took over responsibility for issuing all the bank notes."

"Darn government!" the boy complained. "No wonder we don't have any lumberjacks on our money anymore."

"There's always change, my boy. Look at the banks now. They're among the leaders in technology. In my day there were no automatic teller machines or computers. We didn't even have calculators. We relied on hard covered books with pages of interest tables. Our ledger cards were posted by hand with straight pens."

"I don't even know what a straight pen is," Brendan said.

Linus thought back to the old days. "I'll never forget that fateful day just after the war when our junior brought into the branch a new invention called a ball point pen," he said. "Our manager looked at it with absolute horror."

"What was the matter with it?"

"He was afraid the ink from a ball point would fade," Linus explained. "Can you imagine the trouble our manager would be in if all the customers' signatures on their loans disappeared? That's why we weren't allowed to use ball points."

"Good for the customers, though," the boy said, with a mischievous look on his face.

Linus looked at his grandson over his glasses and suggested, "You should think about opening a savings account for yourself."

"You mean *now*?"

"I happen to know you received ten dollars this month for your birthday," Linus reminded him. It was rumoured to be hidden away in an old shoebox under his bed.

"So?"

"So you could put your money in the bank where it would

be safe."

Brendan frowned at the hinted affront. "My money *is* safe."

"You'd get interest on it," Linus added, sweetening the offer.

"But how do I know they'd give it back to me?"

"That's a good question, Brendan. You'd have to trust them to do that. Canada's banking system is based on trust."

It was a very reluctant young depositor who finally agreed to withdraw his ten-dollar bill from his personal strongbox to commit it to the bank.

The next day Linus strode into the local branch with his grandson at his side to open an account in the boy's name.

They stood together in a short lineup to speak to the savings manager. Brendan clutched his cash in a sweaty, vice-like grip. He certainly had misgivings about handing over his stash.

"Many children today have the mistaken belief that their parents just have to insert a card into a bank machine and out comes the cash anytime they want it," Linus said. "They have no idea that the money has to be put in first."

"Putting the money in first is harder than I thought," Brendan said, glumly. He suspected that he might never see his birthday money again.

When it was their turn to be served, they were introduced to the young manager of the savings department. They followed her to her office and provided her with their names and addresses.

She began to key the information into her computer.

"Our system is a little slow this morning," she informed them pleasantly. "We have new screens for opening accounts and there are a few bugs to iron out. This new system automatically scans and converts the information to digitized images. This provides us with electronic access for all our documents."

Linus and Brendan listened attentively.

"That way all our historic records can be archived and re-trieved online," she continued. "In the old days we had to send our computer printouts to storage."

Linus thought this person seemed very young to be talking about "the old days".

"I'll make a copy of this information for both of you and be right back," the manager said. She then excused herself and walked to the printer.

Linus shook his head. "This is what passes for the old days now," he whispered to his grandson, as soon as she had left. "Can you imagine her definition of 'the old days' is sending computer printouts to storage?"

"You could tell her a thing or two about what the old days were *really* like," the boy whispered back.

"She's too young to even know what carbon paper is," Linus said for good measure.

"She's just a 'johnny-come-lately', Grandpa," the nine-year-old put in.

The pair rolled their eyes, exchanged smiles, and waited.

When the manager returned, she handed a copy of the account information form to both of them. She also handed Linus her pen.

"Would you sign as the trustee for Brendan's account?" she asked the boy's grandfather.

While Linus signed the document, she politely explained to Brendan that he wasn't allowed to sign his own name on the account because he was a minor.

"I see you use ball point pens here," the boy said, by way of a reply. "Aren't you worried his signature might disappear?"

Then turning to his grandfather, he commented, "Too bad it's not a bank loan."

"Whatever do you mean?" the manager asked, baffled by the boy's remark. "Is there something wrong with the pen?"

"When my grandpa worked here, they weren't allowed to use ball point pens," Brendan informed her.

"That must have been a long time ago," she said, and then turning to Linus. "You worked for the bank?"

"I did."

"He even had an account with the *Bank of Ottawa!*" Brendan blurted out with pride.

Her jaw dropped. The Bank of Ottawa? How old must this man be, she wondered? "You must have seen many changes since you were in the bank," the manager said to Linus with reverence. "I can imagine that a great many things were done differently in the days before we had computers, weren't they?"

"We made our own ink," he said, nodding his head sagely.

"You did?" was her only reply. She found herself staring at each of them in turn. She wouldn't forget this pair for a long time.

After the account was opened, Brendan's ten dollar bill sped efficiently through the bank's clearing system. It was well and truly deposited.

As the two of them were leaving the bank, Linus gave his grandson a proud pat on the back. "This was a good day's work, Brendan. Let's take a leisurely walk home and relax."

Brendan smiled at his grandfather. "On the way, let's see how many cartoon characters I can name."

Linus removed a piece of paper from his shirt pocket. "I'll have to write them down," he said. "I wonder if you can break your old record."

"I've been practicing."

"When we get home, we should make roast beef sandwiches for lunch," Linus suggested.

"I'm getting hungry already," Brendan said, with a happy look on his face.

It doesn't get much better than this for a nine-year-old boy.

Something fun to do, someone to do it with, something to look forward to—and money in the bank.

1 9 3 0

My Lou Gehrig Story

An Afternoon at Old Maple Leaf Stadium

LINUS AND BRENDAN WERE ON THEIR WAY TO WATCH A BASEBALL
GAME.

"Have we got everything?" asked Linus, "I've got the tickets. I've got money for hotdogs. I have binoculars, sunglasses...
what else?"

"I've got my glove," Brendan said, pounding the pocket of
his junior-sized trapper. This would be the boy's first Toronto
Blue Jay game and he was ready. "Do you think I'll catch a ball,
Grandpa?"

"Don't forget there will be lots of fans around us with the
same idea."

"But if I do catch a ball can I keep it?"

"Sure," Linus said, "I think you're allowed."

"Can I get it autographed?"

"Well, bring a pen along just in case," replied his grandfather,
"but don't get your hopes up too high. The chances of getting
near a player in the modern stadiums aren't very good. Which
reminds me, when I was a kid..."

"Don't we have a baseball game to go to?" Brendan said, cut-
ting him short.

"We have lots of time. I have a nice little baseball story for you."

"Don't forget you said it's a *little* story," the boy reminded him, knowing from past experience that when his grandfather told a story about the olden days, his coffee always got cold.

"I'll tell you on the bus," Linus said. "You'll like this story."

"Is there a time limit?"

Linus glanced at Brendan, shook his head, and grinned.

The two baseball fans caught the downtown bus and Linus began his story.

"It took place here in Toronto," Linus said. "It was a warm summer afternoon in 1930—July 11, to be exact."

"Boy, you've got a good memory."

"I remember that day as if it was yesterday. My best friend Spencer and I had taken the streetcar to the old Maple Leaf Stadium down by the lake to see our local team—the Toronto Maple Leafs—play the most celebrated baseball team in the world."

"Wait a minute," the boy said. "What do you mean—a baseball team? The Maple Leafs are a *hockey team.*"

"Toronto had a Triple-A ball team then and they were called the Maple Leafs—the same name as the hockey team."

"Oh. Were they any good?"

"Toronto had a very good ball team that year," Linus said. "Triple-A is just below the major leagues."

"So who did you say the Maple Leafs were supposed to play?"

"They were going to play the New York Yankees. The Yankees had come to town on a barnstorming trip. What a lineup they had! The team was called 'Murderers Row' because of all the sluggers they had. Spencer and I were big Yankee fans."

Linus looked at his grandson and asked, "Have you ever heard of Babe Ruth?"

"Sort of," Brendan answered, thinking the name sounded familiar.

Lou Gehrig at Yankee Stadium
The 'Iron Horse' was Spencer's favourite player until 1936, the year a young
rookie named Joe Dimaggio made his Yankee debut.

"Babe Ruth had just signed the biggest baseball contract in history," Linus said, "It paid him $80,000.00 a year, which was an unheard of amount in 1930."

"That's a lot," agreed the boy, who secretly had no idea what those big dollar amounts meant that his grandfather was always talking about.

"Another great player on that team was Lou Gehrig, who was Spencer's favourite player. His nickname was the 'Iron Horse'."

"Did they call him that because he could run so fast?"

"He had that nickname because he played more games in a row than any other player. Lou Gehrig was rated one of the best first basemen of all time."

"He was?" the boy asked, having dreamed of someday becoming a major league first baseman himself.

"Let me tell you about the game we saw," continued Linus. "The Leafs played a double header that Friday afternoon. The first game was a regular season game with the Jersey City Skeeters."

"The Skeeters?"

"Yes, the Leafs beat them 11-1 so you know the Leafs had a good team. Next came the Yankees. Of all the fans in the stadium that afternoon, none was more knowledgeable about the Yankees than Spencer. It amazes me to this day just how much baseball that kid knew. He told me that Babe Ruth might not be well enough to play in Toronto. Ruth had injured his hand by jamming it on the outfield fence at Yankee Stadium a couple of days earlier. But Spencer said that Gehrig would definitely play."

"Had he been injured too?"

"No," Linus answered. "Spencer just meant that Gehrig *always* played. He was the Iron Horse and he *never* missed a game."

"Then the fans would have wanted to see him too."

"They certainly did. When the starting lineup was introduced, Gehrig stepped out to great cheers, but the greatest ovation was for Babe Ruth. Everyone had come to see the Babe. The great Yankee slugger appeared dramatically from the dugout at the last minute. As soon as the fans saw him, they went wild.

Toronto fans always had a huge love affair with the Babe."

"Because he was so good?"

"I think they liked the fact that Babe Ruth had hit his first professional home run in Toronto sixteen years earlier," Linus answered. "They were as proud of him as if he was a hometown boy."

"He must have hit a lot of home runs."

"He hit a lot of them," Linus agreed, "but Gehrig was a great hitter too. Maybe he didn't get as many home runs, but he got more hits."

"That's important too."

"Spencer was a real, loyal Lou Gehrig fan. At first he was worried that he wouldn't get a good look at the Iron Horse because Gehrig played first base and our seats were in the bleachers. But it turned out perfectly, because when the Leafs came up to bat, Lou Gehrig was playing in the outfield and Babe Ruth was at first. "

"How did that happen?"

"They had switched positions," explained Linus. "They do that sometimes in exhibition games."

"Spencer was really lucky."

"Well, we sure saw a great game. I remember when the Babe first came up to bat you could hear a pin drop. It was the second inning and the bases were loaded. The fans wanted a homer and that's *exactly* what they got. The Yankee slugger coolly connected on one and it soared over the Mr. Peanut billboard at centre field and dropped into the parking lot for a grand slam."

"I guess the Mr. Peanut billboard made a good target."

"It sure did. Later he hit another homer with three men on. I can still see the Babe running the bases. He had skinny legs and was getting a little overweight but there was never a player like him for bringing the crowd to its feet."

"It must have been a great game."

"The Babe was definitely the star of that team, Brendan, but Lou Gehrig was the solid worker. Lou had four singles that afternoon on five at bats. Of course, Spencer was on his feet cheering every hit."

"That's what I would have done too, if I'd been there."

"But there was more to Gehrig than just being a good player," Linus said. "He worked hard all the time and never complained. He played through injuries and practiced hard to improve his game. He was the kind of person you'd like even if he hadn't been a baseball star." Linus raised an eyebrow and looked hard at the boy, "And incidentally, when he was your age, he never missed a day at school."

"*I know, I know,*" Brendan sighed. "He was the Iron Horse."

"The Yankees won 16-11," continued Linus. "After the last Leaf had struck out, Spencer made his move."

"What did he do?"

"He turned to me and said, 'Wait here' and then raced down to the right field fence, climbed over it and was onto the outfield."

"Was he allowed to do that?"

"Not really," Linus admitted, "but nobody stopped him and I just sat there watching."

"I bet he got into a lot of trouble for doing that."

"He caught up with Gehrig and ran alongside him all the way across the field back to the Yankee dugout. Then I lost sight of them in the crowd at the far side of Maple Leaf Stadium."

"Then did the security guards catch him?" asked Brendan.

"I don't think they even had security guards in those days. Little kids running onto the field wasn't as big a deal back in 1930 as it is now."

"They'd never let me do that," spoke the boy who never got away with anything.

"Just the same, I was really glad to see him a few minutes

later running back across the park toward me," Linus said. "He was totally out of breath when he returned to his seat."

"Did he get Lou Gehrig's autograph? That would have been the important thing."

"Spencer had wanted to, but he'd been too much in awe of the man to ask. Instead, he just stood there staring up at his hero. Gehrig didn't speak either. He just stared right back waiting for the boy to make the first move."

"That was when he should have asked for his autograph," Brendan said.

"Then the moment came that Spencer would remember all his life. After that prolonged silence, the Iron Horse flashed Spencer the biggest smile the boy had ever seen in his life, touched the peak of his Yankee cap and said to him, 'So long, Kid'. He then disappeared into the Yankee dugout."

"That's a pretty good story. I'll give you two thumbs up."

"That's my Lou Gehrig story, Brendan. I've heard it said that the Iron Horse would never have spent even that much time with the press. Lou was known to be shy with broadcasters and newspaper reporters."

"Maybe he liked kids more."

"Maybe he did," his grandfather agreed. "Lou always had the knack of saying the perfect thing to them."

"Well, he didn't really say all *that* much, Grandpa."

"Look at it this way," said Linus. "Gehrig only said three words, but we're still talking about them more than seventy-five years later."

"So what became of Spencer?"

"He grew up, served with Conn Smythe's Sportsmen's Artillery Battery during the war and afterwards had a long career in public relations before he retired."

"I bet he always wished he'd gotten Lou Gehrig's autograph."

"He often told me that," Linus answered. "It was Spencer's only chance to get Lou's autograph. They never met again. You see, Lou Gehrig later became quite ill."

"And he didn't play anymore?"

"Actually, he kept playing."

"He still played?"

"He was the Iron Horse after all," Linus answered quietly. "He also had an illness called ALS. Those are the initials of its formal name, but we now call it 'Lou Gehrig's Disease'. It's a disease of the nervous system. Gehrig died of it and now it's named after him."

"Do you think that's right? I mean, to name a disease after a nice person?"

"I suppose it's a way of honouring a special man," Linus explained. "It's a reminder. Does that make sense?"

"I guess so," answered Brendan.

"That was a good question," Linus said, giving his grandson a shoulder hug, "but enough talk about the old days. Let's watch a baseball game."

CHAPTER NINETEEN

1 9 3 9

Rinkrats I Have Known

A Morning at Old Maple Leaf Gardens

"THEY'RE ONLY SECOND HAND," LINUS SAID, PRESENTING A PAIR OF SKATES TO HIS GRANDSON, "BUT AT LEAST THEY'RE YOURS."

This was an exciting day at the local rink for Brendan. These were his first real skates. He had never skated much before this; lacrosse had been his game. It didn't seem that long ago that he had worn bob skates, but they were for little kids. This had been the winter that hockey had become Brendan's favourite sport.

"I hope you enjoy skating as much as I have over the years," his grandfather said. "I learned to skate on a rink my Dad made me in our backyard. Like everything else, it's easy to learn when you're young."

Brendan couldn't foresee any problems. "I should be a fast learner," he blustered. "Don't forget I was pretty good on bob skates."

Linus too, had been a good skater in his youth and still enjoyed an occasional lap around the old cushion. His knees and hips were telling him to be careful now and not to push it. He smiled as he recalled that in the old days he had been called 'Flash'. Had it really been that long ago? He stood up gingerly and braced himself. He felt he could still do it. Then he checked on Brendan. Having put on his new skates, the boy sat patiently on the bench waiting for his grandfather. But something about the budding star didn't look right.

"You have your skates on the wrong feet," Linus said. "How in the world did you manage to do that?"

"I have?" The nine-year-old asked, gazing down at his skates with a perplexed look on his face.

"You can't wear them like that, my boy."

"Why not? They're more comfortable this way."

"Because Syl Apps would be rolling in his grave if he saw that."

"What's he got to do with it?" asked Brendan, never having heard of the man.

Linus stroked his chin. "I should tell you my Syl Apps story."

"Is it a long story? I thought we were going skating?"

Brendan was usually a patient listener when it came to his grandfather's stories, but this didn't seem to be the right time. There were already other kids out on the ice.

"This won't take long," Linus said. "Don't worry, we have all afternoon to skate and I promise to buy you some hot chocolate afterwards."

"Remember there's a time limit," Brendan said, as he began to reverse his skates. "So who is Syl Apps anyway?"

"Syl Apps was a hero to every kid who grew up in the thirties," Linus began. "He was the perfect Leaf captain: tall, good looking, a natural scorer, a smart playmaker and a born leader."

"That's a pretty good resume."

"But everybody admired him because he was a clean player too."

"I guess he didn't get very many penalties."

"Apps played the game without taking penalties. Teams don't win games with their best players in the penalty box. And I can tell you, Brendan, in the thirties and forties the Leafs had the best players in the league. Just as an example, Apps won the Calder Trophy, the Lady Byng Trophy and was a five-time All-Star." He then added with pride, "*And* he was their captain on three Stanley Cup winning teams."

"That's a really good record to have."

"*Not only that*—he's in the Hall of Fame."

Now Brendan was very impressed. He knew only the best players were in the Hall of Fame.

Linus wished he had players like Apps in his hockey pool now. "He always averaged a point a game," he said to his grandson, "and those were low scoring days."

"There are *lots* of players who do that today, Grandpa," the young hockey fan pointed out, "but it sounds like he must have been one of the best players—back then, I mean."

"I should tell you something that happened to me in my rinkrat days." Linus said.

"*Wait a minute! You were a rat?*"

"Well, a *rink*rat," Linus explained. "A rinkrat is someone who hangs around the rink."

"Oh."

"There were four of us at the rink that day. There was Bill, whom we called 'BB Eyes'..."

Brendan interrupted his grandfather, "Are you just making this up?"

"No, we called Bill that because he had bright, penetrating eyes. There was also my friend, Jim. We always called him 'Nose' and there was Bert."

"Didn't Bert have a nickname?"

"Bert didn't want one and he said he'd beat up anybody who gave him one," Linus explained. "All the rest of us had nicknames, though. They called me Flash.

The boy blinked when he heard that one. "*Flash?*" he repeated. He was having a hard time picturing his grandfather in his younger days. But he liked the nickname and secretly wouldn't have minded being called Flash himself. But he felt sorry for the boy whose nickname was Nose.

"Back in the thirties," Linus went on, "we couldn't scrape enough money together to buy tickets to see the Leafs play, so one day we decided to head down to Maple Leaf Gardens to watch them practice."

"Were you allowed to do that?"

Linus shrugged sheepishly. "We didn't exactly have their permission," he admitted.

"Why not?"

"Because we were supposed to be in school," Linus answered. "We were afraid if we'd asked, they would have called the principal." As soon as he had said those words, Linus wanted to take them back. He'd never before told Brendan that he'd skipped school. He cleared his throat and tried to explain it. "You see, Brendan, this was a special situation. The Leafs had a home stand and we wanted to see all their great players. *You would have loved them.* They had a great team with players like: 'Sweeney' Shriner, 'Swivel Hips' Langelle, 'Bingo' Kampman, and of course, their great goalie, 'Turk' Broda."

"Don't forget Syl Apps. Didn't you just say he was your hero?"

"Yes, but unfortunately he'd been injured a couple of days earlier on Christmas night at Madison Square Gardens in New York. He'd been hit with a high stick in a goal-mouth scramble. Apps had thought he'd only sprained his shoulder and he finished the game. However, when the train pulled into Toronto's Union Station the next morning, he had trouble getting out of his berth."

"I know what that feels like. I once sprained my ankle and it was so bad I could hardly walk on it."

"It turned out Apps had a fractured collarbone."

"You must have been pretty disappointed to hear that."

Syl Apps with the 1947 Stanley Cup
The Leaf Captain won the Calder Trophy, the Lady Byng Trophy and was a five-time All-Star.

"Still, the Leafs had plenty of other great players who we wanted to see."

"So how *did* you get in?"

"One of us in the rat pack had discovered that the latch on the eastern gate of the Gardens had been left unlocked. That's how we got in. Bert had agreed to be our decoy."

"What did he have to do?"

"Bert had the task of distracting Tim Daly."

"Was he the security guard?"

"Tim was the Leaf trainer," answered Linus. "In those days, trainers used to handle security in addition to all their other duties. I don't think the Gardens had a full-time security guard then."

"No wonder you were able to sneak in."

"I wonder if any Leaf fans remember Tim Daly today," Linus went on. "He was well known back then. He had been the team's trainer since the Leafs' first season in 1927. He looked after their equipment, sharpened their skates and made all the travel arrangements. He was very popular with the players."

"Probably because he did so much work for them."

"Except they didn't like playing cards with him," Linus said with a chuckle. "Tim used to beat the pants off them at gin-rummy. But other than that, he was very protective of his players. During practices, he kept a sharp eye out for sneaky kids looking for autographs."

"Especially for a rinkrat named Flash," the boy said with a big grin.

Linus smiled back. "Tim didn't see me," he said, "but it didn't take him long to spot Bert."

"So did he try to catch him?"

"Actually, Tim wasn't a very good runner. He was a little on the portly side. Instead, he shouted at him, 'Where are *you* going?' But Bert, being a good rinkrat, pretended not to hear him and scampered down the corridor. Tim then yelled louder, 'You can't *go* there'. Bert simply picked up the pace which meant that Tim was forced to break into a little shuffle. He hated that. The Leaf trainer was last seen huffing and puffing down the corridor after him."

"I guess Tim was kind of slow," Brendan said.

"With Tim out of the picture, the rest of us split up. BB Eyes and Nose ran down one corridor and I ran down another. We were all trying to find a safe spot to watch the practice. For some reason I headed in the direction of the Leaf bench. I was taking a chance going there—I knew I might be caught. But I *still* kept going. When I finally reached the boards, I glanced to my left. A man in street clothes sitting several rows up from ice level was watching me. He looked like a movie star and he wore a sling around his arm and shoulder."

"I know who that was," Brendan said. "It was Syl Apps, wasn't it?"

"I recognized him immediately. I'd never seen the man in person before, but I had plenty of Beehive photos of him so I knew who it was. In fact, only the night before I'd glued into my scrapbook a great picture of Syl Apps from the *Telegram*, wearing that same sling. So I took a deep breath, walked over to him and spoke."

"What did you say to him?" asked the boy, wondering what he would say if he ever met Mats Sundin in person.

"I knew he had injured his shoulder so I asked him when he'd be back."

"Was he mad at you for sneaking in?"

"He never said a word about it. He told me his fracture would take a long time to heal and he thought he might be out of the line up for two or three weeks."

"It sounds like he was really friendly."

"I couldn't believe that I was actually having a conversation with *Syl Apps*. I just stood there thinking how often I'd heard Foster Hewitt broadcast that man's exploits every Saturday night." Linus then pretended he was speaking into a micro-phone, "*And now it's Apps leading a rush over the Montreal blue-line...the pass to Davidson...over to Drillon...he scores!*" He put his imaginary microphone down and said, "And here he was sitting beside me in the flesh."

"That was before television, wasn't it?"

"Before television, Syl Apps was *every* kid's favourite player."

"So did you ask him for his autograph?"

"I never thought of it," Linus admitted, having kicked himself ever since for the missed opportunity. However, he had wonderful memories of the encounter. "Can you imagine a famous athlete today taking that much time with a kid?"

Brendan frowned. "Mats Sundin would," he said, referring to his favourite hockey player.

Linus knew that his comment hadn't come out right. It wasn't fair to slight every modern athlete so handily. "You're right— Mats Sundin would," he agreed, being reminded that every generation has its sporting symbols.

"After meeting Syl Apps, I raced to catch up with the other rinkrats. I found them high up in the greens watching the practice, out of sight of the prying eyes of trainer Tim Daly, who had since returned to the Leaf bench in a bad mood. I told everybody how Syl Apps had taken the time to chat with me as if I was a young cub reporter, not some rinkrat called Flash, who had skipped school that day."

"What did they say?" Brendan said. "I bet they wished they'd been with you."

"Bert never liked making a big deal out of things like that. It took a lot to impress Bert. He simply nodded his head and said, 'No kidding?' However, BB Eyes and Nose were both big Syl Apps fans and I had to repeat every word the Leaf captain had said. Toronto fans of all ages in the thirties and forties idolized Apps. He was well known for speaking to boys about accepting responsibility and practicing good sportsmanship." Linus then added as an afterthought, "Boys liked being taught things like that back then."

"Good thing you hadn't told him you sneaked in," Brendan

reminded him.

"I never did it again," Linus said, and he couldn't help adding, "I was getting too old to be a rinkrat anyway."

Brendan put on his gloves and smiled. "I'm glad you learned your lesson, Grandpa," he said, giving him a paternal pat on the back.

"I still look back at Syl Apps with admiration after all these years," Linus said. "I should tell you about some of his later accomplishments off the ice. I bet you didn't know he went into politics and became a provincial cabinet minister."

"Politics?" the boy gagged. "Don't forget about the time limit."

"You're right, Brendan," his grandfather said, realizing that talking politics would only get him into more trouble. "Let's keep this a hockey story."

CHAPTER TWENTY

1935

The Adventures of the Tricky Sons

"He bulged the twine and waited
for his teammate's cheers to come.
But all they ever said was
"Why that's our own goal, you bum."

Anon

IT WAS AN EARLY SPRING DAY. The sun was out and the snow on the streets was melting quickly.

Linus was at Brendan's home paying him a visit.

He was surprised to find his grandson in his room reading a comic book on the bed. The boy should have been out playing road hockey. That's what Linus would have been doing at that age.

"I can't go out until I've cleaned my room," Brendan explained, looking around at all his belongings strewn on the floor. "My Mom has been asking me for a while and I guess it's taking me longer than I thought. I keep finding stuff I thought I'd lost."

"How can you find *anything* in this room?" Linus said, looking around at the chaos. "How can you *be* so untidy?"

Brendan shrugged it off. "It's part of my mystique," he answered.

"You should be cleaning your room instead of reading a comic book. Putting things off is really the very worst habit you can get into."

"Didn't you read comic books when you were my age, Grandpa?"

Linus grinned. "I went right from my grade school reader to Charles Dickens."

"I can't imagine any kid not reading comic books," Brendan said.

"I would suggest you clean your room and get that done first," his grandfather said. "Procrastination is the thief of time, my boy."

"Do you want to see my Mats Sundin card?" the nine-year-old asked, skillfully changing the topic. He picked up a hockey card off the bed and showed it to his grandfather.

"It's a beauty," Linus said, examining it closely. "And it's in really good condition."

"It's his rookie card."

"How did you manage to find it in *this* room?"

"My Mom found it."

"You're lucky," Linus said, thinking back to when he was a kid. "*My* mother never found anything. She only threw things out."

"*Mine* found this under my bed."

Linus carefully returned the card. "Keep it in a safe place, Brendan. Look after your things. I used to have hockey cards of the 'Kid Line' when I was your age. I was careless with them; and when I left home my mother got rid of them. They were my favourite players."

"I thought Syl Apps was your favourite player back then, Grandpa?"

"He played a little later," his grandfather replied. "My all-time favourite player was known as 'The Big Bomber'." Linus was very nostalgic about the Maple Leafs of the 1930's.

"The Big Bomber?"

"That was Charlie Conacher's nickname. He played on the Leaf's Kid Line with 'Busher' Jackson and Joe Primeau—the best line in hockey. The Big Bomber was as famous then as Mats Sundin is today."

"He was?"

"He sure was," answered Linus. "Conacher was a big, rugged right winger who won a couple of scoring titles."

"I never heard of him before."

"The fans loved him. In those days we used to listen to all the Leaf games on radio."

"That's because you never had television back then."

"To hear Foster Hewitt call a Leaf game in the thirties, you would have thought Charlie Conacher was the only man on the ice," Linus said, thinking back to the glory days of the Maple Leafs. "Of course, now he's in the Hall of Fame."

Brendan knew that meant he must have been a very good player.

"His brothers are in the Hall of Fame too," continued Linus.

"They are? How many did he have?"

"There are three Conacher brothers in the Hall. When Charlie was growing up, he idolized his older brother Lionel, who was already an established rushing defenseman, first with the Pittsburgh Pirates and later the New York Americans and the Montreal Maroons in the NHL. They called Lionel 'The Big Train'. He was an excellent, all-round athlete. Today's athletes are all specialists, but in those days a good athlete might play several sports. Lionel was good at baseball, lacrosse, football and wrestling. Sometimes he played two different sports in one day."

"*Two in one day!*" exclaimed Brendan. "That's pretty good."

"The Big Train was voted Canada's best all-round athlete of the half century by the Canadian Press in 1950," Linus said.

"I guess that's a good award to get," Brendan said, but secretly he was only interested in the Hall of Fame.

"Harvey Pulford from Ottawa was another great all-round athlete from the old days," Linus said. "I've heard it said he was every bit as good as Lionel." Having been raised on stories of Black Pete and Larry Frost, Linus always was a big fan of the athletes from the Ottawa Valley. "Charlie's little brother, Roy, broke into the NHL with the Boston Bruins in 1938," he added.

"I bet his brothers were sure proud of him when he made the NHL just like they had," Brendan said.

"Roy established himself immediately as a good goal scorer. In his first year in the league, he scored more goals than any other player."

"He would have won the Maurice Richard Trophy today for that, but they didn't have it back then," Brendan said. The boy was a wonderful source of up-to-date information about the modern era. "That's the trophy for the player who scores the most goals," he added, thinking it was probably too new for his grandfather to have heard of.

"Roy was runner up for the Calder Trophy too," Linus said.

Brendan knew that the Calder was awarded to the best rookie. "Can you imagine what it must have been like growing up in that family?" he said. "You could fill up your autograph book over breakfast."

"Everyone in that family played sports," Linus added. "Naturally, they called Roy 'The Little Train'. He was a big man and a strong skater, and like his brothers he had a great shot. He was a finesse player, but not showy. Roy's problem was that he always played in the shadows of his brothers. Even his nickname of the Little Train reflects that."

"They sure liked to give everybody nicknames back then."

"Well, I certainly appreciate the Little Train now more than I did then."

"Why now, Grandpa?"

"For a long time, I took his career for granted," Linus said. "You see, in 1942, after only three seasons in the NHL, Roy left the Bruins to enlist in the air force. He played for the RCAF team."

"At least he got to play hockey."

"It must have been very difficult for a player to return after being away from the NHL for four years. To me, that makes Roy Conacher a special player."

"Because he was away in the war, you mean?"

"I mean that even though he missed out on his best playing years, he came back and still had some great seasons."

"I guess that would be hard to do."

"He even won the scoring championship."

"He did?"

"Roy wasn't the only one to serve in the war, of course; many NHL players did the same. All the Tricky Sons signed up too."

"The Tricky Sons?" Brendan asked, wondering who in the world they were. "Do you mean suns in the sky or the human kind?"

"That was the name of our road hockey team back in the thirties."

"Are you just making this up?" Brendan asked. "I've never heard of a team with a name like that before."

"Didn't I ever tell you about the adventures of the Tricky Sons?"

"You told me about the rinkrats."

"It was really the same group. They were all kids my age who lived on Paton Street in the Bloor and Lansdown area of Toronto."

"Is that where you played?"

"Only we called it the Paton Street Arena."

"That's pretty good."

"We never had any trouble getting a couple of teams together in those days. Across the street from me lived Johnny Dance. He was a great guy. He had two very pretty sisters whom I liked, Dot and Kay. Next door to Johnny were the Gallaghers. There were nine kids in that family alone. They could have formed their own team. Bert was my age."

"Wasn't Bert the kid that didn't want a nickname?"

"He didn't want one and I don't think any of his brothers had nicknames either. I remember Tom and Carl and Ray Gallagher, but I forget the others. They were a great family. Further down the street lived Jim 'Nose' Bailey, who spent more hours playing road hockey than any of us. Next door to him was Bill 'BB Eyes' Le Fave, who was the biggest sports fan on the whole street. He kept all the stats. Then we had Russ Mailing, the smallest Tricky Son. There was also Cam Sodergreen and Bud Matthews. Bud was the old man on the street at fifteen. I think I've already told you about some of our adventures."

Paton Street, Toronto, 1935
Back row, Johnny Dance, Jim 'Nose' Bailey,
Middle row, Bill 'BB Eyes' LeFavre, Bert Gallagher, Cam Sodergreen,
Front row, Ray Gallagher
Photo taken in front of Hart's Grocery

"Didn't they call you *'Flash'*?"

Linus smiled sheepishly. "I think they meant the opposite. I wasn't that good. I once scored a goal on my own team by mistake."

"Everybody makes mistakes," Brendan said, having made many himself.

"They didn't say much, but I knew the Tricky Sons weren't very happy about it."

"Were you a forward or a defenseman?"

"A defenseman," replied Linus, "a *rushing* defenseman. We had two teams: the Paton Seafleas and the Tricky Sons. I was always a Tricky Son. All our games were played on Paton Street. We went up and down all day long. Kids were always coming and going. It was like being in a marathon six-day bike race. Nowadays the big worry is child obesity with parents trying to get their kids into exercise programs. We'd never heard of that problem. In the thirties we never had *time* to eat." Linus was on his soapbox now and drove his point home by adding, "Eating would have interfered with our fun."

"Even pizza?" the boy asked, finding that very difficult to believe.

"There wasn't pizza back then, and had there been, we didn't have any money to buy it."

"I don't have any money either, Grandpa, but I still like pizza."

Linus considered Brendan's point for a moment. "I suppose we did buy chestnuts from a street vendor from time to time," he admitted. "And we loved fudge. Sometimes we would buy a nickel's worth at Hart's Grocery store at the corner."

Linus had a happy far away look in his eyes—fudge at a nickel; gasoline at twenty- five cents a gallon and three cents to mail a letter. "It was better then," he sighed. "Today's kids are so pampered. Why do they need organized leagues, with heated dressing rooms and regulation-sized nets? Nowadays they all wear full equipment and even have their names stitched on the backs of their sweaters. Some kids even attend hockey camps where coaches give presentations in a classroom. Why does everything have to be so *professional* for them?" Linus shook his head in despair of the modern era. "On Paton Street, our goalies wore Eaton's catalogues as pads and the defensemen strapped on *Liberty* magazines as shinguards. Our goals were two tomato tins and our coach was Nose Bailey, all of twelve years of age."

Brendan responded to all of this with a blank stare.

"We made our own fun," Linus said. "When summer arrived in the thirties, we took our bats and balls onto the same street where we'd played road hockey all spring. Only we just changed the name from Paton Street Arena to Paton Street Stadium."

"We make our own fun too," Brendan said, rising to defend the modern era.

"I'm sorry, Brendan, of course you do," Linus said, realizing how critical he must have sounded. "I suppose I overdo it sometimes about the old days, don't I? Gee, Brendan, am I getting that old?"

"I don't think so, Grandpa," answered the boy, always the diplomat.

"We all thought we had the world by the tail in the thirties," Linus said, pushing all the worst memories of the Depression out of his mind. "It really was a great time to be a baby-faced youth."

"*You* had a baby face?" Brendan asked, trying hard to picture his grandfather as a little kid.

"We all did. We were *all* pink-faced little cherubs," Linus said with a big grin. He then became serious and added quietly, "But the Tricky Sons bid farewell at the end of the 1939 season—The Paton Street League folded."

"That was fast," Brendan said. "What happened?"

"Early in 1940, the military came looking for pink-faced little cherubs. Paton Street Arena provided good pickings."

"What do you mean?"

"Able Seaman Bert Gallagher joined the navy and served on HMCS *St. Laurent*. The *'Sally'*, as that great destroyer was affectionately known, sank two U-boats in the Battle of the Atlantic. Bud Matthews flew with the RCAF but he was killed in Toronto in a tragic streetcar accident at the corner of Bloor and Bathurst in 1947, a year after his discharge. Flying Officer Johnny Dance became a bombardier in the RCAF. His Halifax bomber never returned from a night mission over Germany in 1943 and he was lost at 21. BB Eyes also joined the RCAF and was stationed in Egypt. Cam Sodergreen signed up with the Irish Regiment of Canada. I don't know what became of Nose Bailey. Russ Mailing was too young to serve and I went into the army."

"What did you do in the army, Grandpa?"

"Let's leave that for another day, Brendan. Time you got your room cleaned."

"Don't worry, I will, but *first* tell me about the army."

"I *can* tell you one thing the army taught me," his grandfather said, speaking in a low voice. "This of course, is just between us men."

"It is?" The boy was always pleased to be taken into a confidence. He thought it must have something to do with some secret commando move that his grandfather had learned during the war.

"How old are you now?" Linus asked the boy. "Nine?"

"Nine and a half," was the proud reply.

"Old enough," Linus said, sizing the boy up.

Brendan tried to look indifferent, but secretly he was incredibly excited. He promised himself that whatever he was about to learn, he would use only in self defense.

"What was it, Grandpa?"

"The army taught me to make my bed every day."

CHAPTER TWENTY-ONE

1940

Above Biggin Hill

"Every morn brought forth a noble chance
And every chance brought forth a noble knight,"
quoted by Winston S. Churchill, *Speech*
June 4, 1940

"THERE SURE ARE A LOT OF PIECES, GRANDPA."

The boy and his grandfather had wings, propellers, wheels, decals, glue and other small plastic parts of their model Spitfire strewn all over the kitchen table.

"Let's hope there's nothing missing," Linus said. He had given the model Spitfire to his grandson for Christmas. He had selected a gift they could enjoy together and what better way to spend a wintry Saturday afternoon than to build an old World War Two fighter.

"Is this the plane that won the war?" asked Brendan. "I think my teacher talked about the Spitfire at school."

"The Spitfire was certainly an important plane in the war and for most of us it symbolized the Battle of Britain," answered his grandfather. "It was fast and beautifully designed, but we can't forget the role played by the Hawker Hurricane. It was the unsung hero of the Battle of Britain."

"I've never even heard of it," the boy admitted.

"People forget there were twice as many Hurricanes in the Battle of Britain than Spitfires. We shouldn't forget things like that."

F/O Ross Smither, RCAF,
Killed in action on September 15, 1940, flying Hurricane P3876 during the Battle
of Britain.

"Maybe we should make a model of one the next time."

"I think so too," agreed Linus, "because I don't know where we'd be today if it wasn't for the Hurricane."

"Why did they need two different kinds of planes?"

"Each had a different role to play, Brendan. The Luftwaffe had a fast fighter plane called the Messerschmitt 109. The ME109's job was to protect the German bombers. The Spitfire was almost as fast, so its job was to draw the ME109's away from their bombers and take them on in combat. The Hurricane was slower and it couldn't dive or climb as quickly as the other fighter planes. However, it was sturdier and its main job was to attack the bombers. Both planes did a superb job. One of my best friends was a Hurricane pilot."

"Was your friend in that battle?"

"Yes, he was. I often think of him when I read John Magee, Jr's wonderful poem. Have you studied 'High Flight' in school?"

"I don't think so."

"I have it in a poetry book somewhere," Linus said, getting up and walking over to his bookcase. "We should memorize it together this afternoon after we've put this Spitfire together."

The nine-year-old furrowed his brow. The last thing he wanted to do on a Saturday afternoon was memory work. Saturday was his day off.

Linus found the book he was looking for and began to recite the opening lines from his favourite poem to his grandson:

> "Oh, I have slipped the surly bonds of Earth
> And danced the skies on laughter-silver wings;
> Sunward I've climbed, and—"

"I just found a pizza coupon, Grandpa," the boy said, interrupting his grandfather's reading in mid sentence and holding up a coupon he had pulled from his pocket, "in case we get hungry later."

"*Pizza?*" asked his grandfather. "I thought we were reading poetry?"

"Well, pizza *is* poetry," the boy said.

Linus smiled politely at Brendan. He always felt that "High

Flight" was a wonderful poem for a young person to learn by heart. Its words took Linus back to the summer of 1940. "One of my best friends in pre-war days was Ross Smither," he said. "Ross had grown up on Rathgar Street in London, Ontario. He loved playing hockey."

"Was he a rinkrat?"

"He would have been proud to have been called one," Linus answered, "but he played a lot of sandlot baseball too, and he sometimes got in trouble for doing some other things he shouldn't have been doing."

"Like what things?" the nine-year-old asked, always on the lookout for new ideas.

"It sounds very tame by today's standards, but growing up in a town like London, Ross and his pals liked to play in the railyards," replied Linus. "That was a dangerous place to play, and his father warned him about it."

"Did he get in trouble for it?"

"His father worked for the CNR, so I'm sure Ross got an earful about that more than once," answered Linus.

"Did your friend always want to be a pilot?"

"I think so," Linus said. "Ross came from a military family. His father, Frank, had served in the South African War, and was one of the first to enlist in the Princess Pats at the outbreak of the First World War. His family believed in answering the call of duty. Both sons, Ross and Syd, signed up in the air force. They were a very patriotic family and every country needs patriots."

"I'm patriotic," Brendan said.

"So am I," his grandfather said. "We don't have to be pilots to be patriots."

"But a pilot puts his life on the line, doesn't he?"

"Ross did," agreed Linus. "He signed on with the RCAF as a teenager, and took his initial training at Camp Borden. I didn't see him much after that. He was stationed in Trenton for a while, moved to Ottawa and finally Vancouver. He was a ten-year veteran when the RCAF formed the first All-Canadian Squadron to go overseas. They were called the No. 1 RCAF Squadron. Ross was proud to join men like McGregor, Russel, Corbett and some fellows from Montreal named Nesbitt and Molson to be part of that splendid group. Their squadron leader was Ernie McNab."

"I bet he was a good pilot too."

"Ernie was a steady, reliable commander," Linus agreed, looking inside the empty box for the manual. "When your life is on the line, you don't want a guy leading you who reads a lot of comic books."

"I read a lot of comic books," Brendan said.

"When you get promoted to squadron leader, you'll have to give those up and read Dickens instead," Linus said, reading the instructions for the Spitfire model through a magnifying glass.

"So how did all those pilots end up in the Battle of Britain?"

"The Canadians arrived in Britain in June of 1940 and were immediately attached to RAF Fighter Command as a Hurricane squadron. Those were the opening days of the Battle of Britain, and what a tough summer it was. The Luftwaffe air raids were becoming more frequent and intense. They were pasting the airfields daily."

"I bet the Canadian pilots had to intercept them."

"They were involved in countless scraps. On August 31, during one engagement Ross shot down one ME 109 and damaged another."

"He must have been a good shot," Brendan said.

"I guess he was, but the German bombing continued and by September our airfields were devastated. We forget today just how important it was for us to win that battle and how desperate the situation was."

"Why was that one so important, Grandpa? There were lots of other battles in the war, weren't there?"

"Because if the Luftwaffe achieved air superiority, a land invasion of Britain would have been Hitler's next step."

"But that never happened, did it?"

"That's because at that crucial hour, the RAF got a very lucky break."

"What kind of lucky break?"

"One of the German pilots got lost over south-east England," Linus answered. "He decided to drop his bombs anyway and they hit Central London. This was the first attack on the City of London and Prime Minister Winston Churchill decided to retaliate. A couple of days later he sent some bombers over Berlin. Not a lot of damage was done, but Hitler was *furious*. He even made a speech about it."

"He did?"

"Hitler was in such a rage that he immediately ordered his air force to stop attacking the airfields and concentrate on attacking the City of London instead."

"I wouldn't want to have been in London when that happened," Brendan said.

"The Londoners called it 'the Blitz'. It was a dreadful time for them."

"But they survived it, didn't they?"

"Yes, they did—and it made a huge difference in the war. It may have been the biggest reason that Germany lost the war."

"How come?"

"This change in German tactics was an important break for the RAF. London was now taking the brunt of daily attacks, which allowed the RAF to repair their airfields and get their damaged planes flying again. They made the most of this opportunity. The RAF held the fort and that's why September 15 has been celebrated ever since as Battle of Britain Day."

"I don't get it," Brendan said. "You mean something important happened on that day?"

"You have to remember that when the Battle of Britain began, it had been predicted by the French generals that England 'would have her neck rung like a chicken in three weeks'. Now, after two months of a brutal air war, the RAF was continuing to send up squadrons of defenders. And for the first time since the Battle of Britain began, something else was happening."

"Like what?"

"There was a subtle change in morale. The German pilots first felt it on September 15. They wondered why there were still so many Allied planes in the air. Surely, the RAF should have been destroyed by now. Yet, it seemed to them there were more Spitfires and Hurricanes flying that day than ever before. How could this be?"

"Were the Allies really good at building planes or something?"

"The simple answer is that the Allied Air Command used their forces very well," Linus answered.

"Maybe they were really good at setting traps and ambushes and things like that," the boy suggested.

"The RAF had very capable leaders," Linus said. "Allied Air Command was led by a man named Hugh Dowding. He knew how many squadrons to keep in reserve and when to use them. The RAF didn't nearly have the resources of the Luftwaffe, but what they had, they used to maximum efficiency. Of course, Lady Luck plays a big role in wartime as well."

"But you mean that was the day that the Germans figured out they couldn't win?"

"That's exactly what happened, Brendan. Morale is a very powerful factor in war. When the ordinary fighting man starts to lose confidence in his commanders, it often means the difference between victory and defeat. It was on September 15 that the German pilots became very demoralized over their prospects of ever defeating Britain by air attacks alone."

"It just seems funny that it happened on that day," Brendan said.

"It's well documented so I can tell you exactly what happened in the air that day," Linus said quietly. "On September 15, 1940, there were two major German raids. The first struck late in the morning. Hundreds of enemy bombers and fighters were again filling the skies over London. The No. 1 Canadians scrambled at 11:40 A.M. from their airfield at RAF Northholt. By noon their Hurricanes had broken formation and were fighting a series of dogfights over London. Ross Smither fought courageously, but he didn't see the ME109 attacking him out of the sun. He was killed at 18,000 feet above Biggin Hill."

Brendan had a lump in his throat. "This is one of your saddest stories."

"The price of liberty is 'blood, toil, tears and sweat'," was the grave reply.

The nine-year-old was silent.

"That was how Winston Churchill put it, Brendan. He was speaking about Canadians like Ross Smither. Churchill knew that the survival of civilization depended on the young airmen of Fighter Command. I remember that in one of his most famous speeches to the House of Commons, Churchill referred to them as 'noble knights'."

"He probably meant like the knights of the Round Table," explained the boy.

"There were many acts of bravery and selflessness in those desperate days," Linus said. "The attacks on London continued, but the spirit of the Luftwaffe had been broken. Hitler knew only too well what September 15 meant."

"What did it mean?"

"There would be no invasion of Britain. Hitler decided Russia would make an easier target for him so he looked east."

"And we won the Battle of Britain," the boy said.

"Let's put it another way, Brendan. It would be better to say we survived it. During the summer of 1940, for the first time ever, the most formidable fighting machine the world had ever seen had been turned back."

"You can have this plane when we're finished, Grandpa. You can have it to remind you of your friend."

Linus stood up and walked to his china cabinet. "I have something else to remind me of him," he said, removing a pair of salt and pepper shakers from the shelf.

He handed them to his grandson. "Ross gave these to your Grandma and me as a wedding gift in 1939."

Brendan held the gift gently in his hands. Even at that young age he understood the sentimental value they must have to his grandfather. He handed them back very carefully.

Linus tucked them back in the cabinet. "I have something even more valuable to remember him by."

"You have?" The boy was on tip toes now, peering further into the cabinet. "What?"

"My freedom, Brendan—and yours."

HIGH FLIGHT

Oh! I have slipped the surly bonds of Earth
And danced the skies on laughter-silvered wings;
Sunward I've climbed, and joined the tumbling
    mirth
Of sun-split clouds,—and done a hundred things
You have not dreamed of—wheeled and soared and
    swung
High in the sunlit silence. Hov'ring there,
I've chased the shouting wind along , and flung
My eager craft through footless halls of air....

Up, up the long, delirious, burning blue
I've topped the wind-swept heights with easy grace
Where never lark, or even eagle flew—
And, while with silent, lifting mind I've trod
The high untrespassed sanctity of space,
Put out my hand, and touched the face of God.

John Gillespie Magee, Jr., 1941

This is the poem that Linus and Brendan memorized together that Saturday afternoon. It is the 'correct' version, meaning that it was transcribed from John Magee's handwritten copy which is held in the Library of Congress, Washington D.C.

CHAPTER TWENTY-TWO

1941

Sir Frederick Goes to War

"Comment is free, but facts are sacred."
Charles P. Scott, quoted in the Manchester Guardian
May 6, 1926

"So what have you been up to in school these days, Brendan?" It was late Saturday morning and Linus' grandson had just arrived for lunch.

He placed some crumpled papers on the kitchen table and sat down. "We've been studying diabetes in school, so I had to do a composition on Banting and Best and the discovery of insulin. I was just over at the library."

Linus was very interested to hear that. "Oh, really?" he said. "I'd love to help you. I know a lot about Sir Frederick Banting."

As soon as those words were out of his grandfather's mouth, Brendan knew he had made a fatal mistake. It was a well-cherished schoolboy creed that the less said to adults about school the better. The damage, however, was done, so the boy retreated into a classic defensive position. "You'd be pretty bored with it, Grandpa," he said, folding up his papers and putting them in his back pocket. "Anyway, I've pretty well finished."

"Finished?" Linus asked. "You must have spent a lot of time at the library."

"It didn't take me very long. I got all the information off the internet."

"The internet?" Linus asked. "Is that information reliable, do you think?"

"Sure it is," Brendan answered very quickly. "There's lots of it and it's fast. That's all I care about."

"But how do you verify it? What if the information is wrong?"

"Most of the sites I use are official websites so I know the information has to be right."

"Couldn't it still be wrong even if it's an official site?"

"I guess I could double check the information with other sites to see if the information was the same," Brendan answered. "But the sites I used were good enough for this project." He sounded confident but his grandfather had sown the seeds of doubt. The boy began to wonder if the websites he used really were the right ones. He removed the composition from his back pocket and had a second look at it.

"I'd love to hear what you wrote about Frederick Banting," Linus said.

Brendan began to read his opening paragraphs.

"Dr. Banting's family lived on a farm outside Alliston, Ontario," the boy began. "He was born there on November 14, 1891."

"Are you absolutely certain that's where he was born?" Linus asked. "The information on that website was probably from a secondary source. Are you sure it's correct? What primary source could you use to validate that information?"

Brendan hadn't considered that the information could be wrong. He thought if someone was going to all the trouble of posting information on the net, he must know what he was talking about. He wondered why his grandfather always had to question everything.

"I didn't even know there *was* a difference between a primary source and a secondary source," Brendan confessed.

"Let's say you're going to school and you meet up with little

Johnny, who's your friend, "Linus explained. "Johnny's going fishing and asks you to go along with him. He tells you there's no school today. So you and Johnny go fishing instead. The next day you both are in trouble because, as it turned out, Johnny was a very unreliable secondary source. If you had checked with your teacher, who was the primary source, you would have found out that it was a regular school day."

"Darn that little Johnny," Brendan muttered. "He's always getting me in trouble."

"My point is that when you are looking for facts, you should always try to find a primary source. What do you think would be a good primary source for Dr. Banting's birthday?"

"You mean like his birth certificate?" Brendan guessed.

"Absolutely," agreed his grandfather. "Dr. Banting's birth certificate is definitely a primary source. A birth certificate is-sued by the Ontario Government gives it authority. It would tell us when and where he was born. So what else did you find out about his life?"

"I read that he volunteered in the Royal Canadian Medical Corps in the First World War and that he won a medal for bravery."

"That's good."

"He got it for operating on wounded men during a battle and he was wounded himself by shrapnel."

"What would be a good primary source for that sort of information?"

"The army records?"

"That would be best place to look," agreed Linus. "A soldier's army records would tell us when he joined, what regiment he was with, where he served and any wounds and medals that he received. The army would also have personal information about him such as his weight and height and his date of birth and next of kin."

"Where do they keep the army records?"

"You could try the Department of Veterans Affairs in Ottawa. Banting's army records would probably be there."

Brendan was beginning to realize that although primary sources might be better, they weren't necessarily very convenient to find.

"What did you have to say about Dr. Banting's discovery of insulin?"

Brendan cleared his throat and began to read slowly from his notes: "Diabetes is a disease that happens when there is too much sugar in the blood. In May of 1921, Dr. Banting, assisted by Dr. Best, began to experiment on dogs at the University of Toronto. They injected diabetic dogs with a substance made from the pancreas of the dogs and the dogs soon got better."

Brendan then showed his grandfather the illustrations of dogs he had drawn for the project. Brendan liked to draw dogs.

"Maybe you could draw some people too," Linus suggested. "Many people take insulin. Don't forget that Dr. Banting's discovery helped save the lives of millions of people."

"*And* they said he became world famous," Brendan said.

"Let's look at the reason for his fame. How can we document the tests he and the other doctors performed in their laboratory to learn exactly how the discovery was made?"

"Well," the nine-year-old said slowly, "maybe somebody took down notes in their journals about the stuff they were doing."

"That's good, Brendan. We could look up the old newspaper accounts. There were certainly many reporters writing about insulin, once it was proven to be successful. But I think the best primary source for the research would be Banting himself."

"What do you mean Banting himself?"

"When a doctor is doing experimental research, he must make meticulous notes. You and I could go to the University of Toronto archives and try to find Dr. Banting's original notes.

They may still be there." Linus looked at his grandson over his glasses, "Do you see now what I mean by a primary source."

"That seeing is believing?"

"That a good researcher bases his work on sources like pho- tographs, government records, newspaper accounts, letters and diaries to get to the truth. That's the kind of hard evidence a researcher wants."

"But, Grandpa, I don't think our teacher is expecting us to do all that."

"I'm sure that your teacher wants you to find out as much as you can about Dr. Banting and put his story in your own words," Linus said, in an encouraging tone. "I think you've done a good job on your composition so far but be careful about the information you download from the internet. A lot of sites may be unreliable. I don't want you blindly accepting every- thing you read on the internet as fact."

"I won't."

"That goes for books, magazines, television *and* newspapers."

"I know," the boy sighed.

"So what did you find out about Dr. Banting as a person? Can you flesh him out a little bit?"

"I found out he liked to paint and he liked to go on long fish- ing trips."

"He was a good artist, wasn't he?" agreed Linus. "He painted in the style of the 'Group of Seven'. What else can you tell me about him?"

"He died in a plane crash during the war. That's about it."

"It was in 1941," Linus said.

"Oh."

"He was a passenger on a Hudson bomber that was being ferried to England for war service."

"I think the website said it crashed in Newfoundland," the

nine-year-old said.

Linus remembered that crash very well. "The Hudson was considered a very reliable aircraft back then, but this one ran into trouble as soon as it took off. First the engine failed and then the radio conked out. The aircraft went out of control and crashed in the barrens north east of Gander, Newfoundland. Dr. Banting died from his injuries the next day."

"He must have been very patriotic to fight in the war," Brendan said.

"In both wars, Brendan. Anyone who volunteered for service in both world wars can be considered to be *very* patriotic. I think that when the Second War began he was at loose ends and looking for a purpose."

Brendan decided two could play at this game. He deliberately leaned forward, looked his grandfather in the eye, and asked, "How can you be so sure about that, Grandpa? What makes you think he was at loose ends and looking for a purpose?"

"That's a good question, Brendan. I thought because he was born into a rural Ontario Methodist home and believed in those old-fashioned values that he learned when he was growing up."

"Like what old-fashioned values?"

"Like commitment, perseverance, hard work and frugality— that sort of thing," Linus said. "Those would have been the values important to Banting. Fame would have been at the bottom of his list. Although he became an international celebrity after his discovery, maybe he had doubts about of all the acclaim that he received. That's only my opinion."

"I don't know why you think he'd be shy about it," Brendan said. "Didn't you just say his discovery saved millions of lives?"

"I did. That's why he's a hero to every Canadian today, but I wonder if he might have been disappointed that he couldn't come up with another big discovery to give to the world," Linus said. "Maybe that's why he volunteered in the Medical Corps in 1939, just as he had done in 1915."

"Maybe he thought by signing up for the war he was doing something for a good cause," suggested the boy.

"*And* doing something for his country," Linus added. "That was the kind of man he was. Now let me tell you one last story about Dr. Banting that's not generally known."

Brendan grinned at Linus. "Did you find it on the internet?" he asked.

"As a matter of fact, I don't know anyone else who would know this," his grandfather said.

Brendan gave his grandfather a sideways look. "Are you just making something up to test me?"

"No, this is a true story. Banting enlisted for the Second World War at the Horse Palace at the Exhibition Grounds in Toronto in 1939. Back then the army used one of the administration buildings for enlistment purposes. Each day fresh volunteers would form a line to sign up at the desk. The civilian on the administration desk would take down all the details of the recruits and issue their service numbers. It was standard routine. This one particular day there was a tall, middle-aged man waiting in the line."

Brendan smiled impishly at his grandfather. "I wonder who that man could be?" he asked, knowing full well how the story was going to end.

Linus continued. "The man standing in line had won the military cross for bravery under fire in the First World War, the Nobel Prize for Medicine in 1923 and was an honoured member of countless scientific societies. He had even been knighted by the King."

The answer was so obvious to Brendan it wasn't even funny. "I already know what you're going to say," he interrupted, unable to hold back any longer. "The man in the line was Dr. Banting, wasn't it?"

Linus nodded. "Yes, Brendan, it was indeed Dr. Banting who

was waiting patiently in line with all the others. When it was his turn to present himself, he was asked if he was enlisting in the army. 'Yes, the Medical Corps,' the doctor said to the civilian, and then he added, 'If they'll have me. I may be too old.' Those were the exact words he spoke."

Brendan listened attentively.

Linus paused for a moment and went on. "That story tells me a lot about Dr. Banting at the end of his life. His great discovery was long behind him, but no matter how famous a man he had become, Sir Frederick Banting remained at heart, a modest country doctor, still wanting to do his duty."

"Wait a minute, Grandpa," the boy said, pouncing eagerly on an inconsistency. "That's a neat story and all that, but I don't think that conversation sounds like something we can prove. Remember what you just said about primary sources. So how do you know for sure that Dr. Banting said those words to that man?"

"Because," answered Linus, "I was that man."

1 9 4 1

Operation 'Leg'

"Everywhere you looked there were Blenheim bombers"
Jack Nickleson, quoted in the Toronto Star
August 12,1941

LINUS HAD GROCERY SHOPPING TO DO AND BRENDAN WAS GET-
TING BORED.

He decided his grandfather was taking too long inspecting zucchinis and broccoli, melons and bananas. Brendan had very little interest in fruits and vegetables. He craved sugar. He had been to this store enough times to know it had a bakery counter full of jelly doughnuts to die for. So how, he wondered, could he get his grandfather headed in the right direction?

"When I was in high school, I had a summer job at the Loblaws store at Yonge and St. Clair, " Linus said. "This store reminds me of it."

"What did you have to do?"

"I was a grocery clerk," answered Linus. "I stocked the bins with produce like cabbages and lettuce." He paused for a moment before flashing an impish grin at his grandson. "Those were *heady* days."

The boy stared blankly at his grandfather.

Linus was deflated. That was his best joke. "Cabbages-let-tuce-heads-get it?" he asked.

Brendan *hadn't* got it. He thought it was probably the kind of humour his grandfather referred to as 'a play on words'. That was the kind of humour his grandfather really liked—the kind of humour *nobody gets*.

"I worked with a fellow named Jack Nickleson," Linus said. "He had a summer job stocking shelves too, and we became friends. That was a long time ago." He paused and added. "I miss him."

"I know," Brendan sighed. "My best friend moved away last year too."

Linus' thoughts went back to the summer of 1940. "When I first met Jack Nickleson at Loblaws, he'd just finished high school at North Toronto Collegiate. He'd been captain of both the junior hockey team and the rugby team. He was also the best pal you could have at your back in a fight, but not so good to have to face in a fight."

"Did he get in a lot of fights?"

"I remember once we were having a morning coffee break in the basement lunchroom. He showed me a bloodied hanky and said it was his 'first conquest'."

"He must have been in a fight."

"I guess he had, but I'm sure it would have been for a good cause. It was shortly after that he joined the air force." Linus had that far off look he often assumed when remembering old friendships as he continued, "Jack graduated as a sergeant-pilot from Uplands Airport near Ottawa early in 1941 and was posted overseas to Squadron 18. I remember his picture appearing on the front page of the *Toronto Star* one day. He had been interviewed after returning from a massive daylight raid over Cologne, Germany. Bomber Command had sent fifty-four Blenheim bombers over Cologne with the object of knocking out a couple of huge power stations."

"How can you remember so much?" his grandson asked.

"Because I write things down," he said, taking his grocery list out of his pocket. "For example, a jug of milk, a loaf of whole wheat bread, one tin of clam chowder soup, one pound of lean ground beef. I write things down. That's the *only* way I can remember." He tapped his list and returned it to his pocket. "Somewhere, I must have written down that there were fifty-four Blenheims and two power stations."

"I guess those power stations would have been a lot easier to see during the day, wouldn't they?" asked Brendan, as they headed toward the dairy counter.

"I suppose the pilots could see their targets better in the day, but the problem was that the Germans could also see *them*."

"Oh no," said Brendan.

"They were certainly taking their chances on these missions," Linus said, placing a jug of milk into the cart. "Everyone knew the Blenheims were too slow."

"That would have made it easy for them to get hit."

"*And* they had very little protection. Each bomber only had one machine gun on the port wing and one on the turret."

"So they couldn't defend themselves up there even if they'd wanted to, you mean?"

"That's right. They needed fighter escorts when they went on a mission. Unfortunately the fighters didn't have enough fuel to accompany the bombers past the French coast. Once they had turned back for home, the bombers were on their own."

"I wouldn't have wanted to be one of those pilots, that's for sure."

"Those Blenheim pilots soon learned how important it was to fly under the radar if they were to survive. When you think that flying low was their only defense, you can see how dangerous those missions were for boys like Jack."

"Did they *really* have to fly under the radar, Grandpa?"

"Jack said he often had to fly less than fifty feet above the ground. Can you believe that? I don't know how they found the courage to do that. Twelve aircraft were lost on that one bombing mission alone over Cologne. No wonder they were called 'suicide missions'."

"Did he become famous?" asked Brendan.

"He never became famous but Jack's name was in the news several times," answered Linus.

"He should have been in a war movie."

"There was another write-up about him in the paper because he was involved in another famous bombing mission. It turned out to be one of the most unusual stories of the war."

"It was?"

"A very famous Battle of Britain ace named Wing Commander Douglas Bader had been reported lost in combat over France. This was very demoralizing for us to hear. The news of Bader was all over the radio. He'd been one of the top RAF pilots, but he was also well known because of his determination to fly even though he had no legs."

"He didn't have any *legs*?" Brendan asked, very surprised to hear that. "What happened to them?"

"Bader had lost both his legs in a very bad flying accident in 1931," answered Linus. "He had been very lucky to survive it. The RAF decided he could no longer fly after that. But Bader was a very determined man. He never gave up trying to get back into action and Fighter Command finally let him. He rejoined his squadron and gained great fame as a Spitfire pilot during the Battle of Britain. He was still flying in the summer of 1941, when his luck finally ran out."

"Did he get shot down?"

"Yes, his plane was hit and he had to get out," Linus replied. "Imagine how difficult it must have been for a man without legs to eject from a burning Spitfire."

Brendan tried hard to picture how he must have done it. "I don't know how you jump out of a plane without any legs."

"He somehow managed to bail out successfully, but he lost his artificial right leg in the process," Linus went on. "Of course, he was immediately captured by the enemy."

"With only one leg, it would have been kind of hard for him to get away."

"The Germans were delighted to have captured such an illustrious figure as Bader. They sent word to the British that the famous pilot had been captured, but was alive and well. After Bader had informed his captors that he owned a spare leg which he kept in his locker at the Tangmere Airfield, the Luftwaffe offered the British 'safe passage' if they would deliver it to them."

"That's pretty good."

"The German air force held Bader in very high esteem."

"But how did they think that the RAF was going to get his spare leg to him when there was a war going on?"

"Bomber Command located the spare leg, packed it securely in a box and put it on Jack's Blenheim. They instructed Jack to drop the leg by parachute on his squadron's next bombing mission. On August 17, 1941, Jack set out on another daylight raid over Germany. But first he had to drop his package over the St. Omer airfield in France where Bader was held as a prisoner. And that's how Bader got his leg back—ten days after he was shot down."

Brendan thought that was a great story. "Imagine dropping a spare leg from a plane on a bombing mission."

"And even in captivity Bader still carried on the fight," Linus said. "The Germans were very frustrated with him because he was continually trying to escape. Do you know what they did to him?"

"Tie him up?"

"After his last escape attempt, his guards took away his legs for a while as punishment."

"That's sure not fair," Brendan protested, knowing what a low-down thing that was to do to a man without legs.

"Jack's squadron called their mission 'Operation Leg'," Linus said.

Brendan loved the name of the mission. It also gave him an idea. The story would be a good lead-in to remind his grandpa about a visit to a certain bakery counter.

"Outbound Blenheims"

This painting by Alex Hamilton shows two Blenheims heading towards France.
The Blenheim pilots soon learned how important it was to fly under the radar if
they were to survive. Art print courtesy of the artist.

He announced excitedly, "Let's pretend our buggy is a bomber, Grandpa, and you and I go on a mission. Our squadron will call it 'Operation Jelly Doughnut' and we'll drop a box of dough-nuts off at my house just like Jack did with the leg."

Linus liked doughnuts too, but he didn't want Brendan to take Jack Nickleson's war lightly. He knew, of course, that a nine-year-old boy had no way of relating to those dreadful days of World War Two. And it would only be worse if he told his grandson the rest of the story. Linus wondered if he should tell his grandson that only a month after Operation Leg, Jack and the rest of the crew had failed to return home from a mission over Holland and were never seen again. Was Brendan old enough to be told that Jack Nickleson, who had always been kidded as the 'baby' of the squadron, was now lost at nineteen years of age?

Linus was sensitive about these important stories. He was careful how he worded it. "Those bombing missions are not something you want to joke about, Brendan," he said. "There was an enormous cost in lives both in the air and on the ground."

The boy was silent. He hadn't intended to make light of the story. It was just that his sense of humour was different from his grandfather's.

Linus looked at his grandson thoughtfully. "Jack died on one of those missions."

Brendan was struck by the sadness of the story. He felt even worse for making a joke about it.

Linus was sad too. "Those aircrews were made up of such fine young men," he said quietly. He stood for a moment with his elbows resting on the handle of the buggy. He wanted to express in words something that Brendan could take away from a story like Jack's. "I sometimes think," he said at last, "that I've lived my life knowing that it was a gift from Jack and I'd better live it the best I can. Does that make sense?"

"I think so," Brendan answered, "I guess you don't want to let him down."

"That's exactly how I feel," Linus said, unable to put it better himself. "I don't want to let him down." He then smiled at his grandson and asked, "Are you as peckish as I am?"

Before the boy could answer, Linus swung his Blenheim buggy around. He then set a course for the bakery counter with his grandson happily alongside as copilot, and warm memories of an old friendship in his heart.

CHAPTER TWENTY-FOUR

1944

The Road to Caen

*"I walked among the by-gone scenes,
I knew in olden days."*
—M.J.Shiels, *Memories*

LINUS WALKED DOWN THE HALLWAY TOWARDS BRENDAN'S APARTMENT FOR HIS ANNUAL CHRISTMAS EVE VISIT. There was music in the air.

Brendan recognized that whistle immediately and opened the door. However, he didn't recognize the tune. "That sure doesn't sound like a Christmas carol to me," he said to his grandfather.

"It's *not* a carol at all, Brendan. It's 'Chatanooga Choo-Choo'."

"You mean it's a song about a train?"

"Not just any train," answered his grandfather. "It was about the train that left from track twenty-nine."

"That means you've been visiting your friend in the old people's home," Brendan said, knowing that was the most obvious place his grandfather would have picked up a song like that one.

"I was. My old pal and I spent the afternoon trying to remember the lyrics to all the old songs we had on 78s."

"What are 78s?"

"They were large vinyl records. Back in the forties we used to play them until they wore out," Linus answered.

"You actually wore them out?"

"And when we couldn't play them anymore they were really

good for skipping across ponds."

"Like the first frisbee," said the boy.

"I wish we still had all those old vinyls, but we had a good time today anyway. The only sad thing is that my old war buddy isn't very mobile anymore."

"He isn't?"

"He can't stand for very long. He has a very bad hip."

"A bad hip?"

"I don't think he was feeling very bushy-tailed. He was sitting in the lobby still wearing his dressing gown when I got there. That's always a bad sign."

"Unless he's a flasher."

Linus raised an eyebrow. "Anyway, it's always a great thing to visit old friends at Christmas."

"I love Christmas," Brendan said, very excited about the prospects of what he might find under the tree in the morning. "I love getting presents."

Linus looked at his grandson in a disapproving way. "There's certainly a deeper meaning to Christmas than simply getting presents, don't you think?"

"There's no school," spoke the boy who loved Christmas.

"What about your fellow man?"

"What do you mean?"

"For starters, isn't Christmas about giving and sharing?" Linus asked. "One thing I love about this time of year is having Christmas dinner with my friends and family. Get the idea? Now you come up with one."

"I love having turkey at Christmas," said the nine-year-old.

"That's *exactly* the same thing that I just said." Linus had hoped to hear Brendan express a clear understanding of the spirit of Christmas. "Come, come, my boy," urged his grandfather. "Surely you can think up something you like about Christmas other than eating turkey." This request was accompanied by a gentle nudge.

"Ham, then," the boy replied.

Linus forged on. "Never mind," he sighed. "Today at the old people's home we talked about the Christmases we had during the war."

"I'd hate to be away from home at Christmas," Brendan said. "I'd be homesick."

"I know what being home sick feels like," Linus said. "The Christmas after Normandy was *my* first one away from home."

"That was a big battle, wasn't it?"

"It sure was. The Battle of Normandy was the largest seaborne invasion in history."

"Wasn't that the war against Hitler—the war you were in?"

"Yes, it was," Linus said. "Liberating Europe from Hitler's army began on D-Day."

"What *does* the D in D-Day stand for, anyway?"

"D is for Day, as far as I know," his grandfather replied, "Some people have called it the 'Longest Day'."

"Is that why you joined up?" asked the boy. "So you could be in D-Day?"

"When I volunteered in 1942, everything was leading up to D-Day. I had no choice in the matter."

"Well, you were in it. That's the main thing."

"As soon as I joined the army, I knew that D-Day was coming," Linus said. "While I was training at Camp Borden, Ontario, I heard about the preparations. Then I was sent to Windsor, Nova Scotia. The only thing I knew for sure was that I was getting closer to Europe. "

"Did you have to get more training there?"

"You mean in Nova Scotia?"

Brendan nodded.

"I was a duty driver when I first got there and then they

trained me to drive tanks."

"Is it hard to learn to drive one?"

"I had driven trucks and jeeps and staff cars at Borden," Linus answered, "so a tank was just another vehicle. I learned that the most important thing to know about tanks is how to bail out of one in a hurry."

"I guess that would be hard to do when you're stuck inside."

"I practiced," Linus said, "and I got to know the other drivers' techniques."

Brendan recognized that far away look in his grandfather's eye. He knew he would want paper for a map soon.

"In Windsor, Nova Scotia, I formed a friendship with Carl, a driver from Huntsville, Ontario. Early in May of 1944, I was sitting with him at the soda fountain at the back of a drug store on the main street of town. Neither of us could decide what to order. I remember his pointing to an advertisement of a banana split posted behind the counter and suggesting we both buy one. But it was *forty cents*! I didn't want to spend that much. Forty cents was a lot of money then, but Carl talked me into it."

"He wouldn't have to talk *me* into it," Brendan said. "*I love banana splits.*"

"Carl wondered what I was saving my money for—which was a good question. 'You know where you're going, don't you?' he reminded me. He was referring to the war in Europe. He was right, of course. We didn't know when it would be, but an invasion of France was imminent and we both knew we'd be in it."

"When did you go over there?"

"Less than a week later, I was on the Queen Mary sailing for Scotland, attached to the First Hussars as part of the 3rd Canadian Division."

"That was fast."

"There were many nationalities taking part in the invasion,

such as Poles, Norwegians, Aussies, New Zealanders, Belgians, Greeks, Czechs and Free French, but the bulk of the invading army was British, American and Canadian servicemen. Two American infantry divisions were to go ashore at Omaha and Utah Beaches, two British divisions were assigned to Sword and Gold Beaches and we were to land on Juno. There were more than one hundred and thirty thousand soldiers in the invading force. There were seven thousand ships and five thousand planes."

"That's a lot."

"There were another twenty thousand men from the airborne divisions who parachuted behind enemy lines the night before."

"Behind enemy lines at night?" Brendan shivered. "I wouldn't want to have to do that."

"Nor would I," Linus said, "but H-Hour had arrived and four years of war effort had come down to this. *Everything* was at stake. It was the most frightening moment of my life. A young major hopped onto one of our Sherman tanks and told us we were going into the field. When I heard those words, my first thought was of Dieppe."

"Dieppe?"

"There had been a disastrous raid on the French port of Dieppe two years before. They were mostly Canadian soldiers. The German defenders had been waiting for our men at the seawall and mowed them down." Linus swallowed hard as he recalled that horrible day in Canadian history. "All we could do was pray that wouldn't happen to us."

"That would have been scary, that's for sure."

"We were *all* scared," Linus said, remembering how hard he had tried not to show it. "We wouldn't be human if we weren't scared."

"Were there a lot of soldiers killed on D-Day?"

"Many Canadians were killed," Linus said, "and many more

wounded trying to get ashore. There were also many British and American casualties."

Brendan listened quietly.

"The Germans were determined to push us back into the sea. Some people think that because the enemy was unsure where our attack would be launched, that resistance was low. Nothing could be further from the truth. Germany had a fierce army with one of her greatest generals, Erwin Rommel, responsible for a major part of their Atlantic coastal defense. Thousands of German soldiers, protected by concrete bunkers and pillboxes sprayed Juno Beach with machine gun fire as we landed."

"No wonder so many soldiers were killed."

"That was only the beginning. There were two powerful German Panzer tank regiments stationed inland which would be counterattacking us the next day."

"I wouldn't want to have to fight them—in real life, I mean," Brendan said.

"The one thing in our favour was that their army was spread out. Had they known the date and place of D-Day, I doubt if we could have made it."

"They didn't know about it?"

"It was one of the best kept secrets of the war," said Linus. "German High Command was convinced we would invade at Calais. The Allies did everything they could to disguise from the enemy where they were really going to land. They sent out fake wire messages to confuse them. They created fake planes, fake tanks and even fake ships so that any aerial shots would mislead the Germans into thinking the invasion would be across the Strait of Dover."

"So even their spies never found out?"

"We would never have been successful on that invasion had they known."

"And you might not be here today," said Brendan, giving his

grandfather something to think about.

"And you might not be here either," said Linus, returning the favour.

"I've seen pictures on television of that battle you were in, Grandpa—of the beach and the fighting and stuff."

"I've seen those newsreels, too, Brendan. There's some very good film footage of landing craft, waterspouts, low flying Spitfires and Typhoons, shells bursting on the beach and thousands of soldiers establishing a beachhead. I'm glad someone took a camera with them because I never saw any of that."

"How come—don't you remember?"

"It was just a blur," Linus said. "I was only able to see a hundred yards ahead of me through the vision slit in the tank. I was lucky that I could make out the big house on the beach that we used as a beacon. Once past that, our orders were to keep moving and not look back. We were told not to stop until we found the road to Caen."

"That's where you were supposed to go?"

"We were ordered to block off the German tanks that we knew were on their way to counterattack us."

"Were there a lot of German tanks?"

"They had a lot of them," Linus said. "The Allies had hoped to liberate Caen by June 7, 1944, but it ended up taking over a month. I remember we had stopped to wait for an ammo truck before entering the city. I noticed there were several tankers walking towards us. Their Shermans had been knocked out earlier and they were looking for reassignment. One of the men was Carl."

"The same guy you knew in Nova Scotia?"

"It was the same guy. I hadn't seen him since last May at that soda fountain back home. We looked at each other like long lost friends. As soon as he recognized me, he ran up, shook my hand and told me he was still thinking about that banana split." Linus glanced at his grandson and chuckled.

Juno Beach, June 6,1944,
This Ken Bell photograph shows the tanks of the 1st Hussars and troops of the
Royal Winnipeg Rifles and Regina Rifles landing near Courseulles-sur-Mer,
France on D-Day.

"That's pretty good," the boy said. "I guess it was a happy memory for him."

"Well, the past month had been full of unhappy memories of Germans taking pot shots at him," Linus said. "I don't think anyone realized how difficult it would be once we were in France."

"What was the worst part?"

"The German Tiger Tanks were very difficult to neutralize," Linus said. "That was the worst part."

"Were they a lot bigger than your tanks?"

"Our Shermans were reliable, but they caught fire easily

when they were hit. That's why you had to get out of them fast. The heavy German Tiger tanks were slower but they carried 88 millimetre guns, which was considerably more firepower than we had."

"How did you fight them?"

"We tried not to get hit."

"I'd try to find their nerve centre," Brendan said, having successfully defeated thousands of computerized alien invaders in his day, "then vapourize them."

"That's basically what we had to do. The Tiger tank could only be destroyed from the top or the rear." Linus took a deep breath and said. "I still shudder at the thought of them."

Brendan took a deep breath too. He was glad he wasn't there.

"After the war ended," Linus went on, "we had several reunions with the men who served in Normandy. Sadly, there were many empty seats because of those we had left behind."

"Did Carl survive?"

"I don't know what happened to him. He was assigned to another unit and I never heard anything more."

"Was there a reunion this year?"

"We haven't had one for a few years. There aren't many of us left."

"Except the man you visited today at the old-folks home."

"He's the last one I know."

"That's too bad."

"Here's how it works," Linus said, taking out his fountain pen from his shirt pocket. "I need a piece of paper."

"Are you going to draw a map?" the boy asked, rummaging through his schoolbag for a sheet of blank paper.

"No," his grandfather said, as he drew a long line on the paper and marked the date 1944 on it, "a time line. This was the year of the invasion. Most of the men who fought in the Second War were born just after the First World War ended. Let's make a note of those war years. Now let's mark your year of birth and today's date. My generation lived here; yours here—but you can see there's some overlap."

"You mean the parts where we lived at the same time?"

"That's right. When you're an old fellow, Brendan, you can say you knew someone who served in Normandy. I'm your connection to the Second World War. When I was your age, I was connected to men who had fought in the First World War and the Boer War. I even knew people who had seen Macdonald and Laurier in the flesh. But my old friend Lewis McLauchlan, who had been in the Klondike Gold Rush, has us both beat. He told me one time that when he was a boy, he remembered meeting an old man who had fought in the *Battle of Waterloo*."

"He did?"

"Isn't it fascinating to think that you and I are connected to a man who had actually fought in the Battle of Waterloo?"

"I didn't even know I *was*."

Linus began to work on his time line. First, he wrote the words "The beginning of Canada" and named the Iroquoian tribes of the eastern woodlands followed by the plains and the west coast tribes; then he wrote in Jacques Cartier's name and dated it 1534; then Hudson, 1610; Champlain's trip to Huronia, 1615; Lasalle, in 1681.

"I remember about LaSalle," Brendan put in. "And of course the Iroquois."

Linus marked the names of Joseph Brant, Sir John Johnson and the other Loyalists who came up to Ontario in 1784; then the names of Tecumseh, Brock, Collier, and the other eighteen-twelvers. He continued by adding names and dates of our pioneers, then Confederation in 1867, Sir John Rose's mission to Washington in 1870, the Gold Rush of 1898, the birth of flight and the war years of the Twentieth Century.

"They were pretty exciting days back then, Grandpa."

"It's our national story," Linus said, hoping his grandson would learn to love his country as deeply as he did. "We're lucky."

Brendan studied the time line carefully. Finally he tapped his finger several times on the year 1944 and said, *"This* one's my favourite."

On hearing those words, Linus beamed with pride. It did his heart good to have Brendan single out his Normandy story. What a wonderful Christmas present for an old D-Day veteran, to be rated higher in his grandson's estimation than LaSalle or Brock or even that grand old man, Sir John A. Macdonald. Linus felt as proud as he was the day he first wore the 'Canada' shoulder flash so many years before. "What is it about that Normandy story that makes it so special, Brendan?" he asked, very much enjoying the moment.

The boy's eyes widened. "I'm still thinking about that banana split."

CHAPTER TWENTY-FIVE

1 9 6 3

Out of Lunenburg

In the age of sail

LINUS HAD SPRUNG A LEAK.

It couldn't have happened at a more inopportune time.

He had been looking forward all week to seeing the famous Nova Scotian schooner, *Bluenose II*, which had been on a promotional tour and was now docked in Linus' hometown.

However, repairs to his kitchen sink required a plumber's attention and that took priority. Linus would have to remain indoors. As Linus mulled over his predicament, Brendan arrived and immediately noticed the dispirited look on his grandfather's face.

"What's the matter, Grandpa?"

"It looks like I won't see the *Bluenose* today," answered Linus. "I have to wait for the plumber to show up and fix my sink."

"That's a famous ship too, isn't it? Our teacher said that's the ship on the dime."

"It's been there since 1937," Linus said, selecting a ten-cent piece amongst the loose change he had pulled out of his pocket. "A Toronto sculptor, Emanuel Hahn, designed it. He also designed the caribou on the quarter."

Grand Bank fishing schooner 'Bluenose',
photographed by Wallace McAskill. The Bluenose won the International
Fishermen's Trophy in 1923 and held it until the end of the age of sail.

"I don't think I've ever heard of him," said Brendan, reaching into his own pocket to check if he had any money, but coming up empty.

"My mother worked with Emanuel Hahn," Linus said.

"Was she a sculptor too?"

"No, they worked together in the bookkeeping department of the old Eaton's store in downtown Toronto in 1900. That was back in the days when Timothy Eaton himself was running the company. Manny Hahn was just a teenager then, but he went back to school the following year to study art, and he became one of Canada's best sculptors and a respected art teacher."

"I bet not many too people know that, Grandpa."

"Well, they *should*," Linus said, "Hahn based his work on a photograph of the *Bluenose* taken by Wallace McAskill."

"I've never heard of him either."

"He was a famous Cape Breton photographer. Back in the twenties and thirties, McAskill won many international awards for his marine photography. He was very well known for his seascapes and portraits of fishermen, but his most sought-after work was his portfolio of *Bluenose* pictures."

Brendan and Linus were both peering at the image on the dime.

"The Mint had better not think about taking the *Bluenose* out of circulation," Linus muttered. "It's my favourite coin." He put his dime back in his pocket and added, "It's bad enough that they're always issuing commemorative quarters which I confuse all the time with nickels."

Brendan thought this wasn't the best time to mention that he collected commemorative quarters. "Why is the *Bluenose* on the dime, anyway, Grandpa?"

"She won the International Fishermen's Trophy back in 1923 and held it until the end of the age of sail."

"That's a long time," agreed Brendan, although secretly he had no idea when the age of sail ended.

"Angus Walters was at the ship's wheel in every race," Linus said. "He was the perfect captain for the *Bluenose*. He was born in Lunenburg, Nova Scotia, went to sea at thirteen and developed into a skilled and brave seaman. He skippered the *Bluenose* to record catches of cod on the Grand Banks as well as winning the International Fishermen's Trophy."

"What was the Fishermen's Trophy for—catching the most fish or something?"

"It was a *racing* trophy which was sponsored by the *Halifax Herald*. All the owners of the fishing schooners coveted that prize."

"Then it must have been a good trophy to win."

"Only commercial fishing schooners were eligible to enter the race, so when the *Bluenose* was built in Lunenburg in 1921, she was designed not only to work as fishing schooner but also to race."

"That's pretty good."

"The *Bluenose* had many races with other schooners, but her most famous opponent was a fast schooner out of Gloucester, named the *Gertrude L. Thebaud,* skippered by Ben Pine. The New England ship beat the *Bluenose* in 1930 for a new award called the Lipton Cup, but the *Bluenose* regrouped and defeated her the following year with a stout-hearted defense of the International Fisherman's Trophy. For seven years there were no races. Then, in 1938, the *Thebaud* challenged one last time for the International. That series was the last of the races between the old saltbankers."

"Is that what they called those ships?"

"It was a nickname they used."

"I bet the *Bluenose* was the fastest saltbanker on the seven seas," the boy said with pride, adding a new nickname to his ever-growing collection.

"Maritimers have always taken great pride in the wooden ships they build," Linus said, "You can imagine how they felt about the *Bluenose*. Her fame spread around the world. She's in Canada's Sports Hall of Fame today."

"So why aren't there any schooners around anymore?"

"There were a number of reasons why the days of the working schooners ended, Brendan. Even in the thirties, they were on borrowed time, but it was the war that really ended the age of sail on the Atlantic."

"It was?"

"When war broke out in 1939, all commercial fishing on the Grand Banks was stopped because of the threat of German submarines," Linus answered. "The old schooners were sold off."

"That's too bad."

"There were other reasons too."

"Like what?"

"Progress, Brendan, progress," Linus answered, bitterly. "It's always technology that takes the romance out of life. Happens every time. Ship owners wanted to modernize and increase efficiency so they began using diesel engines on their ships. I admit that diesel power was safer for the crew, but the younger generation also figured they could catch more cod that way. Of course, old salts, who had spent their whole lives on schooners weren't too happy about it."

"I bet the cod weren't too happy about it either," Brendan said.

Linus sighed. "The glorious era of the working sailing ship was over."

"So what happened to the *Bluenose*, Grandpa? Did it go sailing off into the sunset or something?"

Linus was somewhat taken aback to hear his bright young grandson say something like that. He put his hand upon the boy's shoulder. "Why, Brendan, if a ship was sailing out of Lunenburg, she would be sailing into the *sunrise*, wouldn't she?"

"I guess I meant the sunrise," the boy said, surprised that his grandfather paid such close attention to little things like that.

"The *Bluenose* was sold as a freighter to some West Indies trading company and she sank off the coast of Haiti in 1946," said Linus.

"That's a sad ending, Grandpa."

"Actually, the story has a happy ending."

"It does?"

"The people of Nova Scotia loved their heritage so much that in 1963 they built a new *Bluenose*. The same specifications and materials were used. The same designer as the original, Mr. W. J. Roue, was consulted. The original Captain—Angus Walters himself—sailed on the maiden voyage. And that's the ship that's at the dockside right now. "

"I bet it could *still* win the Fisherman's Trophy" said the boy.

"That would really be something."

"She doesn't race *or* fish anymore. She's an ambassador today and only makes promotional tours, but to me, the building of the *Bluenose II* is one of Canada's greatest sea stories."

"I wish I could go and see it," Brendan said, "but one of my friends is having a birthday party today."

"I know," said Linus, wistfully. "That's why I didn't ask you to come with me."

"And now because of your darn sink, you can't go either."

"Well, these things happen," Linus said. "Of course, I'd love to see the *Bluenose*, but more than that, I'd love to sail on her. Think of what it must be like to work your passage on an old fishing schooner like that. I guess it's too late for me now, but that's what I always wanted to do when I was your age." The man then assumed another of his trade mark far off looks. "I had wanderlust."

"You mean you wanted to run off to sea as a cabin boy?" Brendan asked.

His grandfather didn't answer. His mind was elsewhere. Linus had never been a sailor, but he had a kinship with the sea gleaned from many stories read in his youth.

He sat down in his wicker chair smelling the sea air. Ever the romantic, Linus envisioned himself as a youth on board a working fishing schooner exactly like the *Bluenose*, filling the hold with cod. "I tell you, my boy, there's nothing like life on board a tall ship. No gas. No engine. No sound but the lapping of saltwater on the hull, the creaking of timbers and the stretching of canvas. It's the age-old story of man against the sea. There's *nothing* like being part of a ship's company for building a boy's character, Brendan. *Nothing!*"

"There isn't?" asked the boy.

"No question about it," Linus said. "I suppose it's the sea air that does it. They say when a boy goes to sea, he returns a man.

The sea is a powerful force."

"It is?"

"I've felt it."

"You've felt it?"

"I have, indeed," his grandfather said. "You know, the better part of my working life was spent behind a desk. I've never told anyone this before, Brendan, but I often used to watch the sailors from my office tower as they worked on the docks. *How I envied those men!* They'd probably just returned from the China Sea. I wanted to quit my job and go with them to their next port of call. I watched them loading and unloading their cargo and wondered what was inside those huge containers. That would go on all day."

"It sure sounds like hard work to me," the boy said, thinking that loading and unloading cargo all day wasn't something he wanted to volunteer for; especially if it was only to build character. The Iroquois and the voyageurs and the river drivers never had to worry about building character.

"And when their watch was done," Linus went on, his eyes gazing into the distant horizon, "the men would go below and I imagined them smoking their pipes around a pot-bellied stove and swapping stories of their lives at sea. Some were talking about how much they missed home. Others were studying maps. The bos'un in his bunk, was whittling a toy ship out of a block of pine and down the passageway a Truro man was playing his fiddle."

"Are you *sure* about that, Grandpa?" Brendan asked, unable to figure out how his grandfather knew what was going on below decks. How could he see all that from his office window? Was he a psychic—or had he simply put too much kelp on his bran flakes that morning?

"About *what?*"

"That a Truro man was really playing a fiddle?"

The retired bank employee hesitated. He stroked his chin for a moment and furrowed his brow. Finally he said, "Well, it *might* have been an accordion."

Brendan gave his grandfather a sideways look. He was seeing first hand how the sea air could get a powerful hold on a man; a hold that was hard to shake. It's been happening, the nine-year-old guessed, ever since man first set sail. Still, it's always sad when it's in your own family.

"All we need is a steady wind," Linus said, eager to enlist the boy as his first mate.

But the nine-year-old had no interest in a life at sea. Brendan would have been perfectly content watching the tall ships race from shore, but he wasn't all that keen to work his passage on one. Being the youngest member of the crew, he knew he'd be the one picked to peel a million potatoes. And when that was done, he'd be told to swab the deck, clean the heads, load the cargo, raise the sails and then be sent up to the crow's nest for the rest of the day, probably in the pouring rain, "to watch the weather". Jobs like that can tire out a growing boy, especially when there's no other kids your own age on board and you feel like you're coming down with a touch of scurvy. For the moment however, he brushed those thoughts aside. "It's too bad you have to wait for the plumber, Grandpa," he said.

"The *Bluenose* is a national icon, Brendan," his grandfather said. "I'd love to have a look at her."

"What's a national icon?"

"An icon is an image," Linus explained. "A national icon would be an image that represents Canada. That's the best way I can put it. Does that make sense?"

"Like a picture?"

"Yes."

"Because I have pictures of myself in front of Canadian monuments and things like that," Brendan said. "Is that what you mean?"

"Sure. I'd say a national icon is the same thing as a national monument. What pictures are you talking about?"

"I have one of myself in front of Brock's Monument. That was on a class trip."

"I hadn't heard about that."

"I've also had my picture taken at the top of the CN Tower. You took that."

"Oh yes, I remember."

"Then there was our school trip to Ottawa when we had a class picture taken in front of the Parliament Buildings."

"I knew you went to Ottawa but you never showed me any pictures from that trip, did you?"

"I *did* show you. Remember I was standing beside the Mountie?"

"A Mountie?" repeated Linus. "Say! You *have* had a lot of pictures of yourself with our national icons."

"I've even had my picture taken with the *Stanley Cup*."

Now Brendan had gone too far. "You've had your picture taken with the *Stanley Cup?*" his grandfather asked in a tone that suggested that was something he wanted for himself as well.

"I got it as a souvenir when my Mom took me to the Hockey Hall of Fame."

"How in the world do you do it, Brendan? I've never heard of anyone having so many pictures of themselves with so many Canadian landmarks. How come no one's ever taken *my* picture in front of one of them? I pay my taxes."

The boy didn't think it was a big deal and answered with a shrug, "Just lucky, I guess."

"Brendan, if you didn't have that birthday party to go to today and I hadn't sprung a leak, we could have gone together to see the *Bluenose* and you could have taken *my* picture right in front of her."

"I would have taken a great picture of you, Grandpa."

"Having my picture taken with the *Bluenose* would almost be as good as having my picture taken with the Stanley Cup," Linus said, which was high praise indeed coming from such an avid hockey fan.

Brendan agreed. "You *definitely* should have more pictures taken of yourself, Grandpa. I've had more than my share."

"You seem to always have the knack of being at the right place at the right time."

"I guess so," the boy said, scooping up his backpack to leave. "See you after the party."

After his grandson had left, Linus prepared for his long wait for the plumber. No sooner had he made a fresh pot of coffee and opened his newspaper, than the plumber arrived, several hours earlier than expected.

Never had a plumber been in and out of a kitchen as fast as Linus' plumber. It turned out that Linus was completely free to visit the *Bluenose II*.

He grabbed his camera and headed downtown to the harbourfront. He saw immediately where she was docked. The *Bluenose II* had attracted a huge crowd. The onlookers were all appreciating the beauty and the history of the famous ship.

After studying the *Bluenose II* from many different angles, Linus took a series of photographs of her. He wondered how Wallace MacAskill, himself, might have taken the same shots in pre-war days. Linus secretly hoped his photos would be worthy of that intrepid Cape Breton Islander. Those were high standards indeed. With one exposure left, he wondered if perhaps he might ask someone to take *his* photograph in front of the *Bluenose II*. He glanced around for an obliging individual and then talked himself out of it. For some reason, at the very last minute, Linus was too shy to ask.

Instead, he decided to finish the roll with one final dramatic shot of the ship. He stretched from the dock as far as he could and took a photograph of the schooner through the starboard rigging. It promised to be his best one.

On his way home, he dropped off his roll of film at the photo shop and asked the shopkeeper to develop it while he waited.

He was very pleased with the results and couldn't wait to show Brendan.

Early in the evening, the boy dropped by his grandfather's home after his party with some exciting news.

"You're not going to believe this, Grandpa. *I saw the Bluenose today!*"

That was definitely exciting news. "You did?" asked Linus. "How did that happen? I thought you were going to a birthday party?"

"I did, and when I told my friend's father about the *Bluenose* being in town today, he drove us all down to the harbour to see it."

Linus had exciting news for Brendan as well. "Would you believe that *I* saw the *Bluenose* today too? Can you believe the coincidence? If I'd known you were there I would have looked for you."

"I never thought of looking for you either," said Brendan. "So how did *you* end up going?"

"The plumber came much earlier than I'd expected and it only took him five minutes to fix my sink. *Was I ever lucky!* I got down in time to see the ship. There were sure a lot of people, weren't there? But you should see the great photos I took of her. I've already got them back." Linus handed the snapshots to Brendan that he had taken. The boy studied them one by one and when he came to the last photograph, he smiled broadly.

"*This* one's my favourite," he said.

"*Mine too,*" Linus answered happily, "It's my 'McAskill'. That was the last picture on the roll. I really had to stretch to get a good shot of the ship through the rigging and you can see all the faces in the crowd admiring her."

Brendan laughed. "We must have been there at the same time."

"What do you mean?"

Brendan handed the panoramic shot back to his grandfather. "Look closely through the rigging. See anyone you know?"

Linus studied the photo and was astonished by what he saw. Were his old eyes playing tricks on him? Was it a mistake at the photo shop—some sort of double exposure? It couldn't be.

Yet there in the crowd of onlookers in his best photograph, peering through the rigging of the *Bluenose II* was the beaming face of Brendan.

1972

"At the Crease"

Remembering the old clutch goalies

"I'M SORRY THAT I'M NOT GOING TO BE ABLE TO SPEND VERY MUCH TIME WITH YOU TODAY," LINUS SAID TO HIS NINE-YEAR-OLD GRANDSON, "I HAVE TOO MUCH HOMEWORK TO DO."

That was the last thing Brendan had ever expected his grandfather to say. *"Homework?"* he asked with a puzzled look on his face. "What homework are you talking about?"

"I enrolled in a night school class a few weeks ago," Linus replied. "I thought I told you. I've already taken two classes."

"You?" was all Brendan could think of saying, never having heard of anyone his grandfather's age going to school before.

"It's something I've wanted to do for a long time."

"School's harder than you think," spoke the boy whose government forced him to go. "Just so you know."

"I'm taking a pencil sketching class at the local high school," Linus explained. "The location is handy and the cost of the course is quite reasonable."

That didn't sound right to the fifth-grader. The idea of paying for your education was completely foreign to him. "You have to pay them to go to school?" Brendan asked, thinking it should be the other way around. "You mean *you* actually pay *them*?"

"Of course I pay them," Linus replied. "It costs money to

educate a person like me."

"Is there some reason you signed up?" he asked, making it sound like his grandfather had gone back into the army. "I know you like drawing maps."

"I've always been a big hockey fan," explained Linus. "I have some good action shots of players in my old scrapbook."

Brendan had seen that seventy-year-old scrapbook. "It's so old, it's evaporating," he said, smiling at the thought of it.

"You mean disintegrating," Linus said. "But you're right about its being old. I'd better get started drawing those old players before there's nothing left. Learning to draw has been a dream of mine for more than seventy years."

"Do you still have dreams?"

"You're *never* too old to dream."

"You're not?"

"And *my* dream is to draw goalies."

"*Just goalies?*"

"I always loved those old goalies from the thirties, especially the Leaf goalies. I was a big fan of George Hainsworth when I was a kid. He was a small man but a great goalie. He racked up such a long string of shutouts that none of us at Paton Street Arena ever thought he'd be scored on again."

"Is he in the Hall of Fame?"

"He is, indeed," replied Linus. "Hainsworth had the most career shutouts in the NHL until Terry Sawchuck came along. Roy Worters, another Toronto boy, played for the New York Americans. He was another favourite of mine. He was small too. In fact, he was so small, they called him 'Shrimp', but he could sure keep the puck out of the net. He's in the Hall as well."

"I bet he didn't like being called 'Shrimp'."

"He was probably good natured about it. *All* the goalies were small back then."

"How come they were all so small?"

"Managers in those days thought that smaller men were more agile. Worters was only five foot three and weighed 135 pounds when he played. "

"No wonder they called him Shrimp."

"You should see the great photo of Worters and Hainsworth that's in the Hockey Hall of Fame."

"I never saw a picture like that," Brendan said, "and I've been to the Hockey Hall of Fame lots of times."

"It was taken back in 1936 after a game between the Maple Leafs and the New York Americans."

"Poor old Shrimp," the boy sighed. "I really like nicknames, but I don't think they should have called him that."

"I guess sports writers got carried away with nicknames back then. For some reason, all the goalies were given crazy monikers. Lorne Chabot played in two of the longest games of the era. He was another shutout king. Do you know what they used to call him?"

"Not really."

"They called him 'Old Bulwarks'.

"What did they call him *that* for?"

"A bulwark is like a fort."

"Then they should have just called him 'The Fort'," suggested Brendan, no slouch in the nickname department himself. "Or, just 'Fort'. If I was a goalie, that's what I'd want to be called."

"Frank Brimsek, the Boston goalie, was known as 'Mr. Zero'. I saw him play many times."

"With a nickname like that you can tell he must have had a lot of shutouts."

"You probably already know that the most famous goalie of all time was known as the 'Chicoutimi Cucumber'."

"I know who that was," Brendan said, but hesitated. He patted his forehead, but still could not come up with the man's name. "Wait. Don't tell me," he pleaded.

Linus folded his arms and waited for a few moments. "It was Georges Vezina," he said finally.

"I *knew* that," Brendan groaned.

"He was given the nickname The Chicoutimi Cucumber because he was so cool under fire," his grandfather said.

"But didn't something happen to him?" Brendan asked.

"Yes, the great Montreal Canadien goaltender wasn't feeling well after a game and he died several months later from tuberculosis—a terrible loss for hockey. That was in 1925, I believe."

"He sure must have been a good goalie to have a trophy like that named after him."

"Well, he was held in such high esteem by his team that they donated it in his name," Linus said.

Brendan knew all about that award. "The Vezina Trophy is for the best goalie in the league."

"George Vezina is one of those goalies I want to draw."

"Were the goalies better in those days, Grandpa?" asked the boy, "even though they were so small, I mean."

His grandfather hesitated before he answered. "I don't think you can compare the different eras, Brendan. The game has changed so much. The big difference is that in the old days, teams didn't have a back-up, so a goalie would stay in the nets for the whole game."

"But they play the whole game now. What's the difference?"

"Back then if a goalie got hurt, he'd go quietly to the dressing room, take his forty stitches and go back out."

"They didn't wear masks then, did they?"

Linus shook his head. "It's hard to believe, isn't it? Can you imagine a goalie playing professional hockey without a mask?"

"Maybe if they played with a tennis ball like in road hockey, but other than that, I think they should have worn masks."

George Hainsworth and Roy Worters, shake hands in the Leaf's dressing room at Maple Leaf Gardens on April 2, 1936, after the Toronto Maple Leafs defeated the New York Americans in the Stanley Cup semi finals. No doubt these two Toronto boys were congratulating themselves on how fortunate they both were to have steady work during the height of the Depression.

"I want to draw those men; goalies like Hainsworth and Worters and Vezina in their prime. That's my dream, anyway. I know I'm going to have to learn the basics before I start drawing them.

That's why I'm going to school." He glanced quickly at his grandson and wondered if this would be a good time to ask him if he might help him with perspective. "You take art in school, don't you, Brendan?"

The boy hesitated. "I *used* to like drawing," he said after a time, "but not too much anymore."

"I thought you *liked* art."

"It was fun at first."

"What happened?"

"My teacher won't let me draw what I want."

"I know what you mean," Linus said. "I liked our first class too, when we only drew circles and lines, but in the second and third classes we began to study perspective, and that's when everything changed."

"I hate perspective," Brendan said.

"It's hard, isn't it?"

"Pretty much."

"But it's important."

"I guess simple perspective is easy enough," the boy replied, giving the matter some thought, "but when our teacher starts to talk about two-point perspective and three-point perspective, that's another story."

Linus was experiencing the same problems with his class. "But if I don't get the hang of it, my goalies won't look realistic. They'll look like stick men."

"But hockey players *are* stick men," laughed Brendan. "That's what they're supposed to be anyway."

"I meant they won't look real," Linus said with a smile. "That's why I have to learn perspective. I think it's really important to learn it, don't you?"

Brendan frowned. "I don't like having to worry about vanishing points and horizons and stuff like that when I draw."

"I guess it just takes practice," Linus said. "My teacher told

260 RINKRATS I HAVE KNOWN AND OTHER STORIES

me that a man learning art at my age needs a lot of practice drawing perspective."

"My teacher's always telling me stuff like that," the fifth-grader said, "only she keeps saying, 'a boy my age'. Then she gives me this look." The boy then made a face, held it firmly in place, stood up and then walked over to the wall mirror to admire it.

"The worst part," Linus said to him, "is my teacher going from desk to desk at the end of the class critiquing every student's work."

Brendan had been there. "*My* teacher always seems to single me out for some reason," he said. "She's always holds up something I've drawn and then tells everybody not to make the same mistakes I made."

Linus felt he had it worse. "*My* teacher hasn't liked *anything* I've done so far," he complained.

"They're hard to please, Grandpa. What can I tell you?"

They smiled sadly at one another.

"The main thing is not to get depressed," the nine-year-old advised. "Just when things get really bad, remember all those neat maps you've drawn."

"Yes—my maps," Linus said, deciding this was a good time to bring up his idea. "Say, why don't you practice perspective with me this afternoon?"

Brendan was reluctant to be pulled into this project. It sounded too much like work. And Saturday was his day off.

Linus knew he had some convincing to do. He walked over to his bookcase and removed a book entitled *High Realism in Canada* which he carried over to the kitchen table.

"This is where I got my inspiration to draw goalies," he said, opening the book to a painting entitled 'At the Crease'.

"That's a pretty good picture."

"It's a painting by Ken Danby," Linus said. "He painted it in 1972."

"I've seen it before, Grandpa. It looks like that goalie is getting ready for a face off. "

"It's a famous picture," said Linus. "I really like it."

"Do you think it's an NHL goalie?"

"He might be. Or he might even be a goaltender in some industrial league in town."

"He's got a great stance. It sure looks like an NHL goalie to me."

"I wish I could draw like that," Linus mused. "Real artists like Ken Danby use perspective to make their drawings look lifelike."

"I guess so."

"It's funny," Linus said, "but now everywhere I go, I notice the point in the distance where all the roads and telephone polls and the roofs of buildings meet. I never used to see these things before. I guess perspective is a fact."

"It's a phenomenon," the boy said, badly mispronouncing the word.

"Seems to be," agreed his grandfather.

It then occurred to Brendan that they might make a game out of perspective. "I think we should go out and have a contest to see who can find the most vanishing points."

"I can't. I have to stay here and start on next week's class."

"What do you have to do?"

"My teacher told us to draw a picture of a key for homework. It's supposed to be an exercise in perspective. He wants the key to look three dimensional."

Brendan thought that would be a difficult assignment. "I don't know how a key is supposed to look three dimensional," he said critically. "That would be hard to do."

"It doesn't matter," Linus said, digging into his pocket and pulling out a set of keys. Then he said those words that send a shiver down every student's spine. *We're going to be marked on it.*

"You're going to need a *really* good key, then," the boy said.

"I have lots," Linus said, sorting through them. He owned a

lot of keys.

"Some of those keys look really old, Grandpa."

"I don't even know what all of them are for anymore," his grandfather said. "I'm afraid if I don't carry them all around with me I'll lock myself out of something."

Brendan also noticed for the first time what was attached to his keys.

"That's a pretty fancy key-chain you have there."

"This?" Linus asked. Along with his huge collection of keys, he possessed a key chain which was emblazoned with an excellent image of a car manufacturer's logo. "The dealership gave me this key chain when I bought one of their cars a couple of years ago."

Brendan knew all about that clunker. "Isn't that the car you were always taking into the shop to get repaired?"

It was true. Buying that vehicle was not one of Linus' better business decisions. "That was the mid-size I had before I bought my big sedan."

"I remember you always complained about how much money it was costing you."

His grandfather didn't need reminding. "It wasn't a reliable car," he admitted, but because a man has his pride added, "I'm really happy with the key chain, though."

Linus then turned his attention back to his keys. He sorted through them individually until he found one he considered worthy to be drawn. "Now *this* is an interesting one," he said, holding up a very elaborate looking old key. "This is the key to my safety deposit box."

"That must come from a very old bank."

"I've had it a long time," Linus said. "It's from the vault of the old Bank of Ottawa in Carleton Place. I can't even remember what I keep there anymore, I've had it so long."

"Can I hold it?" Brendan asked.

Linus placed the key in the boy's open palm. "It's heavy, isn't it?"

"Actually, I wouldn't mind drawing it," the boy said. Being an old Bank of Ottawa fan, he had finally been won over. "I'm not that good at perspective, Grandpa," he added, "but I'll try anyway."

Linus was delighted they would both draw the key together. "Do you need paper?" he asked.

"I have lots of paper in my bag," Brendan said, removing a brand-new notebook and holding it up. To show his grandfather the importance that he placed on the key assignment, the boy added, "I bought this with my own money."

Linus placed the key delicately on the kitchen table.

The two of them sat back and studied the key from various angles. Never had two artists shown so much concentration on their subject. Every so often, one of them would move the key slightly in the hope of improving the quality of their work.

Linus was the first to break the silence. "Maybe this key will unlock the mystery of perspective," he said in a half whisper. He squinted at the key over his glasses and measured its length with his thumb.

The room became quiet once again.

Brendan had his arm outstretched and measured the key with his pencil. The kitchen took on a solemn atmosphere.

All that could be heard was the sound of HB pencils on paper. After a while, Brendan ripped a sheet from his pad, crumpled it in a ball and tossed it into the recycle bin.

"Darn perspective," he muttered. "That's another fifteen cents down the drain."

"It's not as easy as it looks," Linus said in a quiet voice, having already crumpled up two of his own renderings.

They worked hard on their technique until they broke for lunch.

"I think I'm finally getting the hang of it, Brendan," Linus said, taking a bite out of his roast beef sandwich. "I really want to prove to my teacher that I can do this."

"Your key actually looks pretty good," the nine-year-old said, as they reviewed their final products. "I think you're going to get a good mark."

"It just takes practice."

"Practice makes perfect," his grandson agreed.

"Yours looks real enough that you could actually pick it off the paper, Brendan."

"If it looks *that* real we should go into business," suggested the boy, with an impish grin on his face. "Do you have any clay?"

Linus grinned back. "I don't think we want to go into *that* kind of business."

"Just kidding."

So, after a hard afternoon in the studio finishing their homework, the two artists agreed to meet again the following week, when they might study composition or even texture. In the meantime, Linus would hand in his homework assignment to his teacher.

The following Saturday Brendan visited his grandfather once again. The boy was more anxious than ever to find out how his grandfather's last class had gone. He was confident that Linus had done well.

When Brendan arrived, the man was sitting in his wicker chair at the kitchen table staring at his drawing of the key.

"I bet your teacher was really surprised at how much you'd improved last week, Grandpa. He was probably mad that he didn't have anything to criticize about your key when he came to your desk."

"He didn't seem too mad," Linus said, without looking up.

"So what did he say about it?"

"He really liked my key," Linus said, but the boy noticed there was little enthusiasm in his tone of voice. "He even showed it to everyone—said it was the best one in the class."

Brendan smiled proudly at his grandfather. "You can start your portrait of the Chicoutimi Cucumber now. I bet you even sell it," he said, getting a little carried away with himself.

"I don't know about that," Linus replied.

"You might even open up your own gallery."

"I doubt it."

Brendan could sense something was wrong. "You don't seem too happy about it."

"I would be, if only my teacher had said all those nice things about my drawing."

"What do you mean?" Brendan asked, picking it up for a better look. "I thought you said he liked it."

Linus leaned back from his wicker chair and sighed. "At first I thought he was talking about my drawing, and was complimenting it, but then I realized he wasn't."

"What do you mean he wasn't—?"

Linus drew a deep breath. "He wasn't complimenting my drawing at all—it was the *old key* he liked."

"*Oh, no!*" groaned the boy. "*What are you going to do now?*"

"I'm transferring to another class," Linus said defiantly. "I don't want to draw keys any more."

"Maybe there's some class that specializes in sports figures."

"I've already signed up for a class called life drawing. My first class is next week."

"Life drawing?" asked Brendan.

"Yes, they use live models."

"Live models?"

"I'll finally learn how to draw the human body."

"*Hey—wait a minute!*" exclaimed the boy. "Isn't that the art class where the models don't wear any clothes?"

A small smile began to appear on Linus' face. "Exactly".

CHAPTER TWENTY-SEVEN

1972

The Two-Way Men

With printers' ink in their veins

"WHAT ARE WE GOING TO DO TODAY, GRANDPA?" THE BOY ASKED ONE SATURDAY MORNING.

Linus was sitting at the kitchen table drinking a hot cup of coffee and reading the newspaper. "I really don't have anything planned."

"You know, every time I come over to your house in the morning, you always seem to be reading the paper and drinking a cup of coffee," Brendan observed.

"It's my favourite way to start the day," Linus said. "I love newspapers."

"—and drinking coffee," his grandson put in.

"I've been an avid newspaper reader all my life, Brendan. I like to keep up to date with the news, read the columnists, glance at the weather report, check the hockey standings, attempt the crossword puzzle and when I'm finished doing all those things, I wrap my fish and chips in it."

"You're a real trailblazer, Grandpa," the youngster said, patting his grandfather on the back.

Linus folded his paper. "You're not so bad yourself," he said, giving his grandson a gentle tap with it. "You should become a newspaper reader too."

"I only read the headlines in the paper box outside my apartment building on the way to school," Brendan said. "That's enough reading for me for one day."

"We're lucky in Toronto that we still have a good choice of papers," Linus said. "With the internet and that sort of thing, it's not easy for publishers to put out a profitable daily paper these days. Over the years many good newspapers have gone bankrupt and folded or merged with others. I still miss the *Toronto Telegram*."

"What happened to it?"

"It went out of business years ago after a great publishing battle with the *Toronto Star*."

"I guess that's why I never heard of it."

"The *Telegram* was founded in 1876 by John Ross Robertson. It was a conservative paper. He charged two cents a copy for it."

"No wonder he went out of business."

"The *Tely* managed to stay around for a long time, before it finally closed."

"Is that what they called it—the *Tely*?"

"That was its nickname. It was one of the papers published during Toronto's 'Golden Age'."

"What Golden Age are you talking about?"

"That's my own term for it," Linus answered. "To me, the Golden Age began in 1948, when the *Tely* was bought by a millionaire named George McCullagh. He hired John Bassett as his general manager and the two of them gave the 'Old Lady of Melinda Street', as the paper was known, a new lease on life. Those were exciting days to be a reporter because the *Tely* and the *Star* were always competing against each other for stories. When McCullagh died suddenly in 1952, Bassett carried on the fight against the *Star* alone."

"But I thought you said he lost," the boy said, "and that his paper went out of business?"

"Later it did," answered Linus. "But during the Golden Age, the *Tely* put up a great fight. You see, there were three papers in Toronto at the time. The *Globe and Mail* was the morning paper, and the *Tely* and the *Star* put out the evening papers."

"The *Star's* still around though, isn't it?"

"It's been around since 1892. The *Toronto Daily Star* had been founded as small crusading paper, but after Joseph Atkinson took over as publisher, circulation and advertising increased and it soon became the largest of the three. The *Tely* was always the underdog. Every day the *Tely* and the *Star* raced each other to get late-breaking stories into their final editions before they hit the streets. They were bitter rivals. The news business isn't like that today. Back then it was a war."

"A war?"

Linus nodded. "Most of the reporters employed in that era had fought in the war. That's probably why they covered stories as if they were going into combat. It was very competitive.

"You mean they wanted to be the first ones there when something happened?"

"Yes, exclusives were the lifeblood of the newspaper business so reporters covering big stories would do everything they could to shut out the other guy. They all wanted scoops."

"That's what they call it when a reporter gets the story first, isn't it? Then doesn't the reporter get to be nicknamed 'Scoop'?"

"That's only in the movies, Brendan. I can't imagine a *real* reporter wanting a nickname like that. Everybody would laugh at him."

"I wouldn't."

"That reminds me of a great newspaper story I heard years ago. There was a *Tely* reporter who was covering a major story in a small town in Ontario, who beat a *Star* guy, also covering the same story, in a footrace to the only local pay phone available."

"You mean the *Tely* guy was trying to get a scoop on the *Star* guy?"

"That's right. In those days reporters had to phone their stories to their city editors. A public phone booth was often the reporter's only means of communication. On this day, the *Tely* reporter phoned his story in first, while the *Star* reporter stood outside the phone booth waiting impatiently for him to finish."

"But if he was second in line, he wouldn't be that far behind the *Tely* guy, would he?" asked Brendan. "He'd get his story in almost as fast."

"It took him a lot longer than he thought."

"How come?"

"Because as soon as the *Tely* guy hung up the phone, he unscrewed the mouthpiece from the handset, slipped it into his pocket without being seen and calmly walked out of the phone booth with it. As he passed the *Star* guy, he told him he could make his call now and then ran as fast as he could for a cab."

"They were allowed to do that?"

"Not at all, but remember it was a war," Linus explained. "*Tely* reporters knew the *Star* guys would do the same to them. It was eat or be eaten."

"Eat or be eaten," the nine-year-old repeated to himself, never having heard that expression before.

"Otherwise a reporter wouldn't last," Linus explained. "The newspaper business was a tough profession. Veteran reporters took great delight putting one over on their competition. Another thing they liked to do was send rival rookies on wild goose chases. Woe betide a young cub reporter in those days who returned to the newsroom from an assignment only to have to admit to a hard-boiled city editor that he had nothing to show for it. He could only hope and pray the other papers had come up empty too."

"That's how I feel when I hand in my homework."

"Photographers were just as cutthroat," Linus said. "To get a scoop, they might try to distract a rival paper's photographer so that a potential page one shot would be lost. It really was a war, my boy."

"It sure sounds like it," Brendan agreed, thinking he would have enjoyed being a reporter back in the Golden Age. He figured he would have made a pretty good one too. He wouldn't have minded being nicknamed 'Scoop' either, because that's probably what everybody would have wanted to call him.

The boy was not alone with those sentiments. Linus too, fancied that he would have looked very dapper with a press card sticking out of the hatband of one of his old fedoras. He pictured himself taking page one shots with his old 1950 Speed Graphic and then typing up the stories on his Underwood under his own byline. Of course, later he would have to fend off all those young cub reporters hounding him at the Press Club for anecdotes about how he picked up his nickname 'Scoop'. Being pestered by admirers is always the drawback of being famous. "You know, Brendan, sometimes I wish I'd become a two-way man instead of working all those years at the bank," he said wistfully.

"What's a two-way man, Grandpa?"

"A reporter who also took his own photos," his grandfather said. Having been a camera buff all his life, Linus thought he could do both.

"I wouldn't mind being a two-way man either," Brendan said, never wanting to be left out.

"Anyway," Linus went on, "the rivalry between the *Star* and the *Tely* reached its peak in the '50's and '60's before computers took over. It was just like the Leafs and the Canadiens in the days of the Original Six. Those were the glory days of the broadsheet. It's not the same today with satellites and twenty-four hour news networks and that sort of thing. News gathering was manual work then and a good reporter had to have his ears to the ground. Who knew what might lead to a scoop?"

"All I know is that I'm rooting for the *Tely* guy," said the nine-year-old.

"*Tely* guys were well known for their initiative," Linus said. "There was an old story told of a *Tely* police reporter sniffing around a murder scene one day when the phone rang. Never missing an opportunity, he immediately picked it up, posing as an inspector, in the hope of pumping the caller for information."

"Did he get a scoop?"

"Not really, because it turned out to be another *Tely* guy on the other end also pretending to be an inspector," Linus said. "It took them a while to sort that out."

All these newspaper stories were doing wonders to Brendan's imagination. "We should pretend we're two-way men, Grandpa," he suggested, his eyes lighting up with excitement. "We should both go out into the city and see who can get the most scoops and phone them into our city editors. We could make up press badges just like real reporters and stuff like that."

"You mean fighting each other for stories like the *Tely* and the *Star* used to do?" he asked.

"I'll be the *Tely* guy and you can be the *Star* guy."

"It would be fun," Linus agreed, "but I wonder how we could do it?"

"I can't wait to find a front page story and race you to the phone," Brendan said, throwing down the gauntlet.

Linus pondered the idea. "We could go to the reference library together where all the microfilms of the old papers are kept. Each of us could write down a headline and the lead sentence from a major story from our respective papers. Then our job would be to get that story to our composing rooms. You find a good *Tely* headline and I'll find one from the *Star*."

"But how do we choose a story?"

Linus thought for a moment. "It has to be a real headline story that was actually covered by the *Star* and the *Tely* during their rivalry," Linus said, setting the ground rules. "The microfilms are kept in drawers in date order. We can either look up a story if we know the date or simply scroll through the microfilm until we find a story we like. What do you think?"

"You mean I can use *any* story I like?" Brendan asked, having already thought of a great story that would beat anything his grandfather could come up with.

"As long as it was published in the *Telegram*," Linus cautioned. "That's the only rule. It has to be a real story that appeared in print."

"Don't worry—it is," said the confident *Tely* cub reporter.

"After we get our story," Linus said, "we'll write the headlines in our notebooks and then go back to my place and phone the stories to our city editors."

"Who are we supposed to phone?" Brendan asked. "Who will be the city editors?"

"We can use *my* phone to leave the messages on the answering machine on *your* phone," Linus suggested. "Then we go to your place and play back the messages. That way we can pretend to be the city editors too."

"But the first person to phone his story in wins, doesn't he?"

Linus wasn't keen about that idea. "I think it will be better if we *both* get to file our stories," he suggested, knowing he was never going to beat the young *Tely* guy in a foot race. "It will be more interesting that way. We can listen to both stories and then we can decide who has the best one."

"You mean the guy who phones his story in first might not win?"

Brendan was sure he could get his story in first. He had one obvious advantage. After all, he was nine years old and was one of the fastest kids in his class. His grandfather was in his eighties and had arthritis.

"I think it's better if the city editors decide who has the best story," Linus said. "We can sit down afterwards and talk about the stories. It'll be fun."

Brendan thought that the more they talked about it, the likelier he would lose. Linus was just the kind of wily old reporter who might scoop him.

However, he was still sure he had the best story going. "I guess that's OK," the boy said, anxious to start.

The rules were agreed on, and the two-way men headed immediately to the reference library on their assignment. Linus wore his homemade press badge in the hatband of his fedora. Brendan stuck his badge in his pant pocket with all his other worldly belongings.

Upon their arrival at the microfilming department of the local library, Linus showed his grandson where the *Toronto Telegram* films were kept, by pointing out the various cabinets and the dates of the past issues.

"You can pick a roll and choose a story that way or you can find a specific newspaper if you know the date," Linus explained, taking a roll of *Telegram* microfilm from the cabinet at random and demonstrating to Brendan how to thread the film and focus it on the screen.

Brendan watched the demonstration, but secretly knew he needn't bother with those time-consuming formalities. The boy had already decided what his story was going to be. He knew the date and he knew the headline and as far as the lead sentence was concerned, he could just make that up.

"You see how this works?" asked Linus, continuing to coach Brendan in the use of the viewer. "Do you have any questions?"

The young *Tely* cub reporter didn't have any.

Linus walked over to the cabinet where the *Toronto Star* films were kept and began his own research.

Brendan meanwhile immediately closed the door of the cabinet of the *Toronto Telegram* microfilm, sat down behind one of the microfilm viewers, and wrote down his headline.

"Canada wins Summit Series! Henderson scores with only seconds left!!" he wrote on a piece of paper, adding an extra exclamation mark to make it look official.

Brendan was very proud of his selection. He didn't need musty old *Tely* archives to provide him with a good headline. He already *had* one. *Every* red-blooded Canadian hockey fan knew all about the Canada-Russia series of 1972.

His job was done.

He folded up the piece of paper and put it in his pant pocket. Then he brought out his computer game from the same pocket and began to pass the time. The young *Tely* cub reporter had the news game by the tail.

Fifteen minutes later Brendan's concentration was broken when a flash jolted him from his fantasy world. His grandfather was standing behind him holding his camera. There was a big smile on his face.

"Hey! What's the big idea, Grandpa?" Brendan asked, taken by surprise. "What did you take a picture of *me* for?"

"How about this for a headline? '*Tely* Guy Sleeps on Job'," Linus said. "This might be a great human interest story. My city editor will love it."

"It just so happens, I've already *finished* my story," Brendan countered. "I was just waiting for you."

Linus patted his camera and headed back for his coat and hat. "Eat or be eaten," he said, but to Brendan it sounded more like a chortle.

"That's not really going to be your story is it?" Brendan asked, only beginning to realize how competitive the news game was played.

"Actually, I already have a very good story I found on the microfilm," Linus replied, "I just took this photo to keep you *Tely* guys on your toes."

Never had a *Tely* guy wanted to beat a *Star* guy as badly as Brendan did at that moment.

"This means war," Brendan muttered. He would have said it even louder had they not been in a library.

The two scribes then headed back to Linus' place with their stories. Once through the door, Brendan was the first one to the phone, so Linus waited patiently in the living room.

It was a well-known feature of Linus' living room that one of the last black rotary phones in the city was still in use. It was right out of the 1950's. Brendan had used it many times. He immediately picked it up and dialed. He sang happily into the phone, "Stop the presses!"

Then he cupped his hand beside his mouth and his voice sank to a whisper, "Canada Wins Summit Series, Henderson Scores with only seconds left." He didn't want to be overheard. The last thing he needed was to have his scoop stolen. The old newsman waiting in the living room had been chasing down stories for more years than anyone could remember. If anyone could steal a good story from under the nose of a *Tely* guy, it would be Linus. The man was a bloodhound.

After phoning in his story, Brendan glanced furtively at his grandfather and then turned his back to him. He didn't want him to see what he was about to do. He took a deep breath, unscrewed the mouthpiece from the old rotary phone, slipped it into his pocket and calmly walked toward the door.

"You can make your call now, *Star* guy," Brendan said to his rival as he walked by.

At the doorway, Brendan waited anxiously for his grandfather's reaction once the trick was discovered. The boy was worried how much trouble he might be in for taking the mouthpiece.

In the news game, it was eat or be eaten, he said to himself. It was a risky move, but any good two-way man would have done the same.

A few minutes later, his grandfather walked towards him down the hall. Brendan studied his face, but the man's expression gave nothing away. Linus was obviously taking it better than the boy had first thought. The expected rebuke did not occur. Not a word was said about the missing mouthpiece.

The two walked over to Brendan's home in silence. They politely smiled at each other and made eye contact from time to time—just to keep each other in sight.

As expected, the answering machine was blinking when they arrived.

The boy eagerly played his message.

Sure enough, it was Brendan's voice that was first heard loud and clear. "*Stop the presses,*" it said, "*Canada Wins Summit Series, Henderson Scores with only seconds left!!*"

He could almost see those two exclamation marks, so proud was he of his work. "*You're scooped, Star guy,*" he shouted, his eyes wide open with excitement. "*Don't try to deny it!*"

"Not so fast, *Tely* guy," his grandfather said, with a disapproving look. "I don't know where you got your story, but it sure wasn't from the *Telegram.*"

Brendan's smiling face turned quickly to one of concern. "What are you talking about?" he shot back.

"That story is definitely not within our time limits."

"Sure it is," the boy answered. "You're getting mixed up with the Canada Cup. That came later. I'm talking about the *first* Russia-Canada series."

"I see," his grandfather said.

"It's a well-known fact Canada won the Summit Series in 1972," Brendan explained in a very confident voice.

"I hate to tell you, but the *Tely* closed in 1971," Linus said.

"What?" Brendan almost swallowed his tonsils.

"I'm afraid the *Tely* wasn't around in 1972 to cover your Summit Series."

"It wasn't?"

"You get a big blue editor's line right through your copy."

Brendan's face was deathly pale. He realized he had made a horrible mistake. He was *one year off.* "I'm going to be fired for this for sure," he moaned.

"Sorry about that, Chief," the *Star* guy said, sounding very sympathetic, but secretly happy to see the competition go down one.

Brendan sat down to regroup but was quickly on his feet again. *"Ha!* It doesn't matter anyway because *you* didn't get a story either."

Linus made no response.

At least Brendan had the satisfaction of knowing the *Star* guy wasn't going to win. The blood returned to the young reporter's face. He reached down and dramatically pulled out the purloined mouthpiece from his pocket. "Looking for this?" he asked with a defiant smirk on his face.

Linus was unfazed. Turning once more to the blinking answering machine, Linus said, "What's that I see? There seems to be a *second* message."

There *was* a second message.

Now it was Linus' voice coming through on the phone lines, *"Dateline, Toronto, September 18, 1971 from the Toronto Star. Bassett announces Telegram will fold, 1200 to lose jobs—John Bassett, publisher of the Toronto Telegram told employees today a decision has been made to cease publication of the 95-year-old paper, Canada's third largest daily."*

He turned to Brendan. "That's my lead story. I think you're the one who's been scooped."

"How—?" the boy gasped. Once again the blood began to

drain from his face. Brendan stared sadly at the mouthpiece which he held in his hand. How did his grandfather make the call without it?

"It didn't occur to you that I had a spare?" Linus asked. "I have a kitchen drawer full of old telephone parts. Surely you knew that."

Brendan was crushed. He had gambled everything on his story and lost. His career as a *Tely* guy was over. And the worst part was the *Star* guy had won.

"I guess I wasn't meant to be a reporter," he said glumly.

"I don't know about that, Brendan. I think you're onto a good story."

The boy looked up. His face had a hangdog look. "I am?" he said. "What do you mean?"

Linus smiled at his grandson. "I bet you're the only reporter in history whose paper went out of business just minutes after they fired you." He gave the boy a friendly pat on the back. "Now *that's* a good story."

Credits and Permissions

Chapter 1. Ambush on the Iroquois Trail

LaSalle on His Way to the Mississippi Via The Toronto Portage (Ontario)
Charles W. Jeffreys (1869-1956) Imperial Oil Collection, Library and Archives Canada, C-073678

Chapter 2. Escape from the Mohawk Valley

Sir William Johnson (1715-1774) John Wollaston (1736-1767); ca 1750-52,
oil on canvas, ht. 30 1/16 in., w. 25 in.; Albany Institute of History and Art, Albany, New York, gift of Laura Munsell Tremaine in memory of her father, Joel Munsell, 1922.2.

Chapter 3. The Capture of Johnny McGinnis

Benson John Losing (American , 1813-1891) after Pierre Le Dru (American) photograph after.
Tecumtha (c.1808) Toronto Public Library (TRL) J. Ross Robertson Collection,
T 16600.

Chapter 4. The Story of the Great Anchor

Mackinac, from Round Island, circa 1812, Library and Archives Canada, C-015127.

Chapter 5. Isabella's Lamp

Isabella Hughes and son Robert, photo author's collection.
God of All Nations by Mary S. Elgar, 1927, excerpted from Anglican Book of Praise, 1938
#327, Anglican Church of Canada.

Chapter 6. The Shooting of Frank Lynch

Hon. Sir John A. Macdonald, chromolithograph published by William Brice. Toronto.
Toronto Public Library (TRL):T 13731.

Chapter 7. The Secret Mission of John Rose

Sir John Rose portrait: William James Topley Studios/ Library and Archives Canada,
PA-025959.

Chapter 8. Black Pete's Last Fight

Log Chute-Timberslide High Falls-Mississippi River, Ontario (n.d.) Archives of Ontario, C224-0-0-16-32 AO 7464.

Chapter 9. The Empire Builders

Page - CPR Locomotive Engine 285, 1885, photo courtesy: Canadian Pacific Railway Archives, NS.17735
Page- Hon. Donald A. Smith driving the last spike. Alexander Ross/Library and Archives Canada, C-003693.

Chapter 10. The Sage of Aru

Report of the Trial of the Libel Suit of Dr. G.S. Howard, of

Carleton Place, Ontario. Reprint from the Montreal Star, 1898.

Chapter 11. Doublecross on Eldorado Creek

Line of Klondikers ascending Chilkoot Pass, Alaska, 1898. University of Washington Libraries, Special Collections, Hegg, 207.

Chapter 12. The Order of the Midnight Sun

Front Street, Dawson, Yukon Territory, July 1899. University of Washington Libraries, Special Collections, Hegg, 2333.

Chapter 13. The Flight of the 'Cygnet'

Alexander Graham Bell, 1904/ Parks Canada/Alexander Graham Bell National Historic Site of Canada.
Portion of the fourth verse of "The Earth, the Sky, the Ocean" by Fred Kaan. 1968 Hope Publishing Co. Carol Stream, IL 60188, All rights reserved. Used by permission.

Chapter 14. The Voyage of the 'Nolturno'

Photo author's collection (not the 'Nolturno', but of a similar steamer from that era.)

Chapter 15. Victoria Cross Hill

General Currie and General MacBrien at a practice attack near the Canadian front-September, 1917.
Canada Dept of National Defense/Library and Archives Canada, PA-002004.

Chapter 16. I Flew with Roy Brown

Captain Arthur Roy Brown, D.F.C.
Credit: Howard Morton Brown/Library and Archives Canada/ C-002272.

Chapter 17. J'Avance

The Bank of Ottawa, Print #:03, Date 1880/11/02, Scotiabank Group Archives.

Chapter 18. My Lou Gehrig Story

Lou Gehrig 310185 NBL, photo credit: National Baseball Hall of Fame Library, Cooperstown, N.Y.

Chapter 19. Rinkrats I Have Known

Syl Apps, 1947- photo credit: Imperial Oil-Turofsky/ Hockey Hall of Fame, Toronto.

Chapter 20. The Adventures of the Tricky Sons

Paton Street, 1935/ photo /courtesy of Mr. Allan W. Brown, Cobourg, Ontario.

Chapter 21. Above Biggin Hill

F/O Ross Smither, RCAF portrait /courtesy of Mrs. Marion L. Westhead, London, Ontario.

Chapter 23. Operation 'Leg'

Oil painting, "Outbound Blenheim's" Copyright Alex Hamilton, Essex, England. Courtesy of the artist.

Chapter 24. The Road to Caen

Tanks of the 1st Hussars and troops of the Royal Winnipeg Rifles and Regina Rifles landing near Courseulles -sur-mer, France, June 6,1944.
Photo credit: Ken Bell, Dept of National Defense/Library and Archives Canada/PA-128791

Chapter 25. Out of Lunenburg

Grand Bank fishing schooner Bluenose, W. R. MacAskill, photographer, Nova Scotia Archives and Records Management, W. R. MacAskill fonds, 1987-453/3977

Chapter 26. 'At the Crease'

Title "At the Crease" used by permission/ Ken Danby Studios, Guelph, Ontario.
George Hainsworth/Roy Worters 1936 photo credit: Imperial Oil/Turofsky/ Hockey Hall of Fame, Toronto.

Bibliography

Chapter 1. Ambush on the Iroquois Trail

Costain, Thomas B. *The White and the Gold*, Doubleday Canada. Toronto 1954

Coulter, Tony. *LaSalle and the Explorers of the Mississippi*, Chelsea House, December 1991

Etobicoke Department of Planning and Development, *The Humber Valley Report*, 1948

Frost, Leslie M. *Forgotten Pathways of the Trent*, Burns and MacEachern Limited, Don Mills, Ontario, 1973

Guillet, Edwin C.- *Pioneer Travel in Upper Canada*, University of Toronto, 1963

Heyes, Esther. *Etobicoke—The Borough of Etobicoke*, December 1974

Jefferys, C.W. *The Picture Gallery of Canadian History Vol 1*. The Ryerson Press, Toronto ,1961

Jenness,Diamond. *Indians of Canada*, Ministry of Supply and Services Canada. 1977

Jones, Donald. *Fifty Tales of Toronto*, U of T Press, 1992

Robinson, P. J. *Toronto During the French Regime* , University of Toronto Press , 1965

Royal Ontario Museum-Rotunda, Vol 19 #4 , Spring 1987

Chapter 2. Escape from the Mohawk Valley

Allen, Robert S. *The Loyal Americans-The Military Role of the Loyalist Provincial Corp*, National Museum of Man, Ottawa. Robert. Allen, General Editor, 1983

Brown George W. , *Building the Canadian Nation*, J. M. Dent, Toronto, 1958

Brown, Wallace, Hereward Senior. *Victorious in Defeat, The Loyalists in Canada*, Methuen Publications, Agincourt, Ont. 1984

Guillet Edwin C. *The Pioneer, Farmer and Backwoodsman, Vol 1*, U of T Press, Toronto 1963

Fryer, Mary Beacock. *King's Men*. Dundurn Press, 1980 (pg 68)

Mika, Nick and Helma , *United Empire Loyalists-Pioneers of Upper Canada*, Mika Publishing Co. Belleville, Ontario. 1976

Raddall, Thomas, Edited by Thomas Costain. *The Path of Destiny, Canada from the British Conquest to Home Rule*. Doubleday Canada, Toronto 1957

Rutledge Joseph Lister, edited by Thomas Costain. *Century of Conflict, The Struggle Between the French and British in Colonial America*, Doubleday Canda, 1956

South Glengarry Heritage Advisory Committee Walking Tour pamphlet, Lancaster, Ontario.

Wallace, W. Stewart. *A First Book of Canadian History*, MacMillan Co of Canada, Toronto, 1942.

Chapter 3. The Capture of Johnny McGinnis

Barber and Howe. *Historical Sketches of the State of New York*, 1841

Berton, Pierre. *The Invasion of Canada 1812-13*, McClelland & Stewart , Toronto, 1980

_____. *Flames Across the Border 1813-1814*, McClelland & Stewart, Toronto, 1980

Collins, Gilbert. *Guidebook to the Historic Sites of the War of 1812*, Dundurn Press, Toronto 1998
Historic Sites and Monuments of Canada, *Tecumseh Monument-* Chatham, Ont
Hitsman, J. MacKay. *The Incredible War of 1812 , A Military History*, Updated by D.E. Graves, Robin Brass Studios, Toronto.1999
Musters, Registers of the 41st Regiment, W.O. 12/5407-5417 . W.O. 25/976. W.O. 120/25 London, England
Stanley, Geo. F.G. *The War of 1812, Land Operations* MacMillan of Canada 1983 in collaboration with the Canadian War Museum. National Museums of Canada.
Suthren, Victor. *The War of 1812* McClelland & Stewart, Toronto,1999
Taylor, Scott. *Canada at War and Peace Vol 1*, A Millenium Military Heritage
Raddall, Thomas H. *The Path of Destiny, Canada from the British Conquest to Home Rule* Vol 111 of the Canadian History Series. Doubleday Canada Ltd, Toronto 1957
Wallace , W. Stewart. *A First Book of Canadian History* (authorized by the Minister of Education, Ont) MacMillan Co of Canda, Toronto. 1942

Chapter 4. The Story of the Great Anchor

Berton, Pierre. *Flames Across the Border 1813-1814*, McClelland and Stewart, Toronto, 1981
Campbell, Marjorie Wilkins. *The Nor-Westers, The Fight for the Fur Trade*, MacMillan, Toronto, 1958
Collins, Gilbert. *Guide Book to the Historic Sites of the War of 1812*, Dundurn Press, Toronto, 1998
Fryer, Mary Beacock. *Bold Brave and Born to Lead, Major General Isaac Brock and the Canadas*, Dundurn Press, 2004.
Gough, Barry. *Fighting Sail on Lake Huron and Georgian Bay. The War of 1812* and *its Aftermath*. Vanwell Publishing, St. Catharines,

Ont. 2002

Hannon, Leslie. *Redcoats and Loyalists, 1760-1815*, Canada's Illustrated Heritage , Natural Science of Canada Ltd, Toronto 1978

Jury, Elsie, McLeod. *The Establishments at Penetanguishene*, Bulletin #12, Museum of Indian Archaeology, University of Western Ontario, London,1959

Malcomson, Robert. *Lords of the Lake, The Naval War on Lake Ontario 1812-1814*, Robin Brass Studio, Toronto 1998

National Library of Canada and National Archives of Canada-*Admiralty Lake Service Records* RG8 3A, Vol 1 Admiralty orders 1814-1816 (Receipt signed by John Batice (his mark) acknowledging $35.00 being payment from Captain Collier of HMS Niagara due to him as pilot from Detroit to Michilimackinac, June 2, 1815.)

Vol 2- Commissioner Sir Robert Hall to Naval Storekeeper 1814-1815

Ontario Historical Society-Paper and Records Vol 55,1963. *List of Vessels Employed on British Naval Service on the Great Lakes 1755-1875* , compiled by K.R. MacPherson.

Parkham, Francis. *The Conspiracy of Pontiac and the Indian War* Vol 1, Little Brown and Co, Boston, 1910

Raddall, Thomas H. *The Path of Destiny Vol 3, Canada from the British Conquest to Home Rule 1763-1850*, Doubleday ,Canada, Toronto 1957

Robertson, J. Ross. *Robertson's Lankmarks* C971.354R Fifth Series, 1792-1837, J. Ross Robertson 1908, from Toronto Evening Telegram.

Turner, Wesley B. *The War of 1812, The War that Both Sides Won*, Dundurn Group 2000

Chapter 5. Isabella's Lamp

Bennett, Carol. *Lanark Society Settlers*, Juniper Books.Renfrew,

Ontario 1991

Guillet, Edwin C. *Pioneer Travel in Upper Canada*, University of Toronto, 1963 reprint.

Land Records—Drummond Township Lot 20 , Con 11 Deed Feb 23/52

McGill, Jean. *A Pioneer History of the County of Lanark*, Clay Publishing, Bewdley, Ont 1974

Whitton, Charlotte. *A Hundred Years A' Fellin'*—Runge Press, Ottawa 1942

1837 Census-Ramsay Township

Pesonal Interviews: Katherine Hughes, Oakland California.

Cora Shiels, Toronto , Ont

Ken Robertson, Medonte, Ont.

Chapter 6. The Shooting of Frank Lynch

Creighton, Donald. *Dominion of the North* , MacMillan of Canada, 1957

Graves, Donald, Editor. *Fighting for Canada: Seven Battles 1758-1945* Robin Brass Studio, Toronto 2000

Findlay, D. Letter to T.C. Shiels 1964

Hardy W.G. *From Sea to Sea: The Road to Nationhood*, Doubleday & Co. Garden City , New York 1960

MacKay, Donald W. *Flight From Famine*, McClelland & Stewart, Toronto 1990

Ontario Archives: Land Grants Ramsay Township/Lanark Co 1841

Pullen, H.F. *The Shannon and the Chesapeake*, McClelland & Stewart Ltd Toronto/Montreal 1970

Roby, Yves. *The United States and Confederation*, The Centennial Commission , Ottawa 1967

Shiels, T.C. Interviews

Stokesbury, James L. *A Short History of the Civil War*, Wm Morrow & Co. Inc 1995

Taylor, Scott Editor. *Canada At War and Peace, A Millennium of Military Heritage* Vol 1, Esprit de Corps Books, Ottawa , 2000
Turner, Wesley B. *The War of 1812*, Dundurn Group 2000
Winks, Robin W. *The Civil War Years: Canada and the United States*, McGill-Queens University Press 1998.

Chapter 7. The Secret Mission of John Rose

Bayne, Margaret W. *Centenary Celebration of the First Woman Teacher in Zorra*, Vancouver BC July 1935
Blaine , James G. *The Alabama Claims and the Geneva Arbitration—* from Blaine's "Twenty Years of Congress" Mrs. Walter Damrosch and James G. Blaine copyright 1884
Cantlie, Hugh. *Ancestral Castles of Scotland*- Collins and Brown, London 1992
Clark, Robert Carleton. *The Diplomatic Mission of Sir John Rose*, Pacific North West Quarterly VO 27 #13 July 1936
Creighton, Donald. *John A. Macdonald, The Young Politician/The Old Chieftain*, University of Toronto Press , Toronto 1952
Crook, D.P (University of Queensland-Australia) *Diplomacy During the Civil War*, John Wiley and Son 1975—pg 59
Cushing, Caleb. *The Treaty of Washington*, Harper and Brothers, Franklin Square 1873
Fuess, Claude. *The Life of Caleb Cushing*, Harcourt, Brace and Co New York, 1923 page 213
Hardy W. G. *From Sea to Sea*, Doubleday and Co , Garden City , New York, 1959
Mahin, Dean. *One War at a Time-The International Dimension of the American Civil War*, Brassey's Washington . D.C.1999
McDonald, Donna. *Lord Strathcona,-A Biography of D.A.Smith*, Dundurn Press, Toronto,1996
Morton, W. L. *The Critical Years, The Union of British North America 1852-1873* , McClelland and Stewart 1964
Ottawa Citizen, July 9,1886

Radforth, Ian W. *Royal Spectacle:the 1860 visit of the Prince of Wales to Canada.*
University of Toronto Press 2004
http/css.alabama.com/css.html

Chapter 8. Black Pete's Last Fight

Brown, Howard Morton . *Founded Upon a Rock*, 150th Year Festival Committee Carleton Place 1969
_____.,*Lanark Legacy*, Corp of the County of Lanark, Perth ,KG Campbell Corp 1984
Creighton, Donald. John A. Macdonald, *The Old Chieftain* , MacMillan 1952
Finnegan, Joan. *Laughing all the Way Home,* Deneau Publisher, Ottawa 1984
Forbes, C.M. *History of Lanark Village*, Perth Courier Dec 15,1909-Feb 9,1909
Fraser, J , *Shanty , Forest, and River—Life in the Backwoods of Canada* J. Lovell & Sons 1883
Hughson John W and Bond, C.W. *Hurling Down the Pine* old Chelsea, Que. Historical Society of Gatineau, 1964
Ibbitson, John. *Loyal No More*, Harper Collins 2001
Jamieson, E.L. *The Story of Lanark* Centenary of Lanark Village 1974, reprint of 1962 publication.
MacKay, Donald. *The Lumberjacks* McGraw Hill, Ryerson copyright 1978
Rayburn, Alan. *Naming Canada* , University of Toronto Press, 1992
Shiels, T.C. Correspondence and interviews
Whitton, Charlotte. *A Hundred Years A-Fellin' The Story of the Gillies on the Ottawa* Runge Press 1942.

Chapter 9. The Empire Builders

Berton, Pierre. *The National Dream-The Great Railway 1871-1881* ,

McClelland & Stewart , Toronto, 1973
Cruise, David, Griffiths, Alison. *Lords of the Line-The Men Who Built the CPR*. Viking Press ,1988
Friesen, Gerald. *The Canadian Prairies-A History*, University of Toronto Press, Toronto 1984
Lower, J. Arthur. *Western Canada-An Outline History*, Douglas & McIntyre Vancouver/Toronto ,1983
Hardy, W. G. *From Sea Unto Sea- The Road to Nationhood 1850-1910*, Doubleday & Co Inc, Garden City, New York, 1960
McDonald, Donna. *Lord Strathcona, A Biography of Donald A. Smith*, Dundurn Press, Toronto, 2002
Newman, Peter. *Flame of Power*, Longmans, Green & Co.Toronto 1959
Wallace, W. Stewart. *A First Book of Canadian History*, MacMillan Co of Canada, Toronto, 1942.

Chapter 10. The Sage of Aru

Brown, Howard Morton. letter to the author
Gunston Hall Plantation—official website—10709 Gunston Road, Mason Neck, Virginia, USA
Howard, Granby Staunton. *Report of the trial of the libel suit of Dr. G.S. Howard*, of Carleton Place
Against the Montreal Star, pamphlet published by the Montreal Star 1898
Shiels, T.C. interviews

Chapter 11. Doublecross on Eldorado Creek

Becker, Ethel Anderson. *Klondike '98* , Benfords and Most, Portland 1949
Berton, Pierre. *The Golden Trail ,The Story of the Klondike Gold Rush* MacMillan, Canada 1954
Berton, Pierre. *Klondike*, McClelland and Stewart , Canada 1958
_____ . *column Toronto Star*, Jan 22/94

Bronson, William. *The Last Grand Adventure, The Story of the Klondike Gold Rush and The Opening of Alaska*, McGraw Hill Book Co. New York 1977

Cohen, Stan. *The Streets Were Paved With Gold, A Pictorial History of the Klondike Gold Rush*, Pictorial Histories Publishing Co Missoula, Montana 1977

Dobrowolsky, Helen. *Law of the Yukon*, Lost Moose, 1995

Handy, W. G. *From Sea to Sea, The Road to Nationhood 1850-1910*, Doublday & Co Inc, Garden City, NY 1950

McLauchlan, Lewis, letters to the author, May 26,1962 / July 31/62

Steele, Samuel. *Forty Years in Canada, Reminiscences of the Great North West*, Prospero Books 2000 (original published—Dodd Mead 1915

Temiskaming Speaker, New Liskeard, April, May 1971

Toronto Telegram , May 1964

Wallace, Jim. *Fortymile to Bonanza* , Bunker to Bunker Publishing, Calgary 2000.

Chapter 12. The Order of the Midnight Sun

Brown, George W. *Building the Canadian Nation* , J.M.Dent , Toronto/Vancouver 1958 edition

Brown , Robert Craig /Cook, Ramsay- *Canada 1896-1921* , *A Nation Transformed* , McClelland & Stewart Ltd , Toronto 1974

Chippendale, Richard. *Laurier—His Life and World* , McGraw Hill Ryerson 1979

Creighton, Donald . *Canada's First Century* , MacMillan Co of Canada 1970

Dobrowolsky, Helen. *Law of the Yukon, A Pictorial History of the Mounted Police in the Yukon* , Lost Moose, Yukon Publisher 1995

Hamilton, W.R. *The Yukon Story* , Mitchell Press, Vancouver 1964

Hardy, W. G. *From Sea Unto Sea, The Road to Nationhood Vol 4-*

1850-1910 , Doubleday & Co. Garden City, New York, 1959

Lester, Edward, edited by Brereton Greenhous. *Guarding the Goldfields, The Story of the Yukon Field Force*, Dundurn Press, Toronto 1987

Lindberg, Murray. *The Alaska-Canada Boundary Dispute* , http://www.explorenorth.com/library/weekly/aa103000a.htm

McLauchlan, Lewis—private correspondence

Newman, Peter C. *Caesars of the Wilderness, Company of Adventurers* Vol 2 .Viking Penguin Books Canada 1987, Power Reporting Ltd 1987

Tait, George E. *Breastplate and Buckskin*, Ryerson Press, Toronto, Ontario. 1953

Wallace, Jim. *Forty Mile to Bonanza* , Bunker to Bunker Publishing, Calgary 2000.

Chapter 13. The Flight of the 'Cygnet'

Edwin Grosvenor. *Alexander Graham Bell*—Morgan Wesser, Harry Abrams 1997
(pg141)

Fred Howard,. *Wilbur and Orville*, Ballantine Books , New York 1987

Petrie, A Roy. *Alexander Graham Bell*—The Canadians- Fitzhenry and Whiteside, 1992

Shiels, T.C.—Halifax recollections-1942,

Shulman, Seth. *Unlocking the Sky*, Harper Collins

Chapter 14. The Voyage of the 'Nolturo'

Halifax Ships Manifests (Ship's passenger manifest, R1206-237-0-E (T-
4744) April 11- Apr 24, 1912. Library and Archives Canada

Chapter 15. Victoria Cross Hill

Bindon, Kathryn. *More Than Patriotism-Canada at War 1914-1918*,

Personal Library Publishers, Toronto 1979

Davis, Mat Pvt. *Letters to a friend* (unpublished) Feb/May 1916

Lotz, Jim. *Canadians at War*-Bison Books 1990, London SW3 6RL

Dancocks, Daniel. *Welcome to Flanders Fields, the First Canadian Battle of the Great War: Ypres , 1915 ,* McClelland and Stewart, Toronto, 1988

Morton, Desmond and Granatstein J.L. *Marching to Armageddon, Canadians and the Great War 1914-1918* Lister and Orpen Dennys Limited, Toronto 1989

Morton, Desmon. *A Military History of Canada from Champlain to Kosovo,* McClelland and Stewart, Toronto, 1999

Pedley, James, B. *Only This-A War Retrospect,* The Graphic Publishers, Ottawa, 1927

Stephens, John http://pages.interlog.com/~fatjack/hill70.htmSat Nov 23.02

Chapter 16. I Flew with Roy Brown

Jones, Donald. *Fifty Tales of Toronto,* University of Toronto Press, 1992

Jones, Ira . *An Airfighter's Scrapbook,* Nicolas and Watson, London 1938

McKellar, John D. *Interviews*

Chapter 17. J'Avance

Schull, Joseph and Gibson, J. Douglas. *The Scotiabank Story- A History of the Bank of Nova Scotia 1832-1982-* MacMillan of Canada, Toronto 1932.

Scotiabank Group Archives, 44 King Street, Toronto.

Chapter 18. My Lou Gehrig Story

Evans, Spencer (Spiff) Gaylord, Interviews circa 1992

Robinson, Ray. *Iron Horse,* W.W. Norton and Co. New York

1990
Toronto Daily Star July 1930
Toronto Evening Telegram July 1930

Chapter 19. Rinkrats I Have Known

Brown Allan W. Interviews 2003
Harris, William. *The Glory Years* , Prentice-Hall Inc. Toronto.
1989
Hewitt, Foster. *Hockey Night in Canada* ,Ryerson Press. Toronto
1961
Toronto Evening Telegram—1939 -1940
Young, Scott , *Conn Smythe If you can't beat 'em in the Alley* ,
McClelland and Stewart, Toronto 1981.

Chapter 20. The Adventures of the Tricky Sons

Allison, Les, Hayward, Harry. *They Shall Not Grow Old*,
Commonwealth Air Training, Leech Printing, Brandon, Man
1992.
Brown, Allan W. Interviews.
Graves, Donald E. *In Peril on the Sea, The Royal Canadian Navy
and the Battle of the Atlantic.* Robin Brass Studio. Toronto 2003

Chapter 21. Above Biggin Hill

After the Battle Magazine. *Battle of Britain, Then and Now*, Battle
of Britain Prints International Ltd.
Bashow, David. *All the Fine Young Eagles*-Stoddart ,1996
Bickers, Richard Townsend. *Battle of Britain*-Salamander Books,
Doubleday Canada Ltd. 1990
Bishop, Arthur. *The Splendid One Hundred*- McGraw Hill Ryerson
1984
Churchill, Winston S. Speeches, *Blood, Sweat and Tears*, G. P.
Putnam's Sons, New York, 1941.
Churchill, Winston S. Speech, House of Commons, Ottawa,

December 30,1941.

Dunsmore, Spencer. *Above and Beyond*- McClelland and Stewart, 1996

London Free Press, September,1940, June,1942

Millbery-Halliday. *The RCAF at War*, Canadian Aviation Books, 1990

Price, Dr. Alfred. *Battle of Britain Day*-Sedgewick and Jackson, London 1990

Westhead, Marion L. -interview

Whiting, Charles. *Britain Under Fire*, Century Hutcheson, London 1986

Wynn, Kenneth. *Men of the Battle of Britain*, Gliddon Books, Norwich, Norfolk,1989.

Chapter 22. Sir Frederick Goes to War

Bliss, Michael. *Banting-A Biography* , McClelland and Stewart , Toronto (paperback) 1985

Coles, Russell, Interviews

Harris, Arthur. *Bomber Offensive* Stoddart Publishing 1990 (first published 1947-(Collins)

Hume, Stephen Eaton. *Frederick Banting* XYZ Publishing, Lantzville B.C. 2001

Pratt, Viola Whitney. *Canadian Portraits—Famous Doctors*, Clark Irwin, Toronto, 1956

Toronto Telegram, February 25,1941

Webb, Michael, Editor. *Frederick Banting-Discoverer of Insulin*, Copp Clark Pitman Ltd 1991 Mississauga, Ont.

Chapter 23. Operation 'Leg'

Allison, Les, Hayward, Harry. *They Shall Not Grow Old*, Commonwealth Air Training, Leech Printing, Brandon, Man 1992

Brickhill, Paul. *Reach for the Sky-the Story of Douglas Bader*, Wm

Collins and Sons, Great Britain 1954

Chorley, W. R. *RAF Bomber Command Losses* Vol 2 Midland Counties Publications, Redwood Books, Trowbridge, Wiltshire 1993

Johnson, JE, Group Cap, DSO, DFC. *Wing Leader*, Ballantine Books, New York, 1956

Pringle, P/O Jack. correspondence, 2004

Profile 218; Bristol Blenheim MKIV , Profile Public, Coburg, Windsor, Berskshire

Toronto Star, August 14,1941 , September 14, 1941

Turner, John Frayn. *Douglas Bader*, Airlife Publishing, Shrewsbury, England, 1995

Wilson, Sgt, A.J. *Skysweepers*, Gainsborough Press, St. Albans, Jarrolds, London, 1942

Wynn, Kenneth. *Men of the Battle of Britain*, Gledden Books, Norwich, 1989

18 Squadron , *With Courage and Faith* http://www.f4aviation. co.uk/wattisham/18sq/18sq.htm

Chapter 24. The Road to Caen

Barris, Ted. Juno, Canadians at D Day June 6,1944 , Thomas Allen Publishers, Toronto, 2004

Churchill, Winston S. and Editors of Life. *The Second World War, Special Edition for Younger Readers*, Golden Press, New York , 1960

Copp, Terry. *Fields of Fire*, The Canadians at Normandy, U of T Press, 2003

Heathcote, Blake. *Testaments of Honour*, Personal Histories of Canada's War Veterans, Doubleday Canada 2002

Lotz, Jim. *Canadians at War*, Bison Books Ltd, London SW3 6RL, 1990

Robertson, Ken. Interviews.

Chapter 25. Out of Lunenberg

Jensen, Lathan, B. *Bluenose 11, Saga of the Great Fishing Schooner,* Nimbus Publishing, Halifax, 1994

Jones, Donald. *Fifty Tales of Toronto,* University of Toronto Press,1992

MacAskill, Wallace. *Seascapes and Sailing Ships,* Nimbus Publishing, Halifax 1987

Robinson, Ernest Fraser. *The Saga of the Bluenose,* Vanwell Publishing Ltd. St. Catharines 1989

Chapter 26. 'At the Crease'

Hockey Hall of Fame. *Hockey Hall of Fame Legends "The Official Book"* Viking Press, Opus Productions, Vancouver, 1993

McDonell, Chris. *Hockey All-Stars, The NHL Honour Roll,* Firefly Books, Willowdale, Ontario, 2000

Toronto Daily Star, April 3,1936

Toronto Telegram, April 3,1936

Weir, Glenn, Chapman, Jeff, Weir Travis. *Ultimate Hockey,* Stoddart Publishing Co. Toronto 1999.

Chapter 27. The Two-Way Men

Carroll, Jock. *The Death of the Toronto Telegram and other Newspaper Stories,* Pocket Books, Richmond Hill, Ont 1971

Creighton, Douglas. *Sunburned, Memoirs of a Newspaperman,* Little Brown & Co. (Canada) Ltd. 1993

Gelb, Arthur. *Cityroom,* CP Putnam and Sons, New York, 2003

Robertson, Ken. Interviews.

Sonmore, Jean. *The Little Paper That Grew,* Inside the Toronto Sun Publishing Corp. Toronto Sun, 1993

Toronto Star, - September 18,1971

RR #4

About the Author

DONALD A. "Don" McKellar is a student of the history of Canada, the *people* histories that reveal events as they really were, described by the people who actually lived them.

As a boy, he much preferred his grandfather's tales of the Ottawa Valley loggers, river drivers, lumber barons and yes, even bankers, to the schoolbook history he was taught.

So his weekends are spent roaming historic sites, little corners of wilderness hidden among the high rises and the small greenbelts with the usually-ignored bronze plaques telling of early day communities. And then happy hours of archival delving to flesh out the real stories behind and beyond the scope of the stiff prose of most history texts. His writing reflects the fun and excitement of his quests and the rough and rollicking times that forged our nation. Then, as old Linus, he relates them to a fictional grandson named Brendan.

Don makes his home in Toronto, where he works for the Bank of Nova Scotia, but his heart is in the camps and cabins of Canada's past. And his readers reap the armchair treasures.

ISBN 142511927-1

9 781425 119270